TORN BETWEEN A GANGSTER AND A GENTLEMAN

J-Blunt & Miss Kim

**Lock Down Publications and Ca$h
Presents**
TORN BETWEEN A GANGSTER AND A GENTLEMAN
A Novel by *J-Blunt* & *Miss Kim*

J-Blunt & Miss Kim

Lock Down Publications
Po Box 944
Stockbridge, Ga 30281

Visit our website @
www.lockdownpublications.com

Copyright 2022 by J-Blunt & Miss Kim
TORN BETWEEN A GANGSTER AND A GENTLEMAN

All rights reserved. No part of this book may be reproduced in any form or by electronic or mechanical means, including information storage and retrieval systems without permission in writing from the publisher, except by a reviewer who may quote brief passages in review.
First Edition September 2022
Printed in the United States of America

This is a work of fiction. Names, characters, places, and incidents either are products of the author's imagination or are used fictitiously. Any similarity to actual events or locales or persons, living or dead, is entirely coincidental.

Lock Down Publications
Like our page on Facebook: Lock Down Publications @
www.facebook.com/lockdownpublications.ldp
Book interior design by: **Shawn Walker**
Edited by: **Sunny Giovanni**

Chicago Public Library
Jefferson Park Branch

Customer ID: ********5029

Items that you checked out

Title: Torn between a gangster and a gentleman : a novel
ID: R0464723583
Due: Monday, April 17, 2023

Total items: 1
Account balance: $6.99
3/26/2023 4:51 PM

Items that you already have on loan

Title: Drawing : the only drawing book you'll ever need to be the artist you've always wanted to be
ID: R0413264984
Due: Saturday, April 15, 2023

Thank you for using the Chicago Public Library.

Stay Connected with Us!

Text **LOCKDOWN** to 22828 to stay up-to-date with new releases, sneak peaks, contests and more...
Thank you.

Submission Guideline.

Submit the first three chapters of your completed manuscript to ldpsubmissions@gmail.com, subject line: Your book's title. The manuscript must be in a .doc file and sent as an attachment. Document should be in Times New Roman, double spaced and in size 12 font. Also, provide your synopsis and full contact information. If sending multiple submissions, they must each be in a separate email.

Have a story but no way to send it electronically? You can still submit to LDP/Ca$h Presents. Send in the first three chapters, written or typed, of your completed manuscript to:

LDP: Submissions Dept
Po Box 944
Stockbridge, Ga 30281

DO NOT send original manuscript. Must be a duplicate.

Provide your synopsis and a cover letter containing your full contact information.

Thanks for considering LDP and Ca$h Presents.

ACKNOWLEDGEMENTS:

J-Blunt: The cost of love is never cheap. You can't buy it but you must pay the price of maintaining a relationship. Commitment, faithfulness, forgiveness, serving, and loving through good and bad is expensive. When you find that priceless person or relationship, hold on to it. This book is dedicated to everybody that believes in true love.

Shout out to everybody that's been rocking with me and supporting me throughout my fight with this injustice system. A special THANK YOU to the fans and supporters of J-Blunt. Thanks for the feedback and the reviews. I write because I love to tell stories and entertain. Connect with me us Facebook @ Author J-Blunt MsKim.

Miss Kim: I never thought I'd be an author with my name on a book, but that goes to show that God's plans ain't like ours. Shot out to J-Blunt for creating a platform for us. I got the torch, bro. Watch me run with it. Mommy, I love you more than life. Dennis, thank you for being my father, Daddy, and protector. Honesty, you made me everything that I am. I'm so proud to the woman you're becoming. To all my siblings, which is too many to name because we steadily finding more of us, I love y'all and hope that life gives you everything you deserve. C-Roc, you know you my nigga. I love your hustle. Keep grinding.

Torn Between a Gangster and a Gentleman

CHAPTER 1 - Ray

"Oh, Ray! It feels so good!"
"That's it! Yeah, baby! Take that dick!"
"Is it good, Ray? Tell me it's good!"
"It's good, Kaysha! It's real good, baby!"
"Talk nasty to me, Ray. Talk that shit!"

When it came to fucking, me and Kaysha went at it like we were in a competition to see who could give each other the most pleasure. If I ate her pussy for 30 minutes, she would give me head for an hour. If I made her cum once, she made me bust twice. At this moment she was on top of me, hips rocking back and forth as she rode. My hands had her cakes in a vice grip while my tongue went back and forth to each perfectly perky C-cup breast.

"Work that pussy on daddy's dick, bitch! Yeah! Mmhh. Just like that."

As I gave her the dirty talk she requested, Kaysha got lost in the zone. Her head tilted toward the ceiling and green eyes rolled to the back of her head. I could feel French manicured nails digging deep into the skin of my chest and shoulders, but I didn't care. She was riding me so fast and hard that I couldn't complain about the little pain from her nails. It would've ruined the mood.

So, I slapped her on the ass and talked some more shit. "Is that all you got! Huh? You can't handle me, lil' girl. I'm a grown ass man. You can't handle my dick."

I could hear her juices sloshing around my pole every time she rammed her pelvis into mine. Then she did it. Something I'd only seen in porno flicks. Something I wasn't ready for. Something I didn't even know she could do.

"Awe shit!" I grunted, gripping her sweat-coated hips as her pussy walls squeezed my dick. Felt so good that I just instantly… My body went stiff as my dick spasmed.

"Now, who can't handle who, nigga?" She grinned, continuing to put it on me as I came.

"I. See. You. Was. Holding out. On me," I managed in between breaths.

"I gotta big bag of tricks for you, baby." She smirked, slowing her pace as my dick rapidly shrank inside of her.

Kaysha was a baddie. No ifs, ands, or buts about it. She was a Puerto Rican and Korean cutie known on Instagram as Kay-Kaygotabody. She was twenty-three years old, light skinned, kinky and curly black hair, and had a body that would make Yung Thug start Crip Walking. The icing on the cake was her eyes. They were emerald. The kind of eyes that a man could get lost in. Eyes that could mesmerize you and make you fall in love if you weren't careful. And believe me, I was careful. I wasn't looking for love. Just fun.

"Let me take this rubber off," I said, tapping her on the butt.

"I know you ain't done, old man," she said while giving me a side eye.

I seen the disappointment on her face and could hear it in her voice. She hadn't gotten hers and she wasn't letting me go to sleep until she got her rocks off. Nympho was an under-statement.

"Let me see what you can do to get me back in game shape," I cracked while throwing the spent condom in the garbage beside my bed.

A sexy smile spread across her face as she began placing kisses from my chest to my pelvis. "I told you my trick bag is full."

***

The first thing that I noticed when I opened my eyes was the warm, soft flesh snuggled up against mine. Kaysha was glued to my ribcage. I fought her off several times during the night but she somehow she found a way to tangle herself in my limbs again. I didn't like that. It meant she was getting attached. And that was a no-no. Plus, she didn't fit.

After untangling myself from Kaysha, I hit the bathroom to freshen up. A shower and some Crest on my gums had me reclining in my recliner fifteen minutes later. I used the remote to power on the 42" flat screen and did a quick channel surf. Didn't take long to find what I was looking for. The latest news on the stock market.

Torn Between a Gangster and a Gentleman

Watching greedy people talk about getting richer was my morning ritual. I had invested $70,000 into the stock market so I watched money making shows like fat people watched cooking shows. I never wanted to work another day in my life, so I learned the ropes on investing and took risks that usually paid off.

I was watching my main man Tony "Buy or Sell" Askew when I heard movement coming from my bedroom. Kaysha was awake. I caught a glimpse of her heading to the bathroom.

"Ray, can you order us something to eat?" she called.

"Yeah. What do you want?"

"What about Jimmy John's? They're supposed to be freaky fast, right?"

I grabbed my phone and placed an order before giving Buy or Sell my undivided. He was ready to give his list on the buy or sell stocks for the morning. Maytag, buy. Hewlett Packard, buy. Walmart, sell. Facebook, sell.

Shit. I just bought more shares of Facebook last week.

When Buy or Sell went to commercial, I called my accountant.

"Mr. Preston, good morning," David Levine greeted me.

"Hey, Dave. I want to sell off some sticks and—"

"C'mon, Ray. Buy or Sell is taking a big risk with Facebook. I think you should wait. It'll rebound."

"Dave, I love you like a brother but Buy or Sell knows his shit. Since I've been watching him, he's made me twenty G's and has only been wrong once. I want to sell off Walmart and Facebook and reinvest the sell-off value in Maytag."

"Final answer?" David asked, with uncertainty in his voice.

"Yep. Final answer."

"Okay. I'll get on it and send you an email. Anything else?"

I was about to say something else but forgot my words when Kaysha came sauntering out of the bathroom wearing a bra and panties. Damn, she was sexy as hell. I had to be careful.

"Ray, you there?" Dave asked.

"Yeah. Um, no," I stammered, getting myself together. "I'm good for now. Send me that email."

"I see I came out just in time." Kaysha smiled. "Wanna know what I was thinking about?" she asked, straddling my lap, smelling like Zest.

"Tell me," I said, straining my neck to look around her at the TV. Buy or Sell was back from commercial and was about to give his NASDAQ, S&P 500, and Dow Jones predictions.

"Hello!" she said, palming my face with both hands and forcing me to look in those hypnotic green eyes.

I broke the spell, pulling her hands away from my face and craning my neck to see the TV. "C'mon, Kaysha! You about to make me miss it."

"Ray!" she yelled.

"Okay. One second."

Dow Jones expecting minimal gains. NASDAQ expected to climb. S&P 500 expected to lose.

"Okay. I'm all yours," I said, giving those green eyes all of my attention.

An *I always get my way* smile spread across her pretty mouth. "So, that's how it is? You want to put your boring money shows over your sex kitten?"

"C'mon, Kay. Money makes the world go round. And since I'm not in school getting a fancy degree like you, I have to be able to take care of myself."

"How did you get into this boring stuff anyway?"

"You actually want to know about my boring life?"

"Yeah, Ray. Stocks are boring but you're interesting."

"Whatever." I shrugged. "But I'll humor you. I took a financial literacy course about five or six years ago that touched on stocks. It was interesting so I looked into it some more. Found out you could make a lot of money if you knew where to invest. Then, a couple years later I got my money and jumped in headfirst."

"So, was it scary in prison?"

"C'mon, Kaysha. I don't want to talk about that. How about you tell me what you were thinking when you walked out of the bathroom."

Torn Between a Gangster and a Gentleman

She looked like she wanted to protest but didn't. "I was thinking we should do something today. I don't have to go to school, and I wanted to spend some time with you."

I didn't like where this was going but I decided to hear her out. "What did you have in mind?"

Her eyes lit up. "I was thinking we should do something romantic. Like his and her spa treatments."

I shook my head. "Nah. Not feeling the spa thing."

A look of hurt flashed across her face. "Why not?"

"Because it's romantic. I don't do romance. You're not catching feelings, are you?"

Her eyes became misty. "I don't know. I guess. A little."

"C'mon, Kaysha. I thought we was just kicking it. Having fun. Don't complicate this."

"But I really like you a lot. I don't care that you're older than me or that you just got out of prison."

"But I already told you that I'm not looking for a woman. I can't be your man."

She got mad. "So, you just want to keep fucking me, but you don't want to be with me?"

"Look, Kaysha, I'm not trying to hurt your feelings and I don't want to lead you on either. I told you what I was looking for, and what I want hasn't changed. I think you're cool, and I like you. I just don't want to be in a relationship."

She studied my face for a moment, the wheels churning in her mind. "Is it me? Am I not doing something right?"

I shook my head. "No, Kaysha. It's not you. You're... Perfect."

She searched my face again, trying to figure out why I didn't want to be with her. "Is it because you just got out of prison?"

It wasn't a major factor, but since she brought it up, I decided to roll with it. "Yeah. I've only been out six months and I'm still trying to figure out life. I'm not sure what I want or what I like. I just did thirteen years in a box. I still have so much to figure out and that takes time. I need time."

Her face softened a bit. "I guess I can understand that. If I did thirteen years, I'd probably feel the same way. I would just want

13

friends, too." She paused, her eyes squinting into lust-glazed green slits. "With benefits!"

"Right," I agreed, leaning forward for some tongue action.

We kissed and rubbed each other's bodiess, ready to get in a round of morning sex. I hit the recline lever on my chair as she was reaching into my boxers. Then I heard someone messing with the lock on my front door. I tilted my head back just as the door opened. In walked my 15-year-old son.

"Hey, Junior. You over here kinda early, ain't you?" I asked, giving him an upside-down smile.

"Hey, dad. Um... Sorry. I didn't know you was..." He stuttered nervously, eyeing me and Kaysha in our underwear.

"It's okay, man. Come in. Close the door. This is my friend, Kaysha."

"Hi." She smiled.

My son looked like he wanted to say something more. His eyes were wide and he kept looking outside like someone was coming.

"What up, man? Is Brittany out there, too?"

"Uh, no. Mom's coming."

I was stuck. Wasn't sure how to respond to that. But I knew one thing for sure is that Kaysha wasn't moving. I wanted my kids' mother to see this super baddie sitting on my lap. And before I had a chance to get in a better position, Brianna walked in. When she seen Kaysha sitting on my lap, shock and anger flashed in her cinnamon brown eyes. The look on her face was priceless.

"Ray!" Brianna gasped.

I couldn't contain my smile. "Hey, Brianna! What do I owe the pleasure?"

I was only being a little sarcastic when I asked the question because since I had been out of prison, Brianna had only been in my house once and I had never been in hers. By choice. She usually dropped the kids and waited outside until they were inside. When I picked them up or dropped them off, I did the same.

"I need to talk to you, Ray," she almost demanded.

Torn Between a Gangster and a Gentleman

I flipped the lever, sitting the chair upright. As I spun the chair around, I made sure to put a hand on Kaysha's perfect booty.

"What's up?"

"I don't want to talk with her around." She mean-mugged.

I wasn't about to let her come in my house and make demands. "C'mon, Brianna. You not about to come in my house and tell me what to do. What do you want?"

"I need to go put some clothes on," Kaysha said, sensing the hostilities between me and my kid's mother.

"Okay, baby," I said, watching her blue pantied booty jiggle as she walked away.

"Dang, dad!" my son uttered, also watching Kaysha walk away.

"Junior!" Brianna admonished, giving him the evil eye.

"Good taste, man." I laughed.

"You need to be ashamed of yourself." Brianna sneered. "Where did you find this one? The high school bus stop?"

"And if I did, so what? Why you worried about my sex life?"

"I'm not. I just don't want you teaching our son to be a hoe."

"Is that why you came over? To see if Junior has my taste in women?" I asked, ready for her to be gone. I didn't like being around her for any longer than necessary. If it wasn't about the kids, we didn't need to speak.

She gave me an angry and disgusted stare, looking like she was ready to spaz out. Her eyes blazed anger and her top lip twitched. But she controlled herself in front of our son. "I need you to keep Junior for the weekend. I have to be in Madison with Benny and won't be back until Sunday."

"Cool. Where is Brittany?"

"She's by my sister's house. Junior wants to stay with you."

"Alright."

"He has a game tomorrow night. Here, let me give you some money, Junior," she said, sitting her purse on my weight bench and bending over to dig inside.

I checked her out while she surfed through the purse. Brianna's body was banging. The white jeans clung to her frame like they were painted on, showing wide hips and thick thighs. The heels she wore had her butt sitting high in the sky like it was the sun. The snug fitting black T-shirt clung to her upper body, showing off her small waist and 34Ds. And to top it all off, my baby mama was bad. Her mother's Creole and her father's Jamaican gene pool gave her skin a bronze tint. High cheek bones, almond shaped eyes, juicy lips gave her that wow factor. And the length of her hair made some women hate her on sight.

"And why don't you do—" she was saying but stopped.

Damn. She caught me looking at her ass.

A sly smile spread across her face before being replaced by the mean mug. "And why don't you do something with your house like buy some furniture? Didn't your father leave you some money?" she asked, twisting up her face as she looked around my spot.

I didn't have any furniture in my living room except a recliner, TV, and weights. My kitchen had a microwave, stove, refrigerator, and a few dishes. And my bedroom had a bed, radio, and dresser. I had learned to get by with just the necessities. "I got everything I need. You worried about the wrong thing."

"Where is Junior going to sleep?"

"On the air mattress in the other room. I got room for Brittany, too."

"Psst. Whatever," she said, blowing me off and turning to Junior. "Be good, okay? Don't cause your father problems. Call me if you need anything. Love you." After kissing Junior on the forehead, she turned to me like she was about to say something then changed her mind. Instead of speaking, she gave me a stank look and left.

"Yo' moms is a trip, man." I laughed.

CHAPTER 2 - Brianna

I hate Ray's guts! That's all I could think about as I stormed to my white Lexus truck. He knew what he was doing when he kept that girl on his lap. And he tried to further incite me when he rubbed her booty.

"Grrrr!" I grunted, slamming the doorway harder than I meant. I really wanted to go back in the house and punch him in the face. Him and that little girl were lucky I didn't condone violence, otherwise I would've left that unfurnished living room looking like a crime scene. His body parts and her green eyes would've been spread all over that house.

I pulled away from Ray's house thinking violent thoughts when my phone rang. "Hello!" I snapped.

"Well, hello to you, too. Looks like somebody in a bad mood."

"Sorry, mom. I didn't mean to snap at you like that. Ray just... Gets on my nerves."

Mom laughed. I didn't find anything funny. "Is Ray by your house? Tell him I said hi," she crooned. Hearing the affection in her voice for Ray made me want to hang up the phone. She loved ray like she birthed him. Always said Ray was her *real* son in law, not my husband.

"No, I'm not at home. I just dropped Junior off at Ray's house."

"What are you so mad about? You just dropped Junior off, right?"

"He had some underage-looking girl sitting on his lap."

"Well, it's his house. So, what?"

"That's not the point, mama. I'm his kid's mother. He should have more respect for me than to be rubbing her booty while I'm standing right there."

"He rubbed her booty?" She laughed.

"Yes. And they were almost naked."

"How did she look? Was she cute?"

The young woman's green eyes flashed in my head. "Yeah. Kind of. But she can't hold a candle to me."

Mom laughed again.

I wondered what was so funny. "Why are you laughing?"

"You. You're jealous," she said, laughing again.

"What! Please. I'm not jealous."

"Yes, you are. You don't have to lie to me, Brianna. I know you better than you know yourself."

"Whatever," I mumbled, going silent.

"You still love him, huh?"

I didn't answer. Focused on driving.

"Well, honey, both of you have moved on with your lives. Just be happy that he's out and gets to be with the kids. He's a good father. Y'all don't have to be together to get along. Just—"

"Mom, I need to go. I have to meet Benny in Madison. Do you need anything?" I asked, cutting her off. I was tired of hearing her talk about Ray.

"I'm not the one you're mad at so you need to lose the attitude. And since you acting all stank, I'll just call Ray and have him take me to the store."

Click.

"Grrrr!" I grunted again, throwing my phone on the passenger's seat. Everybody was getting on my nerves this morning.

As I drove home, thoughts of Ray flooded my mind. I didn't want to think about him, but I couldn't help it. Every time I seen him or heard his voice, a video reel went on in my head and memories of us flooded my brain.

We met when we were teenagers. He was 16 and I was 14. I was carrying a bag of groceries up the stairs of my sister, Tamar's, house and he was blocking my way. He looked good but I didn't like him like that. He had a pretty thug kind of swag and I was a shy schoolgirl. After giving me a few compliments, him and his friends helped carry the groceries in the house. I ended up spending the weekend by Tamar's house and he spent most of it trying to get my phone number. I eventually gave in. After several weeks of talking on the phone everyday, I gave him my virginity. The first time we had sex, I swore he was my soulmate and that I had known him in another life. I got pregnant with Junior when I turned 16. Two years later we had Brittany. Fast forward 13 years and now we were in a

Torn Between a Gangster and a Gentleman

place where we barley even spoke. I tried to fix it, but he didn't want to put in any effort. It took some time, but I eventually accepted that our relationship would never be the same and focused on being a good mother to my kids and a good, supporting wife to my husband.

"Forget, Ray, Brianna," I told myself in the rearview mirror. "That part of your life is over. Bigger and better, not smaller and bitter."

After giving myself the pep talk, I found a song to fit the mood. K. Michele's *Miss You, Goodbye* hit the spot like a sip of ice-cold water on a hot ass day. By the time I got home, I was feeling like a lady boss. Home for me was a $600,000, 5.5 bathroom, 3,500 square foot Victorian on Lake Shore Drive. We moved into the house 8 years ago and I didn't plan on ever leaving my suburban getaway.

After letting myself in the house, I dashed to the room to touch up my make-up and get dressed. I was expected at a fundraiser that started at noon. It was almost 9 o'clock. I needed to change into my dress and make the two-hour drive to our state's capitol so that I could be by Benny's side when the shindig started. I stripped from the jeans and T-shirt, slid into the gold and black Alexander McQueen evening gown, and did a few twirls in the mirror. I wasn't a conceited woman, but I know I look good. My mama's mixed heritage gave me a full head of thick and curly hair that fell past my shoulders. My lashes were on point, blush had my cheeks popping, and no woman could ever go wrong with red lipstick. When I was satisfied with my look, I slid into my Alexander McQueen heels, hopped in my truck and began the two hour trek. During the transit to Madison, I busied myself ruining every song on Muni Long's *Public Displays of Affection* album.

When I pulled up to the Four Seasons, I was greeted by a young, handsome, dark skinned valet.

"Enjoy your evening, madam." He smiled, taking my keys.

Charming.

The event was held in the hotel's ballroom. After checking in at the front desk, I was escorted to the ballroom by Boris Kojoe's no nonsense looking twin brother. Once inside the ballroom, I began looking for Benny. The place was filled with stuffy looking rich people who all probably thought that Lil' Wayne was a real gangster. Lawyers, judges, politicians, CEOs, and business owners were spread out everywhere. They mingled while sipping flutes of champagne and ate expensive delicacies from trays that were being carried around by waiters dressed in black tuxedos. The event was a luncheon to raise money for a Republican senator candidate, Tim Michaels. I wasn't a fan of politics, especially Republicans, but my husband was devoted to conservativism.

"Brianna!"

I spun around searching the crowd until I found him. Didn't take long. Benny was literally the blackest man in the room. And he was standing with a group of pale skinned white men that made him look even darker.

"Hey, sweety," I said, walking over to peck him on the lips.

"Hey, dear. These are the fellas. Dan West, David Legume, Robert Allmedniger, and the Honorable Judge Sylvester Gableman. Gentlemen, this is my lovely wife, Brianna," Benny introduced us.

All the men smiled like Cheshire cats.

"Hi, guys." I waved.

"Wow, Benny. You're a lucky man," David Legume grinned, undressing me with his eyes.

"Thank you." I blushed.

"I know. Brianna is a remarkable woman," Benny beamed. "Honey, we are seated at table eight. I'm going to wrap this up with the boys and join you in one moment," Benny said, kissing me on the cheek.

I was delighted to leave. I didn't want to stand around and listen to their boring conversations and get ogled by the white men. After grabbing a flute of champagne, I went to find our table and play the role of a good wife. And this was the part of our privileged lifestyle that I hated. Benny's boring social gatherings. He hung around boring people that talked about boring things and he wanted me to tag along as arm candy and smile for the people. I hated it. This wasn't my crowd, but I did it because it was important to Benny. He had an image to uphold. So as much as I would rather be at home watching some housewives of whoever, I had to suck it up and take one for our team.

"Hey, Brianna!" I looked to my left and seen Emily Schmidt approaching fast, carrying a flute of champagne in one hand and a whiskey on the rocks in the other. Emily was the wife of a local businessman that frequented the same events as Benny. Emily was also an alcoholic that wore too much makeup to cover up the effects of alcohol induced ageing and too much perfume to cover up her smelling like a liquor store.

"Hi, Emily." I smiled.

"I'm so glad you came. I can't stand being around all of these stuffy people with sticks stuck up their asses," she griped while sitting at the table.

"Is that why everyone walks so stiff?" I laughed.

"Yeah, sticks up their asses and little dicks makes white men stiff as ironing boards. But I bet you don't have that problem with Benny Boston, huh? Mandingo!" she cracked, raising her eyebrows and taking a sip of the whiskey, and chasing it with champagne.

"Is that all you think about is sex and the size of a man's penis?"

She looked at me like I was from another planet. "Yeah. What else is there to think about? Have you seen my husband? Not only is he hideous, but that little pinky he calls a dick can't satisfy me. I need something like that." She pointed. "Now, that's a real man!"

I followed her finger to the Boris Kojoe looking brother that escorted me to the ballroom. "Yeah, that is definitely a man," I admitted, comparing the man to my Benny.

I loved Benny. He was a good man. And he was handsome in a distinguished kind of way. Big bright eyes, a perfect smile, a shiny bald head, bushy eyebrows, and big soft lips. At 46, he was still in good shape. We met 11 years ago at a popular nightclub. Ray had been gone for 2 years and I had been jumping from man to man trying to find the reincarnation of him in someone else. When I met Benny, he swept me off my feet, literally. Everyone in Milwaukee knew of Benny Boston. He was a legend. Respected by everyone in the community from corner hustlers to the small business owners. He was best known for hiring ex-cons that just came home from prison. I felt special that he chose to speak to me that night.

After we hit it off, he introduced me to a life that I had only seen in movies. Trips to islands, designer clothes, diamonds, and expensive cars. And he was wonderful with Ray Jr and Brittany. Didn't take long for me to fall for him. And since I knew that Ray was never coming home, when Benny proposed, I said yes. We got to live in an expensive house, the kids went to good schools, and money wasn't a problem. I also went back to school and got two degrees— a bachelor's in business administration and an associates in childcare. Couple years later I opened 2 daycare centers.

"I'm gonna go slip him my number and see if I can get some of that dark meat later tonight. Talk to you later," Emily said before sashaying away.

I shook my head and watched as Emily approached the man. She openly flirted with him, grabbing his bicep. Seeing her touch his muscles made me think of seeing Ray a few hours ago. Even though he was 33-years-old, he still looked like he did when he was 20, minus the cornrows. Prison had preserved him well. Really well. I knew he was in good shape but I never imagined he would look like he had this morning. He wasn't a big man, maybe 6'1" and 200 pounds, but he was solid. Very fit and muscular. His skin was the color of caramel, his dark eyes mystic and piercing, a strong African nose, full lips, and his hair was freshly cut with brushed waves. My baby daddy was sexy enough to have a very popular Only Fans page, and I would definitely subscribe. Just thinking about him made me wish I was that girl on his lap this morning. What I wouldn't give to feel—

"Hey, sweetheart. Are you enjoying yourself?" Benny asked.

I didn't hear him approach. I was flushed but recovered quickly. "You know these are not my people, baby. I'm here to support you."

"Thank you for suffering me to all these uptight functions. I really appreciate it. I will make it up to you. How about for our next vacation we go to the Virgin Islands? Get down with some of the islanders for a few days." He smiled.

Torn Between a Gangster and a Gentleman

"Now, don't try to flake on me at the last moment like you did when we were supposed to go to Europe. I want my island experience."

"I promise, baby. Oh, hold on. Tim is about to speak."

***

We spent the rest of the day between the luncheon in the ballroom and a cocktail party at some rich politician's mansion outside of Madison. By the time we got back to the hotel, I was bone tired. After taking a shower, I sat on the bed in my panties and bra to put on lotion.

"Did you call the kids?" Benny asked, taking off his glasses and sitting the stack of papers he was reading on the nightstand.

"Yes. Brittany acts like she's having the time of her life by Tamar's house. She says she wrote two new songs that she can't wait for me to hear."

"That's good. That girl has some serious pipes. I may need to take her to a studio and get her signed. And how's Junior?"

"He's fine. Him and Ray are playing video games," I said dryly.

"That's a good thing that Ray came home, don't you think? He's a different man now. Responsible and mature. I think Junior needed that, you know?"

"Yeah, that's good," I mumbled, letting out a yawn and reaching for the sheets to slide under them.

"Wait a minute, young, lady. You act like you're the one in their forties," Benny said, rolling on top of me.

"Hanging out with your boring friends wore me out," I said before yawning again.

"Oh, well. I'll just have to do something about that." He grinned, lowering his head to kiss me while his hands traveled under the sheets.

I liked where this was going. "You playing doctor tonight?"

He stood and took off his shirt, giving his best Barry White impression. "Oh, yeah, baby. Tonight, I'm your love doctor!"

I threw the sheet aside, no longer tired. "Get on over here, love doctor, because I need something for this wet spot between my legs," I said, taking off my panties and throwing them at him.

Benny caught them midair and took a big sniff. "Mmhh! Smells like kiwi."

"C'mon and get you some of this forbidden fruit," I moaned, touching myself while he took off his underwear. We hadn't had sex in weeks and I was dying for some licking and sticking.

Benny approached the bed slowly, watching me like a hungry animal stalking prey while stroking himself hard. "You want this big, black snake?"

Watching him masturbate was sexy as hell and I couldn't wait to feel him inside of me. "Come and give me my medicine, love doctor."

"Say it again," he requested while positioning himself between my legs.

I grabbed hold of his dick and pulled it inside of me. "Fuck me, love doctor."

"Damn, you feel so good," Benny moaned, stroking me deep.

"So do you, baby. Keep it going! Right there," I moaned, egging him on.

"Oh, baby! You feel so good. I'm about to bust!"

Alarms and bells went off in my head. It couldn't be over. Not yet. "No! Wait. Slow down. Not yet," I begged. It was just starting to get good and I needed more.

"I can't! Uh-ahhhh!" he grunted, plunging deep inside me and coating my insides with his sperm.

I was so disappointed. This was another part of our relationship that I hated. Without any sexual stimulants, Benny was a 2-minute brotha. And not only that, but we barley had sex. His sex drive wasn't that high, so we had sex 4 or 5 times a month. He was usually too tired, too busy, or not in the mood.

"I'm sorry, baby. I didn't bring my pills," he breathed, rolling onto his side of the bed.

"It's okay. I'm going to take a shower. You want to join me?" I asked, hoping to get in another round.

Torn Between a Gangster and a Gentleman

"I'm sorry, honey. I have to get up early and I need to rest. Big day with the judge tomorrow."

I left the room without another word. After turning on the shower and setting the temperature, I climbed in. My thoughts quickly turned to Ray. I thought about how good he looked in that chair this morning. When my hands found their way to my clit, I fantasized that I was riding Ray on that recliner. Came twice.

Torn Between a Gangster and a Gentleman

CHAPTER 3 - Benny

"Ciarra, I need to see you in my office for a moment."
"Be right there, Mr. Boston."

After turning off the intercom, I cleared my desk of miscellaneous paperwork while waiting for my secretary. I was sitting behind the desk in my office at B & B Global. I began the trucking company 5 years ago. It was here that all the connections I made over the years were finally paying off. For a fee, I shipped products all across the country. If it fit into the back of one of my rigs, then it was shipped professionally and discreetly. The company proved to be a wise business opportunity. Not only did it pay well, but I also got to meet interesting people.

"You wanted to see me?"

I looked up as my secretary stepped into the office. Ciarra Reed was a 35-year-old brown skinned woman that had been with me since before I started the trucking company. She stood 5'10", was as skinny as a runway model, with big ass 36DD titties. She had small hips and a tight little ass that I loved spanking whenever I was in the mood. And to top it all off, she was gorgeous. Full lips, a little pointy nose, nice white teeth, with her hair in a slicked back weave ponytail. She looked the part of a professional dressed in the white blouse, teal skirt, and heels. Ciarra had all the gifts to go far in the business world. Great worker. Never complained. Worked long hours. Went above and beyond her duties when needed. The only problem with Ciarra was that she didn't know her potential. But that was okay because I did. That was the reason I rescued her from the Projects and sat her ass at my receptionist's desk.

"Secure that door and come and help me with something," I told her.

After locking and closing the door, she walked over and stood in front of my desk. "What do you need help with?"

"I'm having trouble with this. Would you take a look?"

She looked down at my empty desk and then at me. Confusion lit her eyes. She was about to speak until I shoved my chair back a little, revealing that I was naked from the waist down. When she saw my hard dick pointing in the air like a missile, her blue eyes, contacts of course, turned into mischievous little slits.

"Now I see the problem. Looks like somebody ain't being taken care of at home," she said while kneeling between my legs.

"That's right, baby girl. I have a big problem and I need someone with your skills to fix it."

"You wouldn't have these kinds of problems if I was your wife," she commented while wrapping a hand around my pole. "You know that should be my house and ring."

"You know you mean more to me than a house and a ring," I confessed, shivering when she began placing kisses up and down the length of my dick.

"Then make it official, daddy. Put her and her kids out."

"Give it time, baby girl. Give it time. The Great Wall of China wasn't built over night. But I don't want to talk about my wife right now. In fact, I don't want to talk at all. Make me cum."

"Yes, daddy."

Those were her last words before taking my pipe down her throat. My eyelids closed and my eyes rolled to the back of my head as I enjoyed the best head in the world. Man, Ciarra could suck the hell out of a dick. If there was a dick sucking contest anywhere in the world I would drop everything and jump on a plane with her and the deed to my business and place everything I own on her oral skills. She knew when to go deep, when to use her tongue, when to play with the balls, and when to jack you off. She had turned oral sex into a form of art. A beautiful, pleasurable, mind blowing form of art. And it only took a few minutes for me to experience the pleasure.

"Oh shit! Damn!" I moaned as she sucked the juice out of me.

"Is that better, daddy?" she asked, looking up at me with those big, fake blue eyes.

"I feel so much better. Thank you, baby."

"I bet Brianna don't suck your dick like that," she commented while standing and straightening out her clothes.

Ciarra was damn right about that. Brianna couldn't touch Ciarra when it came to sex. Ciarra had grown up in the hood. Highland

Torn Between a Gangster and a Gentleman

Housing Projects used to be her stomping grounds. She learned how to trade sex for money at a young age. Her mother was a crackhead and her daddy was dead. It was either use her body or starve. Sleeping with the local drug dealers for money made her a pro by the time she turned 18. Brianna, on the other hand, was a different breed. When I met her in the nightclub all those years ago, I immediately recognized her potential. And my gamble had paid off. Now she was a college educated business owner and a great piece of arm candy to take to political events and conferences. She was well spoken, had tact, and the etiquette of a southern belle. Marrying Brianna was a good social and political decision. Keeping Ciarra around was a good business and pleasure decision. But I couldn't explain all of this to my side bitch at the moment. She was emotional when it came to me and would never understand.

"How about we leave Brianna out of our mouths for the rest of the day. Besides, your mouth is much more talented. But right now, we need to focus on this next move. I need you to take a trip with me to Green Bay. Can you find a babysitter?"

"Yeah. I'll have my sister watch the kids."

"Good. Make us hotel reservations. We'll spend the night and drive back in the morning. Now, get back out there and look pretty while I make some calls."

"Okay, daddy. I love you," she squealed while heading for the door.

"Love you, too, baby."

When she was gone, I called my wife to inform her of my trip.

"Hey, sweetheart," Brianna answered.

"Hey, baby. Listen, I just got a call and I have to make a trip. Got some business in Green Bay. Probably won't wrap up until tomorrow. Gotta next with some senators about a new prison reform bill that we're trying to get signed."

"Okay. Do you need me to come with you?"

"No, I'll go alone. I don't need a tag along this time. I'll give you a break since you spent the weekend with me in Madison. I know that was tough on you and I don't want to put you through that again so soon."

"Tough on me is an understatement, love." Brianna laughed. "But I'll do it again if you need me. I got your back, husband."

"Awe, thank you, baby. But I can handle this one alone."

"Okay. And I still want my island experience! I haven't forgotten."

"Give me a few weeks and we'll be soaking up some sun on the beach. But I have to go. Love you."

"Love you, too, baby."

After the call with my wife, I made a call to rent a limousine. I gathered Ciarra along with my trusted worker, personal security, and driver, Sergio. He had done prison time in 4 different states and knew to keep his mouth closed. He was one of my *high risk* drivers. High risk drivers were the ones that made *special* deliveries. I only had a hand full of them and I made sure I took care of them because they were the backbone of my business.

After piling in the limo, we left the city around 5 o'clock and arrived in the parking lot of Exclusive Gentlemen's Club in Green Bay, Wisconsin around 7. The upscale strip club was frequented by sports figures and entertainers. It was one of the hottest spots in Green Bay besides Lambeau Field. It was also my favorite spot to do business when I was in town.

Most of the lights were dim except those upon the stage. That part of the club was lit up like a football field. A sexy two-woman show was in full effect. Sergio headed in that direction while I craned my neck to check out the action as Ciarra and I headed toward the private rooms. A tall and beefy bouncer wearing a little black T-shirt was protecting the hallway.

"Which room is Clyde in?" I asked, palming him a 50-dollar bill as we shook hands.

"Room three." He nodded, allowing us to pass.

I found the room and walked in.

"B.B. King! What's up, nigga?" Clyde smiled, flashing a single gold front tooth.

I knew Clyde from back in the day. Back when we were both small time hustlers. Since the days of old, both our fortunes had

Torn Between a Gangster and a Gentleman

multiplied. "Smooth glide Clyde!" I grinned, giving my friend a hug and pat on the back.

Clyde was 51 years old and wore his thinning grey permed hair in a short ponytail. He was light skinned, almost red complexioned, average height, with a chubby build. "C'mon in here, nigga! And I see you brought company. She work here?" he asked eyeing Ciarra.

"Nope. She's with the company and there is a strict hands-off policy."

"Oh, shit. A keeper, huh? I ain't mad at chu, nigga. I only wanted to keep her for the night," he cracked.

"What you been drinking?" I asked as we had seats.

"Only the best, nigga. Have some of this Black Label," he said, handing me a bottle of Whitley Neill premium dry gin. There was also a plate on the table with about a quarter ounce of cocaine on it and a box of condoms.

"Pour us some glasses, baby," I said, handing Ciarra the bottle of liquor. "So, Clyde, tell me why you had me drive two hours to see you. What's on your mind?"

"I need your trucks, man. About three of them. I need some shit shipped from a spot in Indiana out to Bakersfield, California."

"You want to tell me what's being shipped?"

"Some high-tech shit, King. Classified government shit."

I normally set my prices at 5 grand for high risk shipments. But since we were talking, I was jacking it up. "I need fifteen thousand a truck."

"Eight," he countered.

"Twelve."

"Ten."

"Deal." I smiled.

He smiled too, showing the gold tooth. "Deal. Shit, I was willing to pay twenty a truck 'cause I need this shit moved yesterday. But ten is a damn good deal."

"I'll remember that next time. Get me the pick-up and drop-off information and we'll get those trucks rolling in the morning."

Clyde sat up, clapping his hands and rubbing them vigorously. "Good. Now that the business is over, let's get the party started. Get you some of that White Girl off that plate and I'mma call in some girls."

While he reached for the phone, I reached for the plate of cocaine. I made two nice sized lines and used the rolled up 20-dollar bill to treat my nose. It was good dope, so the effects were instantaneous. In less than 30 seconds I was high as a muthafucka! I passed the plate to Ciarra and let her get a taste. She was snorting her lines when there was a knock on the door. Clyde opened it and 3 women walked in. Two Asians and a white girl. All of them had toned and athletic bodies that they proudly showed off in bikini tops, thongs, and heels.

"I got yellow fever!" Clyde laughed, snapping his fingers and two stepping around the Asians.

The women began dancing with him, rubbing his body and grinding their little booties on him. The white woman came to me. She was very pretty with long green hair, green eyes, and studs in both cheeks. She also had some big ass titties that looked like they were about to bust out of the little bikini top. She danced in front of me for a moment before lowering the bikini top and flashing those big ass titties and big pink nipples.

"I like her, daddy," Ciarra purred, reaching out to rub the stripper's breasts.

The girl giggled, turning her attention to Ciarra and putting those big ass titties in her face. Ciarra flicked out her tongue and teased the woman's nipples. I liked what I was seeing. The cocaine had me high as an eagle and I was ready for some action.

"Show me how much you like her, baby," I said, encouraging my girl to show me a good time.

Ciarra stood and stripped from the blouse and skirt. When she was naked, her and the white woman began grinding on each other and kissing. They sat on my lap for a moment, each one sitting on a knee, taking turns kissing and rubbing me while helping remove my jacket and shirt. When I was bare chested, they went back to kissing and freaking one another. A moment later they were on the couch next to me in the 69, licking each other's pussies. The white woman on top. I watched them for a moment, loving the sight and sounds

Torn Between a Gangster and a Gentleman

of two women eating pussy. When my dick started hurting and it felt like my balls were about to explode, I stripped from the rest of my clothes, grabbed a condom from the box, and joined the party. I aimed my dick for the white woman's shaved pink pussy and slipped inside. Ciarra continued eating her pussy while I fucked her from behind. She was hot and wet. Felt good. So good that I started pounding that pussy. I was causing too much motion for Ciarra to keep eating her pussy, so my girl did other things. Like moving her head back a little more and sticking her tongue out. Every time I pulled out and thrust forward, Ciarra's tongue licked me from my ass crack to nut sack. I don't ever remember something feeling so damn good. And right when I was on the verge of busting, she shoved her tongue up my ass.

"Oh shit!" I groaned, filling the condom with my seed and falling back on the couch. "Y'all go ahead. I need a moment."

Ciarra and the stripper got right back to eating one another while I watched. When I looked toward Clyde, he was laying on his back while both Asian women took turns giving him head. Watching the women pass his dick back and forth made me want to get my dick sucked by 2 pair of lips. I grabbed the plate to do another line when I heard Clyde groan. I looked up as the women drank and shared his nut. Clyde looked paralyzed with pleasure. I definitely wanted next!

"Oh, B.B. I meant to tell you something," he panted as he sat up. "I caught a word about that nigga, Red Fox. Remember him?"

I paused to match a name with the face. "Yeah. We had some good times back in the day. What's up with the old pimp?"

"Word is he locked up in Vegas. Say the Feds try'na charge him with taking a minor across state lines for prostitution."

"Damn. Didn't he already get a rap for that a while back?"

"Yeah. He came from under that one. Word is he worked with the police to solve a murder."

That caught my attention. "Really?"

"Yep. And they say he try'na work out another deal. So, if you got loose ends that he might know about, make sure you tie them up."

I reached for my clothes. "C'mon, Ciarra. We gotta go!"

CHAPTER 4 - Ray

"R-Sun! What up, fool!"

"C'mon, Cray. You know it's just Ray. The old me is dead and gone," I said, quoting the throwback T.I. song as we shook hands.

"You know I'm just messing with you, brotha. I know you're a big-time stock investor now. Who would'da thought that you would stop robbing people and start investing and I would stop trafficking and open a couple of bars? Only in America!"

I laughed it up with my oldest friend as I took a seat at the bar. Cray was a 50-year-old ex-drug trafficker that I had known since I was a boy. He was average height with a husky build. His dark brown skin looked leathery from all the years of drinking and smoking. The short graying afro made him look like the twin brother of Red Fox.

"Yeah, man. Only in America. Why don't you pass me one of those Budweiser's," I said eyeing the bottles of beer in his cooler.

"No, problem, man. First one is on the house. So, what brings you by? What you been up to?"

"Nothing much. Just stopped by to say what's up. Junior at Faded getting his hair cut and I thought I'd check in on you."

"Oh, word? The little one is next door getting cut up? Man, I haven't seen him in a nice little while. Is he still playing ball?"

"Yep. One of the top players in the state. Got a game later tonight against Rufus King. I told him to come over when he's done getting cut up."

"Well, alright! I can't wait to see lil' man. That's good that he's taking hoops serious and not getting involved in them streets. I see that Brianna did right by him while you were gone."

I gave Cray a serious look when he mentioned my kids' mother.

"Shit. I forgot. I won't say her name no more."

I acknowledged Cray with a nod while taking a sip from the brew to wash away the mention of Brianna.

"What I meant to say was it's good that he's focused on positive things despite you being in prison most of his life. You know, most kids without a father end up in prison."

"Yeah. Or it could go the other way. I was raised by my pops and still ended up in prison."

"Your situation was different, Ray. You got dropped off on his doorstep by your mother. Hell, Reggie didn't know nothing about taking care of kids. He just got out of prison his self. He didn't have no education or plan. All he could do was give you a roof, food, and clothes. I miss that fool. Reggie was a good nigga."

"I know. I hate that he passed away while I was locked up. I would've loved to kick it with the old man one more time."

"Yeah, that cancer is a beast. But he fought 'til the end, Ray. And he did a good thing leaving you the money. If you think about it, your father's passing is what got you out. You got to buy a good lawyer. That was his hope. That the money would help you get out and give you a chance to start over and live a good life."

"I think about that all the time, Cray. I owe him and the only way to repay him is by being successful and not going back to that cage. He made sure I was taken care of and I love him even more for that."

Cray smiled at me. "You look just like yo' daddy, boy! Big nose and everything!" he cracked, bringing humor to the sad moment.

I shook my head and took another sip of beer. "So, how you been, man? How's business?"

"Same ol' thing. When you run a bar, you always got problems. Nothing I can't handle though. The problems I can't seem to handle are the ones with Irene. Think we headed for a divorce."

I was surprised to hear Cray speak the D word. "Divorce? Seriously? After fourteen years?"

"Yeah. She's tired of my cheating ways. Caught me with another woman about two weeks ago. Moved out of the house and in with her sister."

"Damn, Cray. This what? The fourth or fifth time?"

"Seventh."

All I could do was shake my head. "That's why I can't get married, man. Too much ass out here to settle for just one. I need variety."

Torn Between a Gangster and a Gentleman

"If I would've done all that time locked up like you, I would feel the same way. But I did two years in Camp Cookie back in '08. Irene was there for me and I felt like I owed her the ring for all her support."

"Yeah, I hear you, old timer. Had to do what you had to do. But I'mma tell you, man, life as a bachelor is not that bad. I like sex with no strings attached. I can dive in some new skins every day of the week if I want. And I don't have to worry about getting caught."

"Yeah, well, it looks like I'm headed in that direction. I just never pictured being a bachelor when I'm fifty."

I gave him a wink. "It's never too late to get back in the game."

"You're right about that." He nodded. "So, whatever happened to that green-eyed thang you was dealing with? The IG model?"

"You talking about Kaysha."

"Yeah, that's her. Girl finer than frog booty hair."

"Frog booty hair?" I laughed.

"Yeah, nigga. That's a different kind of fine right there. Rare."

"A'ight." I shook my head. "But you can hit her up on social media and give her a wave. I'm good on all that."

Cray looked shocked by my comment. "What happened, man? How you let a broad that fine get away?"

"She was getting clingy. Starting to develop feelings."

"Well, yeah. That's how women are. Emotional creatures."

"That's why I had to let her go. The only woman that had my heart broke it and I ain't going through that shit again. I don't deal in emotions."

Cray let out a sigh. "Yeah, I hear you on that, Ray. I don't like repeating the same mistakes either. What we gon' do?"

"I don't know about you, but I'mma finish this beer and order another one. Then, if you want, I'mma take you over to one of those pool tables you got and show you the fine art of billiards."

Cray looked at me like I insulted his mother. "You beating me at pool is like Oprah fucking Donald Trump. It'll never happen."

***

"Hey, Brittany. What you up to?" I asked my beautiful 12-year-old daughter as we chatted on Facebook Live.

"Hi, Daddy. Me and Sabrina just finished recording our new song."

"Oh, for real? When can I hear it?"

"It's not done yet. I'll send it to you when it's finished."

"Bet. Make sure I get to hear it first. I got the ear, remember?"

"I got you, Daddy." She giggled, looking just like a young Brianna.

"Cool. I'm at the mall with Junior. Do you want me to get you something?"

Her eyes lit up. "Yeah! Can you buy me some Fendi shoes to go with my jacket? It's white, black and gold."

"Fendi shoes?" I scoffed. "You think I'mma ATM? What happened to a pair of Jordan's or Air Max?"

"Please, Daddy! I need these shoes or I'mma die! Please!" she whined.

"You lucky that you are cute. I got you, baby girl. I'll drop them off later."

"Thank you! Love you, Daddy."

"Love you, too."

I had just hung up the phone when someone caught my eye. A pretty woman with blonde hair walked by and gave me a look that let me know she wanted me. She wore royal blue sports leggings and a sports bra that showed a nicely toned body. She also had a basket full of vitamins and supplements that told how serious she was about her health. I craned my neck to follow her through the store, hoping that we would bump into each other on the way out.

"I'm killing 'em at my game tonight, dad. Ja Morant numbers. I'm going ham!" my son bragged.

"What you say?" I asked, my attention distracted by the woman.

"I'm going for a triple double tonight. Twenty, ten, and ten."

"Those are pretty good numbers. You sure you can do that?"

Junior looked at me like I had spoken another language. "You probably can't do it, but I can."

Torn Between a Gangster and a Gentleman

I returned the look that he had given me. "Better watch your mouth before I take you to one of these courts and ruin your self-esteem. I ain't those kids you play against. Your arm too short and your legs too small."

A challenge flashed in his eyes. "What! Let's leave right now. Only reason you won the last time was because you cheated. I can beat you, dad. You know it and I know it."

The gleam in my son's eyes let me know that he wouldn't rest until he beat me. He was hungry and determined. The day would come when he would beat me, but I was going to hold him off for as long as I could.

"Let's go up to this counter so I can pay for my vitamins. I'mma show you that it's only room for one Mandingo in our family."

As we headed toward the cashier, I seen the woman that had given me googly eyes already standing in line. When she noticed me approaching, she gave me the flirty look again, her eyes dancing over the form fitting compression shirt I wore.

"Who is that?" Junior asked, noticing the woman stalking me.

"I don't know. But we're about to find out."

"You like white girls?" he asked, sounding a little surprised.

"Quick life lesson, son. Never judge a book by its cover. All blessings don't look the same. The only way you will figure out what you like and what you don't like is to give it a try. Feel me?"

"Yeah." He nodded. "I feel you."

"Good. Now watch the master in action." I held eye contact with the woman as we approached, her blue eyes holding me in a mini trance. "Good afternoon." I smiled. "How are you doing?"

"Fine. Just making a vitamin run? You?"

"I'm good. I was just telling my son how an ordinary day can turn into an extraordinary one in a matter of moments. You agree?"

She smiled with her lips and eyes. "I do."

I extended a hand. "My name is Ray and this is my son, Ray Junior."

She placed a small and soft hand in mine. "I'm Amanda. Nice to meet you guys."

"You look like an Amanda. And I mean that in the best way possible," I joked.

"And you guys look like Ray's. And I mean that in the best way possible, too." She laughed.

After sharing a laugh, I nodded to her basket. "You have a lot of supplements in there. What do you do?"

"I'm a yoga instructor. Keeps me young."

"And limber." I winked, giving her body a head-to-toe look.

She smiled again. "Yes. And limber, too. Very limber."

I needed to hurry up and get her number before we violated my son's ears. "I've been thinking about getting into yoga for a while but I never could find a class or instructor. Can I get your information and schedule a lesson? Maybe you can show me how to do a proper downward dog."

"Yes, I would love that," she said pulling out her phone. "I think you would love to see my downward dog."

"What's a downward dog?" Junior asked.

"A yoga position that you don't know nothing about, son."

After getting Amanda's number and paying for my vitamins, I took Junior to the nearest basketball court. Ended up at McGovern Park on Silver Spring Drive.

"Alright. We playing to seven. Behind the three-point line is worth two points. Make it, take it. Take around is the free throw line. We shoot for ball," I said, going over the rules of play.

Junior put the ball in my chest. "We don't need to shoot. Your ball, dad. You need all the help you can get."

I laughed at my son's bravado. He was a confident kid that toed the line of cockiness. But I guess when you were 15 years old, averaging almost 20 points a game, and one of the best players in the state, you could be cocky. As he stood in front of me to defend, I sized him up. He was well built at 5'10" and 180 pounds. He wore a size 10 in shoes and hands were big enough to palm the basketball.

"Remember what I said, lil' nigga. It's only one Mandingo in our family," I repeated as we checked the ball.

"I'm the Mandingo, dad." He grinned, passing the ball back.

Torn Between a Gangster and a Gentleman

When I got the ball, I wasted no time getting to work. I outweighed him by 40 pounds and had a 4-inch height advantage. I used that advantage to back him down into the post and muscle up a lay-up. "One-zip, Mandingo," I bragged.

"You charged me and used your shoulder. But it's all good. Let's go."

I went back at him with the same move, but he was ready this time. When I banged into him and attempted the layup, he absorbed this contact and stripped the ball.

"Let me get this, old man," he talked smack, stepping back to the free throw line.

I went out to defend and he let off a shot in my face. Nothing but net.

"One-one." He smiled.

After checking the ball, he pump-faked like he was about to take another jumper. I bit and attempted to block the shot. He went right around me and did a high-flying two-handed dunk. "Two-one, my way," he said.

After his display of quickness and agility, I decided to play off him to stop him from attacking the rim. He made me pay by sinking 2 jumpers in a row. He missed the third one and I grabbed the rebound.

"One-four. That's it for you, lil' man," I said, stepping back to the 3-point line. He tried to chase but I got off the shot before he could close out. Made the net go *swish*. "Three-four, your way," I said, calling out the score before making my way to the 3-point line again and firing another one. "Five-four, Mandingo's way. If you say sorry, I'll forget about the challenge and keep this between us."

"Yeah right, old school. I got you right where I want you," he said, refusing to back down.

After a check ball, I drove to the rim hard, using my size and strength to get an easy basket. Unfortunately, Junior wasn't giving up anything easy. I jumped for the layup and he jumped with me, except he jumped higher. When his hand blocked the ball, it sounded like someone being slapped.

41

"Get that garbage outta here!" he yelled, sending the ball flying. He moved quickly to grab the ball before it went out of bounds. His next two scores were attacks at the rim. Each time he shook me with the dribble and got past me for a layup. "Six-five my way, dad. You okay? You look kind of tired. You want to call it quits right now? I won't tell nobody you quit."

My son was good at ball and he knew it. If he kept the drive and determination to get better, there was no doubt that he would be playing professional ball one day. It wouldn't be long before I wouldn't be able to beat him. I had to get my wins in now.

"Let's go, talker. All you do is talk. When you miss, game over."

Junior gave a sinister smile while dribbling the ball toward me. I held my ground, ready to steal the ball if he was careless. He dribbled right and then left. When I thought I had the ball bounce timed, I went for the steal. Junior did a quick crossover, changing direction in an instant. My momentum wouldn't allow me to stay in front of him. He took off toward the rim and all I could do was watch as he took off for another high-flying dunk. Which he missed. The ball bounced off the rim, flying a few feet away from me. I tracked down the peel and raced to the 3-point line. I wanted to end the game now. This was my opportunity. Junior raced toward me as I set up for the shot. He jumped to block the ball, his fingertips just a few inches away as the ball left my hands. The shot was high arching and seemed to float in the air forever. When it found the orange cylinder, it went right in. Nothing but net.

"I told you its only one Mandingo in our family, lil' nigga!"

CHAPTER 5 - Ray

"Hey, mama!" I grinned, giving the only woman I ever called mom a hug and kiss on the cheek.

"Hey, Ray! Hey, grandson! What a pleasant surprise!" Mom beamed, accepting our hugs and kisses. Mom was Brianna's mother. Misses Earlene Swear. She was a 52-year-old, big boned, Jesus-loving Creole woman from New Orleans. Mom only stood 5 feet tall, but what she lacked in height she made up with her many other talents. Cooking was my personal favorite talent of hers and why we showed up.

"We just came from my game, Granny. I killed 'em. Twenty-three points, thirteen rebounds, and nine assists," Junior bragged as we walked in the house.

"That's good, baby! I'm so proud of you. You gon' be the next Kobe Jordan!"

"Kobe Bryant or Michael Jordan," I corrected.

She gave me the, *boy, don't correct me look*. "I don't care about they names, and you know what I meant. Either way, my grandson is good. Y'all hungry? I was just about to put the food up."

"I see we showed up just in time!" I smiled, rubbing my stomach.

This was the reason we came over. To eat some real food. I had been eating fast food for the last couple of days and was starving for a home cooked meal. I knew Mom always had leftovers. Cooking is what she did. It was her hobby.

"Where is Brittany?" Mom asked as she made plates.

"At home. I have Junior with me for a couple of days," I explained. "Did Brittany tell you about the new song she recorded with Sabrina?"

"I heard it yesterday. It was a really good song. My granddaughters are so blessed with those voices. I want to get them in my church choir so their voices can be nurtured. Brittany must've got that voice from somebody on your side of the family because can't nobody on my side hold a note." She laughed.

"I don't know about that one. Pop wasn't a singer. He could barely sing the ABC song."

"Oh, you're so wrong, Ray!" Mom laughed. "You know I liked your father. He was a good man. And that was the right thing to do by leaving you that life insurance policy. I called and got a policy for myself the other day. I want to leave something to my girls when I go."

"That's the right thing to do," I nodded. "Pops never even told me about the policy. One day I'm sitting in my cell and the guard come talking about a lawyer visit. I go see him and he shows me the policy and has me sign for a hundred thousand dollars. I couldn't believe it."

"I wish grandad could've lived long enough to see me play," Junior cut in.

"Me, too. He would've been proud of you, man."

"What about your mother? Where is she?"

"I don't know, man." I shrugged. "I don't know nothing about her except her name. Pop said she dropped me off on his porch when I was three and never came back. Pop did the best he could to raise me, but he didn't know how to raise a kid. Buying me clothes, feeding me, sending me to school, and keeping a roof over my head was about all he knew to do. He never graduated high school and spent most of his life in and out of prison, and hustling so he couldn't tell me that much about the real world. By the time I turned fifteen and started running the streets, he let me go. And because of what I went through with my dad is why I'm making sure that you're doing what you're supposed to do."

"You don't gotta worry about me, dad. I'm going to the NBA. I don't care about try'na be hard or being in the streets. I want to be rich and have my own shoes."

"I know that's right!" Mom cut in. "Your daddy tried that thug life and you see where it got him."

"Nowhere but a cell box. I'm so glad that part of my life is over." I sighed.

"We are, too. The Lord works in mysterious ways, son. I always told you that you were coming home. Didn't I? Told you to just

Torn Between a Gangster and a Gentleman

keep this faith," Mom said as she placed two plates filled with food on the table. Baked chicken, dressing, biscuits from scratch, candied yams, and collard greens.

"Yeah, you did. And I had just about run out of faith until that lawyer showed up. A technicality, Mom. I'm sitting in this kitchen with you and Junior because of a technicality. The appeal attorney that I hired found out I was issued bogus jury instructions. Now, I'm here."

"It wasn't a technicality, son. It was God," Mom corrected.

"Yeah, dad. It was God. We used to pray for you to come home all the time. God heard us, huh, Granny?"

"That's right, baby. He's always on time. So, what are you doing with your money?" Mom asked while we stuffed our faces.

"I'm playing with the stock market for now. That's how the politicians get rich. Gotta have a diversified portfolio. Only pay fifteen percent taxes on capital gains."

"Well, whatever you just said, I wish you luck. Sounds like you did a lot of reading while you was locked up."

"I did. Read everything from Socrates to Egyptian mythology. I'm trying to tell Junior that girls love smart guys with swag. Wish I would've known that when I was fifteen."

"My drip is super saucy, dad. I'm a swag surfing three-point-o student. Act like you don't know," Junior bragged.

"You want to impress me, get that GPA up to a four-point-o and then you would be untouchable."

After filling our bellies with the best food on the planet, we gave Mom hugs and kisses before heading back to my place. During the drive, I decided to get in Junior's business.

"So, what's up, man? You still a virgin?"

"What?" he asked, raising an eyebrow and voice rising a few octaves.

"You heard me, nigga. You got any cuddy yet?"

My son was handsome. Basically a light skinned, better looking version of me. And the fact that he had a promising hoops career made the girls flock to him like pigeons on breadcrumbs. I had accidentally snuck onto his Facebook page a few times when he left it up. Some of the comments left by his fans and groupies were too mature for TV. The girls were a lot faster than they were when I was 15.

"C'mon, dad. I don't want to talk about this with you," he said, shifting nervously.

"Why not? You supposed to have these conversations with me. I'mma tell you the truth. So, what's up? You smashing yet?"

"Dad!" he whined.

I continued to press. "Don't 'dad' me. Tell me, man."

"Okay. No, I never did it before. I'm still a virgin."

"That's cool. Nothing wrong with that. But you won't be a virgin forever. Just make sure you strap up and wear a condom when you do. You have a lot of potential to be great. There are some girls out there that will try to trap you with a baby to get a free ride. You have to make sure you wear rubbers and don't slip up. Okay?"

"Yeah, I know. Mom told me."

"That's good. So, do you got a girl yet?"

"Nah. I just have a lot of girl friends."

I waved a hand at him. "Yeah, right. You don't have girls sweating you like that."

"Uh huh! I got plenty of game. More game than you."

"Is that a challenge? You seen how I got at Amanda in the vitamin store."

"That wasn't nothing, dad. She was definitely a thotty. Anybody could've got that. But I bet fifty dollars that I got more game than you."

I looked over in the passenger's seat to see if he was joking. His stare was unblinking and serious. "Man, I'm about to take all of your allowance money." I laughed. "Okay. This what I'mma do. I'mma point to a girl and you gotta get her number. You do the same to me. We go until somebody get shot down."

"Bet," he accepted.

I had been driving for about 5 minutes when I spotted the first girl for him. A brown skinned teenage girl was standing on the bus stop alone. "There she go." I pointed before pulling into the gas station across the street.

46

Torn Between a Gangster and a Gentleman

"Too easy." He grinned, hopping out of the truck and strolling confidently across the street. He approached the girl and they began talking. When she smiled, I knew Junior was getting her number. A few more words and then he pulled out his phone. Looked like she was saying her number while he punched it into the phone. A few more words and he was strolling back toward the gas station. The smile he wore spread from ear to ear.

"Lelani. Here go her number," he said, flashing the phone number in my face.

"Okay, okay. You did your thing. Now you get to watch the master in action, again," I said, about to pull out of the gas station.

"Wait!" he stopped me. "You gotta get her number."

I looked to where his finger was pointing. A blue Hyundai had just pulled up to a pump. The woman behind the wheel looked familiar but I wasn't sure if she was who I thought she was because of the glare of the gas station's lights on her window. When she got out of the car, I was able to see her face. I recognized her immediately. "Nah, man. Not her. Pick somebody else."

"No, dad. You gotta do who I pick. You made the rules."

"But I know her."

"Well, that should make it easy."

"C'mon, man. That's my P.O."

He looked surprised for a moment. Then the surprised look was replaced by dollar signs in his eyes. "Get her number or give me my money."

I gave a pleading look, hoping he would change his mind. "C'mon, man."

He stuck his hand out, wanting payment.

"Lil' busta," I mumbled while climbing from my F-150.

I knew that I was taking a big risk by trying to spit game at my P.O. If she wanted, she could fry my ass for this. But I couldn't back down to my son. I had to give it a shot. I studied my parole officer as I approached from her blind side. She had crazy curves. Figure 8 like a race car track. Stacked on the top and bottom. Her skin was dark as hell, what we used to call blue-black when I was growing up. She wasn't all that attractive in the face. The big forehead and nose made her look like she could be Serena Williams sister. Her hair was cut low into a curly sandy brown afro. But what she lacked in beauty she made up with her style and sex appeal. And her giant booty.

She was already pumping gas, oblivious that I was ogling her body.

"Miss Abo? Hey, how are you?" I asked, acting like I just noticed her.

"Mr. Preston, how are you?" she asked with a heavy East African accent.

"Good, good. Let me help you with that," I offered, taking the gas pump and pumping her gas.

"Oh, you are so nice. What're you doing here?"

"I was on my way home. Just came from my son's game," I said nodding toward the truck. Junior watched us like we were a Netflix show.

"Awe! He so cute. Look just like you. Hi!" She waved.

Junior waved back.

Now was my moment to put up or shut. "Um, so listen, Nilanti. I was wondering if we could get a bite to eat sometime. Maybe discuss my case file, you know?"

The surprise at my request flashed in her eyes. Then she blushed, turning a shade darker. "Mr. Preston, are you hitting on me?"

"Um, kind of," I said nervously. I wasn't nervous about her response. I knew that all she could do was accept or reject the offer. But what I was nervous about was whether or not she would take offense and report me. That wouldn't look good on my record.

"I'm very flattered, Mr. Preston, but I cannot date a client. It would be unethical."

"Not a date, just a meal," I clarified.

She giggled. "Ahh, Mr. Preston, I tink you are a very charming and handsome man, but I cannot."

I shrugged off the rejection. "Okay. Cool. You can't blame a brotha for trying. It's just, I've always wanted to visit the motherland," I said, letting my eyes travel down her body.

Torn Between a Gangster and a Gentleman

"Ha!" she laughed. "You are very charming. Finish your parole. Den we will see if you are serious about my motherland."

There was something about the way she said those last words that left an impression on me. When I walked back to my truck, I left without her number. But I did do something else. I created an opportunity.

"Gimmie my money, dad!" Junior said, sticking his hand in my face when I climbed back in the truck.

Torn Between a Gangster and a Gentleman

CHAPTER 6 - Brianna

"Hey, Brianna. What are you doing over here?"

"Well, hey, Tamar. I'm happy to see you too, sister," I sassed while standing at the screen door, waiting to be allowed inside.

"Stop playing, girl. You know it ain't like that. I'm used to people calling before they show up. I wasn't expecting you. C'mon in."

My sister Tamar was 5 years older than me but swore she was 10 years my senior. As far as a relationship, we were closer than close. We told each other everything and were each other's best friend. Like me, Tamar also had 2 kids. Sabrina was 14 and Sarita was 1 year old.

"Look at the little baby! Hi, little mama!" I gushed, picking my niece up from the carpet.

She smiled and laughed as I got a slobbery kiss.

"Don't you want to take your niece for a couple of days and give me a break?" Tamar asked, running a hand through her wild mane.

My sister was a very pretty woman. Light brown skin, long hair, brown eyes, and curves that demanded everyone's attention whenever she entered a room. But today she looked beat. Her hair was wild, she had bags under her eyes, and the holy sweatpants and dingy t-shirt did nothing to help her cause.

"I love you like cooked food, big sister, but I'm not taking any babies home. Teenagers cost more but are less maintenance. But you can drop her off by the daycare anytime you want. Better get your tubes tied and then enjoy the rest of your thirties."

"I'm surely thinking about it. But I want to keep my options open for when I find my Mr. Right. I want the baby and the ring."

I gave her a look that let her know I wasn't buying the bullshit she was trying to sell.

"Don't look at me like that, girl. I know you talking about Armani. He was a mistake that gave me my blessing. But he ain't shit. That's why I need one more go at it with the right man. Plus, your tubes ain't tied so don't try to give advice that you won't take for yourself."

"I don't need to do that. Benny got a vasectomy."

"Benny ain't the one you gotta worry about getting pregnant by." She smirked.

My eyes popped and mouth dropped open. "I know you didn't just go there!"

"Girl, stop playing. Ain't nobody in this house but me, you, and Sarita. I know you still love Ray. You know you still love Ray. And if Sarita could talk, she would say exactly what I'm saying. Hell, Ray might even still know that you love him."

I sighed and sat my niece back on the carpet as I flopped onto the couch. "You ain't no good, you know that?"

"You know it's all love, baby sis. I just never experienced the kind of love that you have for Ray. I love Sabrina's father to death, but if I lived in a half million-dollar house and was married to a millionaire, Damon would be the last man on earth that I would think about."

"But Ray was my first everything. First love, first orgasm, kids, and all that. I mean, don't get me wrong, I love Benny. He's an amazing man and husband. But I still feel connected to Ray. I think he's my soulmate."

"See, that's what I'm talking about. That soulmate shit. I never felt that. I want that. That's why I won't get my tubes tied."

Hearing my sister cheer for soulmates and love while thinking about Ray made my mood take a nosedive. "You wanna know what the worst feeling in the world is?"

"What? And why do you sound like the world is about to end?"

"I went by Ray's house to drop Junior off a couple weekends ago because I needed to go to Madison with Benny. Well, I put on my good white Louis Vuitton jeans and was oozing sex appeal. I was hoping to get in a few words with him and figure out what's the problem between us because ever since he's come home, he acts like he hates being around me. Won't even step a foot in my house. I wanted to talk to him to see if we could at least be friends. Well, when I walked in the house, him and a little green-eyed bitch was sitting on the recliner half naked. Seeing him with another woman

Torn Between a Gangster and a Gentleman

felt like I had been stabbed in the heart. I had never been so jealous in my life. I wanted to decapitate her and castrate him."

Tamar bust out laughing.

I gave her the look.

"I'm not laughing at you, Brianna. I'm laughing because I can't believe you got so mad that you wanted to kill her and cut off his balls! Damn. That sounds worse than when you got dressed up in the red dress to meet him at Junior's game and he ignored you."

I rolled my eyes. "Yeah, thanks for reminding me about that."

Tamar bust out laughing again.

"Laugh it up, Tickle Me Elmo."

"I'm sorry, Brianna. I am. I can't help it. I'm sorry."

"Forget you. I'm leaving," I said, getting up from the couch.

"No, no! Don't leave!" she said, grabbing my arm. "I won't laugh no more. I promise."

After giving her a stare that let her know I would cut her if she laughed again, I sat back down. "I wish I would've stuck by his side when he went to prison. I was just so young and confused."

"Plus, he got all that time. I didn't think he was ever coming home again. I would've left his ass too. You can't put your life on hold just because he got locked up. He was the one robbing those people, not you."

"It still don't feel right. I seen the judge give him a hundred years for those robberies. I was eighteen years old with two kids. I never thought he was coming home. I thought he was going to die in prison, and I didn't want to suffer with him. I had to leave him to keep my sanity. I went five years without talking to him and fell in love and married Benny. Then one day my phone rings and it's him. Just hearing his voice made me fall in love with him all over again. But he didn't want to talk to me. He said he called to speak to the kids."

When Tamar saw the pain in my eyes and heard it in my voice, all of the humor was gone. "Damn, Brianna. You never told me about that phone call. C'mon, we can go castrate his ass together. I'll hold him down."

That made me laugh. "You so damn crazy!"

53

The doorbell rang, interrupting our sisterly moment.

"That was right on time because you about to have my ass up in here crying with you and Ray's love story. Let me see who at the door."

While my sister went to answer the door, I got on the floor to play with Sarita. I was shaking a block shaped rattle at my niece when I heard Tamar arguing with a man. I picked up Sarita and went to investigate. The door was slightly open with Tamar blocking it from opening all the way.

"Who is it?" I asked.

"Armani's no-good ass," she yelled to me before turning her attention back to him. "Get off my porch, nigga. If you ain't got no milk, money, or pampers for my baby then you ain't coming in."

"Let me see my daughter, Tamar! Quit playing and open this door before I kick this mu'fucka in and fuck you up!"

Hearing the threat of violence put me on edge. Armani was crazy and I didn't want to experience the craziness.

"Why don't you let him come in for a few minutes, Tamar?" I asked, trying to keep the peace.

"Hell nah! His no-good ass ain't shit. He ain't did nothing for my baby since she was born. His ass—"

She was cut off by Armani trying to push the door open. "Bitch, open this door! Open this door right now!"

Tamar held her ground, keeping him from getting in the house. I joined in, helping her close the door. "Fuck you, Armani!" Tamar screamed.

Armani went crazy kicking at the door and Sarita started crying. I was torn between two choices: call the police or Benny. I chose my husband.

"Hey, honey bunch. How you doing?"

"Benny, we need help. I'm by Tamar's house and Armani is trying to kick the door in. We—"

Boom!

The sound of him kicking open the door scared the hell out of me. I turned my head just in time to see Armani charging into the house with a gun.

Torn Between a Gangster and a Gentleman

"I told yo' ass to open this mufuckin' door! Who you on the phone with, Brianna! That bet not be the police!" he yelled, snatching my phone and hanging it up.

"What the fuck are you doing, Armani? Get out!" Tamar yelled.

"Shut the fuck up, bitch! Get y'all asses in the living room!" he yelled, forcing us to sit on to couch. "I came over here to see my daughter and y'all gon' sit there while I spend time with my princess."

I stayed quiet and allowed Armani to take Sarita from my arms. He was on some crazy shit and I didn't want him to start shooting. Tamar, on the other hand, didn't feel as threatened for her safety as I did.

"I can't believe you kicked in my door and pointed a gun at me, nigga. I swear to God I'm calling the police when you leave. And I'm telling them you raped me, too."

He pointed the gun at her. "If you call the police on me, I'mma kill yo ass. Think I'm playing? I'll kill all of us right now."

"No, Armani!" I screamed. "I won't let her call the police. I swear to God. Go ahead and spend some time with Sarita."

"Whose side are you on?" Tamar snarled at me.

"I'm trying to make it home to my kids. Just let him see his daughter. At least he's trying."

"That's right, Brianna. Tell that bitch. I'm try'na do the right thing but she won't let a nigga."

Tamar mugged him. "Call me another bitch and I'mma fuck you up," she promised.

Armani smiled. "Bitch."

I tried to grab Tamar but she was quicker than I expected. She jumped up from the couch and ran at her baby daddy like a wild woman. He pointed the gun at her but didn't shoot. And that was his mistake. She punched him in the jaw before a wrestling match ensued. Sarita was caught in the middle.

"Stop, y'all!" I yelled, reaching for my niece. After sitting the baby on the couch, I ran back to the fight to break it up. I grabbed Tamar around the waist and pulled as hard as I could. We ended up in a pile on the floor.

"Stupid ass bitch!" Armani yelled, pointing the gun at us, about to squeeze the trigger.

"Yo, Armani! What's up, brotha?"

I recognized the voice instantly. And so did Armani. He froze in his tracks like a statue as we all turned toward the door. In walked my husband in a charcoal gray tailored suit and one of his drivers. Anger lit his eyes on fire, his face serious as I've ever seen.

"Oh shit! Benny Boston! What's going on, brah?" Armani asked humbly, sounding like he was addressing Barack Obama.

"You what's going on, Armani. Why do you have a gun and why is my wife on the floor?" he asked before turning to me and helping me and my sister from to floor. "Baby, you okay?"

"I'm fine. Just a little scared."

"Uh... Me and Tamar was arguing," Armani stammered. "We having some problems about our daughter. I just wanna see her. I didn't touch yo wife, man. My bad for scaring her with the banger," he apologized, tucking the gun.

"You realize that kicking in doors and pulling out a gun won't help you to see your daughter, right? These are women and this is a child. No need for guns, brotha," Benny admonished, speaking to Armani like he was a son.

I was surprised to see the wild and violent man so humbled by my conservative business owning husband. I knew Benny had respect in the streets, but I had never seen it. Until now.

"You, right, Benny. But I didn't touch them. Ask 'em."

Benny turned to Tamar. "What happened?"

Armani attempted to answer. "I told you, Benny. It was—"

"Be quiet, nigga. I'm talking to Tamar," Benny said firmly.

I half expected Armani to start cursing, casting threats, and pull out his gun. But he didn't. He lowered his head and kept quiet.

"He ain't shit, Benny. Fuck him. He kicked my door in because I told him don't come over if he don't got shit for my baby. He don't do nothing for her. I'm calling the police on his punk ass. And he better pay for my door!"

"Everything is fine, baby," I spoke up. "He didn't hit us. Just kicked in the door and scared us."

"Alright. Chill out, Tamar, and I'll take care of everything. No need to call the police. Will have somebody fix the door? You just take care of that cute little daughter of yours and I'll take care of the rest. Brianna, I'm going take a ride with Armani and get all this sorted out. Why don't you stay with your sister until my guy comes to fix the door? He shouldn't take that long."

"Okay, baby," I managed as me and Tamar looked at my husband like he was the cure to all the diseases in the world. Watching him save the day was so damn sexy. Just thinking about what I was going to do to him when he got home got my panties so wet that it felt like I peed.

J-Blunt & Miss Kim

CHAPTER 7-Ray

"Twenty-one, twenty-two, twenty-three. Urrr, twenty-four. Twenty-five!"

After finishing another set of handstand pushups, I pushed off the wall and grabbed a fifty pound weight plate. I was in the middle of a grueling workout. 25 Handstand pushups, 25 sit ups with the 50-pound plate on my torso, 25 weighted squats, and 50 jumping jacks. I was 2 sets in, aiming for 10.

"You're so hot," Amanda commented, watching me from the recliner.

It was still early, around 8:30. I'd been awake for an hour. I had to watch my boy Buy or sell and Amanda was an early riser, so we lounged around the living room in our underwear and listened to stock advice. Afterwards, the workout.

"I thought you were supposed to be stretching. What happened?" I asked, sitting on the floor and beginning the weighted sit-ups.

"I was, but you're distracting me. You have a great body. I ever told you that?" She smiled, showing off Crest strip whitened teeth.

"You might've mentioned it a time or two."

Actually, she complimented my body a lot. It had been a couple weeks since I met her in the vitamin store. Every time we got together, she constantly touched and complimented my body. Still wasn't sure how I felt about it yet.

"I'm just so... I mean... I... Look at what you're doing to me. I can't even get my words out." She laughed.

"I tend to have that effect on the ladies." I smiled, giving her a wink while finishing another set of sit-ups. I burned through sets of squats and jumping jacks while Amanda did yoga stretches. Her stretches were sexy as hell and she wasn't self-conscious about showing her body. She positioned herself so I could see all the goodies and so she could watch me as well. I flipped into a handstand, the heels of my feet against the wall to keep balance as I did more upside-down pushups.

"I have an idea." Amanda smiled, crawling toward me like a sexy white cat. Her breasts jiggled and nipples poked through the fabric of her bra, hard as diamonds.

"Wait. We gotta finish the workout first," I said, wanting to finish exercising before getting in a morning round.

Amanda ignored my words, kneeling in front of me and pulling my dick through the hole in my boxers. When she sucked me into her mouth, I closed my eyes for a moment, loving the feeling of being down her throat. Amanda ignored the sweat as she devoured my piece like a delicious treat.

"Damn, girl! You don't know how to take no for an answer," I moaned, struggling to hold myself in the handstand.

One of the many things that I liked about Amanda was her love of giving head. Could literally suck me for hours and not get tired of it. She was a pleaser. It gave her pleasure to make me feel good. While her head bobbed back and forth, I tried to ignore the small fires building in my arms and shoulders. A few minutes later, my body was shaking uncontrollably from the stress that my full bodyweight was putting on my shoulders. And on top of that, I was about to bust.

"Amanda, stop. I need to get down. I'm about to fall."

She ignored my words, holding me against the wall as she continued sucking. I could feel the blood rushing to my head as my balls began to spasm.

"Awe shit!" I groaned, exploding in her mouth as my shoulders gave out. I collapsed to the floor, lightheaded as hell as my seed sprayed everywhere.

"Damn! That was so fucking hot! I'm so turned on right now."

"Yeah, well I'm about to wreck your shit. You gon pay for that," I said, struggling to get up. My arms felt like rubber.

Amanda pulled off her panties and kicked them across the room. "Oh yeah, Ray. I've been so fucking bad. Spank me," she purred, crawling toward me.

She put a dip in her back, pushing her firm cheeks high in the air. As I approached her from behind, her shaved and wet pink pussy winked at me. I loved hitting her from the back because she didn't

Torn Between a Gangster and a Gentleman

have that much ass so nothing was stopping me from getting deep in them guts. But before giving her the D, I had to inflict some pain before pleasure.

"You been a bad girl this morning," I said, caressing her ass before giving it a slap.

"Oh, yes! I'm a bad girl. So fucking bad," she moaned. "Spank me some more, Ray."

I gave her what she wanted, turning that ass pink with my handprints before getting in a round of sex on the floor and another in the shower. When we were finally able to pull ourselves apart, we got dressed and headed to our vehicles. I had to go check in with my P.O. and she had to go to work. She owned a yoga studio.

"Can we get together again in a couple of days? I have to go up north with my parents for a couple of days. Thirtieth anniversary," Amanda was saying as we walked down my walkway to her red Toyota Avalon.

"Wow! Thirty years. Gotta be a record nowadays."

"That's nothing. My grandparents were married sixty years."

"That shit sounds foreign. Sixty years with one person? I don't know," I scoffed.

"Oh, stop, Ray. One day you'll meet somebody that'll make you turn in your player card. Might've already met her," she winked.

"I don't know what a player card is. You be on social media too much."

She stopped to look in my eyes. "What happened? Did she cheat on you?"

I knew what she was talking about but I didn't want to get into it. "What are you talking about?"

"I'm talking about the woman that broke your heart. That's why you don't want to settle down. You don't want to feel that heartbreak again. I felt like you when I found out my husband and my best friend were fucking around. But the pain eventually goes away."

I stared into her blue eyes for a moment, identifying with the pain of betrayal reflecting inside her irises. "Call me when you get back in town," I said before pecking her lips.

61

She smiled at my side stepping the emotional conversation. "You will heal in time, Ray. I'll be in touch. Need some more of that bow-chica-wow-wow!" She giggled before giving me a hug.

After parting ways with Amanda, I hopped in my truck and headed to my P.O.'s office. I checked in with an older black woman at the front desk before taking a seat in the small waiting area. As I waited for Nilanti to come and get me, I thought about our run in at the gas station a couple weeks ago. She told me to finish parole and then she would see if I was serious. I still had 2 years left. I wondered if there was any way to expedite the process.

"Mr. Preston?"

I looked up as seen Nilanti standing in this doorway to my right. She was looking good in the beige blouse, form fitting jeans, and heels. "Good morning," I smiled while walking over.

"Good morning to you, too. How are you?" she asked, her accent heavy.

"I'm good. Looking forward to my monthly meeting with the best P.O. in the world."

"Best P.O. in da world, huh?" She laughed. "You are still trying to charm me, huh?"

"If the truth is charming, then I'm guilty."

She shook her head. "Follow me."

We walked through the door and down a hallway filled with small offices the size of cubicles. During the walk, most of my attention was on her giant bouncing booty. I wanted to grab it so bad.

"We will see—" she was saying, turning around and catching me looking at her booty. Her eyes squinted, face frowned, and she shook her head. She didn't say another word until we were standing face to face outside her office door. "Still worried about my motherland, huh?"

"It's a big, beautiful continent," I complimented.

She laughed. "Come and sit down. Let us talk about what has happened since we met last month."

I followed her into the office and sat in the red plastic chair in front of her desk. She didn't have many personal effects around the

Torn Between a Gangster and a Gentleman

small office except a diploma from the University of Madison on the wall.

After sitting behind her desk, she picked up my file from a stack and opened it. "Buy any-ting new? Get a job? Start a business? Police contact?"

"No, to all of those."

"So, do you want to work? I know you have a lot of money, but maybe you should do some-ting wit your time."

"I'm doing some investing right now. I've been thinking about signing up four school and getting a degree. I'm also thinking about starting a business. I'm torn between a recording studio or buying into a franchise."

"A recording studio?"

"Yeah. My daughter and her cousin are really good singers. I'm thinking about investing in them."

"Hmph. Okay. Keep me posted on what you decide."

"Will do," I said, letting my eyes roam over her face. Nilanti had a feminine cat look. Like a sexy ass jaguar.

"Do I have something on my face?" she asked.

"Ah, no. I was just... Nothing," I said, blowing off the thought.

She squinted her eyes. "You are going to get in trouble."

"Do I look like trouble?" I smiled.

Her eyes roamed my face and upper body. When I flexed my chest muscles, her eyes popped and jumped back to mine. "Yes. You look like trouble. A lot of trouble." She swallowed.

"Everybody needs a little danger in their lives, right?"

"No, no, no. American Black men are all players. You want hoes and bitches. Too much trouble."

"Damn, you painting with a big ass brush, ain't you?"

"If the shoe fits."

"What if it doesn't? What if you're wrong?"

"I'm not wrong, Mr. Preston. You have been out of prison for six months and don't have a girlfriend. Why? Because you don't want to settle down, right? I think my big brush has painted a good picture. I am fine."

"But what about those?" I asked, looking at her chest. Her nipples were poking through her blouse like 2 little fingers.

"Mr. Preston!" she shrieked, crossing her arms and covering her chest.

"Let me take you to eat. Lunch. Dinner. Your choice."

She looked flustered while searching her office to find something to look at. "I'm sorry but we have to end this meeting."

"Nilanti?"

"What?" she answered, refusing to look at me.

"Nilanti?"

Finally, eye contact. "What?"

"I'm not a player. I just want to take you out."

"Mr. Preston, please. I cannot," she whined. Her mouth said no but her body and eyes were saying something different.

"Just one meal."

"I cannot."

"Yes, you can."

"No, I cannot," she whispered weakly.

I leaned in close, keeping eye contact. "Yes."

She shook her head no and gave another weak protest. "Nooo."

"I'm sorry, Nilanti, but I can't take no for an answer. You are one of the most striking women I've ever met. I like everything about you, and I would like to kick it with you on a personal level. I'm a good guy. Give me a chance to show you. I promise you won't regret it."

She just stared at me, mulling my request over in her mind. "Just once. One time. No more."

I smiled victoriously. One time was all I needed. "Can I have your number?"

"No. I will call you. Now get out of her before I change my mind."

I stood. "Ohhh. I like bossy."

She just stared at me.

"No hugs or handshakes?" I asked, extending a hand, hoping to get another glimpse at her nipples.

"No. Just leave."

Torn Between a Gangster and a Gentleman

"Alright, Nilanti. If that's how you want it. I don't mind being dominated. I will do anything you want," I sang, heading for the door. On the way out, I paused for one more look.

She shook her head at me. "You are going to get in trouble."

J-Blunt & Miss Kim

Torn Between a Gangster and a Gentleman

CHAPTER 8-Brianna

I left Building Blocks early, walking across the parking lot to my Lexus truck. I normally stayed until the daycare closed at 8:00 so I could lock up. But today I was allowing my assistant manager to close up so that I could go check on my mother before it got too late. It had been about a week since I'd last seen her, and I wanted to hang out with her for a little while and see if she needed anything. My mother was my best friend. Didn't have to worry about Mom being jealous of me, judging me, or telling my secrets if I made her mad. Plus, Mom gave the best advice. And I missed her. I was a mama's girl. Have been for as long as I could remember. Had no reason to be a daddy's girl since he chose another family over us when I was 5. Hadn't seen him since. Didn't care either.

As I drove to Mom's house, I snapped my fingers and sang along with Snoh Allegra and DVSN. Their duet *Between Us* was one of my favorite R&B songs. I was halfway through listening to the song for a third time when I turned onto 67th and Hampton. Halfway down the block I seen something that made me forget the words to my favorite song. For a moment I considered not even stopping. Seeing Ray's truck parked in front of mom's house had me flustered. Didn't know if I should come back later or walk in and act like everything was cool. Like being around him didn't excite me and make me nervous. Like I didn't notice how he acted like he didn't want to breathe the same air as me. But that was my mother's house. I couldn't let him dictate when I saw my mother. I was going inside. If he didn't want to be around me, he could leave.

After parking behind his truck, I gave myself a once over in the mirror. Had to make sure I looked good. I wanted to remind him what he was missing. Remind him that Brianna Boston was still that chick! When I was satisfied that I didn't have nothing in my teeth or in my nose and that my hair wasn't out of place, I got out of my Lexus and climbed the stairs to the house I grew up in. I was about to put the key in the lock when my nerves started getting the best of me. My stomach started flipping, heartrate increased, and I got the jitters.

"Hell, no, Brianna! Get it together, girl," I whispered, giving myself a pep talk while sticking my key in the door. "Mommy!" I called, walking through the living room.

"We're in the kitchen!" she responded.

When I walked past the bedroom that Ray and I made so many memories in, goosebumps popped up on my skin. Memories of the good ol' days flooded my brain and I was gripped by nostalgia. The closer I got to the kitchen, the faster my heart beat. When I walked past the threshold, the first person I noticed was Ray. He sat with his back to me, the muscles in his shoulders showing through his T-shirt. My mother sat across from him and there were bowls, pots, and plates all over the kitchen.

"Hey, baby!" Mom smiled, excitement flashing in her eyes as she got up to hug me.

"Hey, mama. I see I came just in time."

I absolutely adored my mom. She was born in Baton Rouge, Louisiana but migrated to Milwaukee, Wisconsin after she met my father. After 12 years together my father split, leaving my mother for his mistress. Left my mom to be a single parent of 5 and 10 year old daughters. Mom became a do-it-all kind of mother. Worked, cooked, cleaned, corrected homework, taught us the Bible, took us to church, and most importantly, taught me and my sister to be independent women. She was only 5 feet tall but her short stature never stopped her from being my biggest support and greatest inspiration. And my mom was beautiful. Not beauty queen pretty but more down to earth and pretty girl across the street look. Light brown skin, dark brown eyes, a round face, and long pretty salt and pepper hair. Mom was also what me and my sister affectionately called "pleasantly plump". Big breasts, big hips, big legs, big...everything. And she wasn't ashamed of her thickness. She loved and embraced every curve. Swore that something was wrong with girls that wanted to be skinny.

"Yeah, you did. Me and Ray was just chatting."

I looked at Ray. His plate was covered in Mom's cooking and he was chewing a mouth full of food. He also didn't even look up to acknowledge my presence. "Hey, Ray." I waved.

Torn Between a Gangster and a Gentleman

"Sup?" He nodded, giving me a quick glance before focusing on the plate of food again.

I wished I would've kept on driving.

"Sit down, Brianna. Let me make you a plate," Mom said, grabbing my arm and forcing me to sit down.

"Don't be trying to fatten me up, mama. Took almost forever to lose the weight I gained over the holidays last year."

"See, that's what's wrong with you girls today. Always worried about y'all figure and staying skinny. Don't no real man want no bag of bones. A real man want a woman with some meat on her bones. Ain't than right, Ray?" Mom asked while fixing my plate.

"Yep," he agreed, keeping his attention on his food.

"That's right." Mom grinned. "So, what brings you over? Everything okay at home?"

"Yeah. Everybody's fine. I just wanted to come over and see how you were doing."

"Well, I sure feel special. Ray said the same thing," she fawned, rubbing his back.

I really hated how close her and Ray were.

"Yeah, well, you're special. Only one of you, mom." I smiled.

"I know that's right!" she sassed, walking my plate over to the microwave. "Oh, Ray told me that he was thinking about investing in a record label so that he could help Brittany and Sabrina."

I looked at Ray. "Really?"

He didn't respond.

"Mmm-hmm," Mom jumped in, picking up the conversation."Ray was just telling me this right before you walked in. I think it's a good idea, don't you?"

"Yeah. It's a good idea. Got anything to add, Ray?" I asked, trying to engage him in conversation.

"Nope. Mama just told you," he said before working the last bit of food into his mouth.

I wanted to grab him and shake him. Two minutes ago, he had a plate heaping with food and now it was clean. He was acting like I had the plague and he was in a hurry to get away from me. I just stared at him in frustration while he took a loud and long drink from whatever was in his cup.

"Mama, that was delicious!" he said before shoving his chair away from the table and taking the dishes to the sink. "I'mma have to find me a woman that can burn like you."

"Wait. You can't leave yet, honey," Mom protested.

"Gotta go, mama. Something came up. I'll stop by and see you again tomorrow."

"Wait. First you gotta taste this cobbler I made. It tastes just like mana from heaven, baby. I know how much you love my peach cobbler," mom said, smiling up at him lovingly.

I wanted to throw up. They were really getting on my nerves.

"Okay," he gave in. "Let me hit this bathroom real quick."

"Y'all make me sick," I told my mom when he left the kitchen.

"Oh, look at Mrs. Boston getting jealous." She laughed, grabbing my plate from the microwave.

I rolled my eyes. "Whatever."

When mom sat the plate in front of me, my eyes popped. Rump roast, scalloped cheesy potatoes, glazed carrots, and biscuits made from scratch. I went for the roast first. The meat melted in my mouth. "Oh my God, Mom! This is so good!" I moaned, having a foodgasm.

"You know he still loves you, right?"

I stopped chewing and looked at my mom. "What are you talking about?"

"Stop playing, Brianna. You know who and what I'm talking about. I know you still love Ray and he loves you, too."

I tried to suppress the grin that was spreading across my face but couldn't. "How do you know? Did he tell you?"

"No, he didn't. Won't even talk about you. And that's how I know. The feelings are still there, baby, but it's underneath the hurt. He really loved you and you left him. Under all that animosity and hate is love. You can't hate someone that you don't love."

"But he won't talk to me, mama. Won't even look at me."

Torn Between a Gangster and a Gentleman

"You should've seen his face when you called me from the living room. I swear I seen him smile for the tiniest moment right before he went stiff as a board."

"But he—" I was saying but stopped talking when I heard the bathroom door open.

Mom busied herself fixing the dessert while I toyed with the roast. No one spoke when he walked back in the kitchen. Me and Mom were acting guilty.

"I stuck my foot in this, baby," Mom said as she brought him a slice of peach cobbler.

His eyes got as big as balloons. "Dang, mama! You gon' make me move in."

"Wait. Let me get you some ice cream for that." She had just grabbed the box of vanilla ice cream from the freezer when her phone began ringing from her bedroom. "I'll be right back," she said, putting the ice cream on the table and leaving me and Ray alone.

Silence engulfed the kitchen. He got up to get a spoon, and while he scooped ice cream onto his plate, I picked at my food and thought of something to say.

"That's a good idea buying a studio for Brittany and Sabrina."

"Yeah," he mumbled before taking a big bite of cobbler and ice cream.

"I was just talking with Benny about that a few weeks ago. Great minds think alike, huh?"

"Hmph," he grunted.

I was tired of the games. I dropped my fork and stared him down. "What the hell is your problem, Ray? If you got something to say, say it."

He lifted his head slowly until we locked eyes. Anger flickered inside his dark irises but he kept quiet.

"Why won't you talk to me? Can we be cordial? I'm sorry for what I did but not talking about it won't fix it."

He continued staring at me, eyes smoldering with rage. Then he spoke slowly and calmly. "How do you fix the last thirteen years?"

J-Blunt & Miss Kim

I didn't have a good answer for that. "I don't know. We can't change the past. All we can do is move forward."

"You left me, nigga," he mugged, raising his voice a little. The words sounding more like a charge than a statement.

"What was I supposed to do? I was young. I had the kids. I was confused."

"You was supposed to stay and support me. We was supposed to figure it out together. You not supposed to turn your back on somebody you love and then marry another nigga. You think I'm supposed to be cool with that? You think that's something that I'm supposed to just get over?"

I didn't want to cry but I couldn't stop the tears from flowing. "It was killing me, Ray. I saw the judge give you a hundred years. I didn't want to watch you die in prison. I was dying inside without you. If I held on to you, I was going to lose my mind. The kids needed me."

"What about what I needed? I died a little more inside every day that I was locked up. Did you think about that? Do you have any idea how it feels to be buried alive inside a little ass box? You knew what I did when you met me. You knew I robbed niggas. You knew it was a possibility that I could go to jail. Why didn't you leave before I got locked up? If you loved me so much, why did you leave when I needed you the most? Why didn't you leave me before I went in?"

That was a stupid question.

"Because I loved you, Ray."

"Did you stop loving me when I got locked up? Did your love for me suddenly disappear when the police came and got me?"

"No, Ray. I never stopped loving you."

He looked down at my hand. "That ain't my ring on your finger."

Ouch!

"What was I supposed to do? You left me with two kids and no way to take care of them. What about how I felt? What about my needs? What about me?"

Torn Between a Gangster and a Gentleman

He mean-mugged me for a moment before shaking his head and turning his attention back to the cobbler.

I reached out a hand to grab his. "Ray, I'm—"

"Don't touch me!" he yelled, snatching his hand away. He continued to stare at me angrily, chest heaving, nostrils flaring. "I used to pray to God that you would come back to me. Even when I was calling the kids and didn't want to talk to you, I was still praying for there to be an us. I know mama taught you the Bible. You remember what it says about love? Love endures. Love suffers. Love believes in hope when all hope is lost." After saying his piece, he left the table without finishing his food. I didn't bother trying to stop him. There was too much hate and animosity between us. Based on the way he felt, I wasn't sure we'd ever be on speaking terms again.

"What happened?" Mom asked, running into the kitchen.

"Ray hates me," I mumbled, wiping away tears.

"Baby, what I just seen was love and pain on his face. Catch him before he leaves. Trust your mother. Don't let him leave without telling him how you feel."

I took a moment to think about what my mother said. I loved Ray. Probably always would. I wasn't sure that telling him how I felt would change anything. It was clear that he hated my presence. But what if it was all a front? What if under all of that hate, there was still love?

Throwing caution to the wind, I jumped up from the table and ran through the house like it was on fire. When I got to the porch, Ray was just stepping off the curb. "Ray!"

He stopped, turning to look at me.

I tore down that porch, ran across the lawn, and right into his strong arms. "I'm sorry that I left you, Ray. I am. It's one of the biggest regrets of my life. I'm so-so-so sorry," I cried.

He held me for a long moment, allowing me to cry on his shoulder. "I know," he grunted, sounding like the words came from deep inside.

I tilted my head to look in his eyes. "And I never stopped loving you, Ray. I still love you."

For a brief moment, he smiled. It was the kind of smile that said more than words. The kind of smile that fills you with hope of better days. The anger in his eyes disappeared and I could see his true feelings. But instead of expressing them with words, he showed me. When his face moved toward mine, I didn't think about it. I closed my eyes and met him halfway. Our lips touched before parting, allowing our tongues to slip against on another's in a forbidden yet familiar dance. I could taste the ice cream and peach cobbler as we exchanged intimacies from the depths of our souls. And just when it was getting good, he pulled away.

"I gotta go, Bria."

I didn't know what to do. The kiss left my emotions a mess. All I could do was stand there and watch as he hopped in the truck and drive away.

CHAPTER 9- Benny

I sat upon the stage watching the hundreds of faces in the crowd as they listened to Wisconsin Senator Leah Dunlap. Leah was a tall blonde haired white woman in her late 40s that really knew how to rally a crowd. She was also a proud Republican from Lacrosse, a small city in northwestern Wisconsin. The event she was speaking at, of which I was a keynote speaker, was a symposium on hiring ex-convicts called 2nd Chance. Several of Wisconsin's who's who had shown up to add their 2 cents and smile for the cameras. Since most of my workforce were felons, I was asked to be a keynote speaker. I readily accepted the invitation, looking forward to the opportunity to further establish myself in the business and political community. After getting a nod from the symposium's host sitting a few seats away, former mayor of Milwaukee Tom Bennett, I turned my attention back to Leah. It was almost my time to speak.

"We know that with the help of this community, these men and women who have paid their debt to society can gain back their dignity and respect and become upstanding members of the great state of Wisconsin. I ask that my constituents and the rest of the voting people of Wisconsin continue to press the legislators as well as businessmen and businesswomen to help out these vulnerable men and women that very much need our help. Now I want to turn the stage over to a man that has become a champion of helping and hiring ex-offenders. What he does is a remarkable act of kindness and charity. Ladies and gentlemen, please give a warm welcome to Benny Boston!"

I stood, smiled, and waved to the sea of people as they applauded. After giving Leah a hug and kiss on the cheek, I took the podium. *Yeah, I was about to milk this shit!*

"Good afternoon, ladies and gentlemen. I want to begin by quoting a few verses from the good book that were instilled in me by my parents and grandparents. 'For all have sinned and fallen short of the glory of God, and in all labor there is profit, but idle chatter leads to poverty.' Ladies and gentlemen, those verses sum up what Second Chance is all about. Nobody is perfect. And I mean nobody. We've all done foolish things that could've gotten us in trouble, but by the grace of God we were spared. A lot of these men and women who need these second chances are mothers, fathers, sisters, brothers, aunties, uncles, grandparents, sons, and daughters. They are more than the crimes they were convicted of. They are people with souls who deserve a second chance. And the worst thing we can do to these precious souls is leave them idle. According to my late mother, 'an idle mind is the devil's playground.' This is a serious topic for me because all of the businesses I've opened up have been mostly employed by felons. I have a special place in my heart for those needing a second, third, or fourth chance. And today we are asking that more people give these men and women the opportunity to make something of themselves."

After speaking for 10 more minutes, I got a standing ovation as I headed back to my seat. The event was over an hour later and the panelists went to mingle with the crowd. I had managed to wedge myself between Representative Paul Carlson from Milwaukee and Representative Jason Crewe from Madison. Carlson was a bald headed brown skinned man in his 50s that smiled too much. I was skeptical of people who smiled too much. You never knew their true intent because they hid it under their smile. Jason was a short and pudgy white man in his late 30s who reminded me of Porky Pig. I had cornered the men because I had gotten word that they were the brain children behind a bill that would give businesses that hired felons a tax break. I wanted in the loop.

"Terrific speech, Mr. Boston. You ever think about getting into politics?" Representative Carlson asked, wearing a wide grin.

"I'm a man of many talents, Mr. Carlson, but trying to please an entire district is not one. I'll leave the politics to you and Mr. Crewe and lend my support from the sideline." I laughed.

"You are a wise man, Benny. Nowadays, politics is a blood sport. More about the party than the people. That's why this event is important. It's about the people," Representative Crewe said.

"I couldn't agree more. Hey, since I have the two of you together, I wanted to ask you fellas about a bill giving tax incentives to businesses that hire felons."

Torn Between a Gangster and a Gentleman

"You must be a mind reader, Benny, because that's exactly what we wanted to talk to you about."

I nodded, giving him my undivided attention. "I'm listening."

"Next month we are introducing a bill on the floor to get a vote on it. We actually want to put your name on the bill and give you some press coverage. You know, get you a couple of interviews to gain public support. What do you think?"

I was so happy that I wanted to attempt a back flip and do the splits. But I thought better, not wanting to hurt or make a fool of myself in front of my peers. "I think that would be an honor, gentlemen. The people of the great state of Wisconsin need this. Count me in." I shook hands with the men at exchanged smiles.

"Great. We'll keep in touch. Keep some open dates on your calendar so that we can set up some press dates." Carlson smiled.

"Alright. Will do," I said, pulling the vibrating phone from my pocket. "Excuse me, gentlemen. I need a moment to take a call." I couldn't wipe the smile from my face as I walked away from the politicians. The exposure I would get from this bill would be huge! And I was going to make it pay off. They didn't call me B.B. King for nothing! After putting some distance between me and the fellas, I checked the screen on my phone. It was my lawyer, Donald Warren. Seeing his name on the screen made my gut bubble. I hoped he had good news. I was feeling on top of the world right now and I was hoping that his news would take me a little higher. "Donald, tell me something good, my man!"

"I'm sorry, Benny, but I don't have any good news."

The good feeling I was riding disappeared like a crack head's paycheck. "What do you have, Donald?"

"You may have to prepare for a legal fight. I'll do what I can but just know that a fight is probably coming your way."

***

"This nigga is gon' be the death of me. I came too damn far to lose to a pedophile street pimp," I vented, pouring another glass of Scotch.

"What happened when your lawyer went to see him? Did they get the chance to talk?" Clyde asked.

"Nah, they didn't get the chance. Said they got some shit going on where nobody can talk to him unless they're on some special list. I got a bad feeling about this, Clyde. My lawyer says we're in for a fight," I said before downing the drink. The warm liquor burned on its way down my throat but it did nothing to remove the pain in my head.

"Well, ain't nothing you can do but wait and see what they got, B.B. You never know. He may still have some loyalty to you. Some of those snakes are funny like that. Real selective on who they bite."

"I shoulda killed that nigga back on '06." I immediately regretted saying the words as soon as they left my lips.

"Well, that's my cue to get the fuck off this phone. Wish you the best of luck, partner," Clyde said before hanging up.

"Fuck!" I yelled, slamming my cellphone on the desk.

Red Fox had me spooked. After almost 30 years of scheming, masterful planning and manipulation, I was finally able to live a comfortable life. I had a trucking company worth 1.2 million dollars, lived in a half million dollars home, had a beautiful wife, and popular name in the community. Now it was all in jeopardy because of a low life pimp. A piece of shit that I should've let die.

Boom!

A noise jarred me from my thoughts. It sounded like someone had driven a car into my house. I jumped up from the desk and grabbed my .45 from the wall safe. I crept out of my home office, the .45 cocked and ready. I was walking down the hall when I heard the commotion. Lots of feet were stomping through my house. When Brianna and Brittany began screaming, I raced down the stairs where the voices became audible.

"Where is Benny Boston!" a man yelled.

"We have a warrant for his arrest!" another one yelled.

Shit! Red Fox sang!

I thought about running and hiding. Leaving the state. Fuck that, I needed to leave the country! In all my days in the streets, I had never been to jail. Never even got a traffic ticket. And now at 47

Torn Between a Gangster and a Gentleman

years old, I was about to be arrested. As much as I wanted to, I knew I couldn't run. I had a life, a name, and a family. I had to face the music. This is why I kept company with judges, politicians, and businessmen. I had done them favors. Helped finance their campaigns. And now I needed to cash in on some of the favors I had racked up. So, I put the gun in my pocket and made myself seen.

"Gentlemen, there is no need for weapons," I called out to the 4 tactically dressed officers who were brandishing handguns.

A tall white cop who looked like he hated successful black men addressed me with a sneer. "Benny Boston, we have a warrant for your arrest."

"Benny, what is going on?" Brianna asked, staring at me through wide eyes. Brittany stood close by giving me the same look.

I was going to kill Red Fox's was for this shit.

"It's okay, baby. Just a misunderstanding," I said, trying to remain calm. I didn't want the family to see me sweat. They knew me as a mover and shaker, not a coward.

"You are being taken into custody for the murder of Tracy Brown," the lead officer said, watching me with hawk-like eyes as I descended the stairs.

When I got to the bottom of the stairwell, the officers grabbed me roughly and put on the cuffs. "There is a firearm in my pocket. It's mine. Registered. I have the paperwork upstairs in my office," I informed them.

"Got it," said one of the officers, taking my gun after a pat search.

"Benny, what is happening? Who is Tracy?" Brianna cried.

"Dot answer any questions. Call my lawyer, honey. This is all a mistake."

"We're going to take your gun with us. Have your lawyers bring the paperwork," the lead cop said, escorting me from the house. "You have the right to remain silent. Anything you say can and will be used against you in the court of law. You have..."

I stopped listening to the cop's Miranda rights as visions of cells and orange jumpsuits filled my mind. I couldn't believe Red Fox had done it. Even though I saved his ass all those years ago, he had bitten me on the ass. I looked back toward my house as I was led to a police car. They were standing on the porch huddled together, sadness and confusion upon their faces. Some of my neighbors also stood on their porches watching me being carted away like a common criminal. I felt the shame descend upon me like storm clouds. I was going to kill Red Fox's ass even if was the last thing I did.

Torn Between a Gangster and a Gentleman

CHAPTER 10-Ray

"In my country, Sudan, it is the men who have all the power. Dat tis why I left. Men get corrupted with power. It goes to deir head. Dey abuse it. Dat tis why I like America. Lots of powerful women," Nilanti explained before taking a sip of Chardonnay.

I liked watching her and listening to her speak. She was very sexy. Everything she did oozed sex appeal. The way her lips moved, the way her voice sounded, and especially the way she looked at me during a point of contention. Her eyes dimmed into sexy slits and she licked her lips like she was hungry or planning to bite. *Sexy indeed!* We were at Mr. Nash, a popular upscale restaurant in downtown Milwaukee. This was our second date.

"And you don't think women abuse their power? Do you see how many scandals we have in America involving men and women?"

"Yes, but men in power far outweigh women. And dere are more men involved in dese scandals dan women."

"How do you know that? You got stats? And even if you were right, suppose that just as many women had the same amount of power as men. Are you saying that women wouldn't have just as many scandals as men?"

Her dark eyes flickered in the restaurant's dim lighting. "Yes, dat is exactly what I am saying."

"Bullshit," I challenged.

"No. Women are creators. Nurturers. Life givers. We sustain and support our communities and one another. We share our power to bring each odder up. We don't abuse it." She smiled at me like she had proven her point me. And while she did make some good observations about women, her point was far from proven.

My retort would put the ball back into my court. "Well, how do you explain Martha Stewart going to prison for insider trading, Hillary Clinton being investigated by the Feds for all kinds of shit, and the infamous Jezebel in the Bible? Three women with three different scandals. All of them abusing their power." After presenting my question, I sat back in the chair awaiting her response. As far as I was concerned, no comeback could erase these powerful women's scandals from the history books.

And the way Nilanti paused to gather a comeback told me that question had her stumped. "Dat was good, Ray. But da one ting you fail to realize is dat all dese women were corrupted... By men."

I bust out laughing. "That's bullshit and you know it. You are one of those hardcore feminists that blame all the world's problems on men but don't accept responsibility for the personal choices that women make that contribute to their own issues. It's that kind of thinking that won't allow women to experience true power. If y'all keep blaming men for y'all issues, y'all won't ever gain control of your own destiny. Taking responsibility is the first step on the stairwell to controlling your own destiny."

She gave a smirk. "You make some valid points. And I'm not a hardcore feminist but I do support all women in every ting dey do." She shrugged before taking a bite of the braised cabbage and carrots.

My retort was lost in the back of my mind as I watched her. She intrigued the hell out of me. Her mannerisms were proper and feminine, like she went to etiquette school. Used the knife to cut her food. Ate small bites. Wiped her mouth after every bite. Didn't talk while she chewed. She also expected me to be chivalrous. Open the door, pull out her chair, stand whenever she left the table. Of all the women I've dated, I had never met anyone like Nilanti. She was a black diamond.

"What?" she asked, catching me staring.

"Who hurt you?"

Vulnerability flashed across her face for an instant before disappearing. "Why do you ask me dat?" she asked, reaching for the glass of wine.

"Because you bash men too much. Someone hurt you. Who?"

A faraway look shown in her eyes. Like she was remembering. "It was a long time ago. I am over it."

"Will I always have to fight him? Will you ever let anyone undo what he fucked up?"

Torn Between a Gangster and a Gentleman

She stared at me for a few moments, reading me. "You are good, Ray. You know just what to say and how to say it. And when."

"That's because I'm real."

"We shall see."

I was about to respond when my phone began ringing. I pulled it out, ready to ignore the call until I seen the number. "I'm sorry, Nilanti. It's my daughter. I have to take this."

Nilanti gave a nod.

"Hey, princess. What you up to?"

"Daddy, the police took Benny!"

I had to make sure I heard her correctly. "What are you talking about?"

"The police kicked in our door with guns out. They took Benny."

I couldn't believe what I was hearing. "When did this happen? Where is your mom?"

"It happened a few minutes ago. Mama downstairs. Can you come over? I'm scared."

I looked to Nilanti. She stared back, the expectation of bad news showing in her eyes. "Um... Yeah. Give me a few minutes to wrap up what I'm doing. I'm on my way."

"Is everything okay?" Nilanti asked when I hung up the phone.

"Nah," I breathed heavily, signaling the waiter. "The police just arrested my kids' stepfather. My daughter said they kicked the door in and pointed guns at them. She's scared. I'm sorry but I gotta take you home."

"No. I understand. She needs you. I imagine dat is very terrifying for a little girl."

"How may I help you, sir?" the waiter asked.

"I need the check. We're leaving."

"One moment, sir," he said before disappearing.

Nilanti and I stood to gather our things. While she smoothed the wrinkles from her form fitting white dress, I couldn't help but wonder what our night could've been had Benny not ended up in jail. I hated to end the night without attempting to explore her motherland.

83

But my kids needed me. When the waiter brought the bill, I dropped $120 on the table and gathered my date.

Drake's voice filled the cab of my truck during the ride to Nilanti's house, but I couldn't focus on the certified lover boy's lyrics. Instead, I was thinking about Benny. What the hell could he have done for the police to kick in the door and point guns at my kids? I'd heard his name ringing in the streets before I went to prison, but since we didn't run in the same circles, I didn't bother digging too deep. There were whispers of him being involved in some black mafia kind of shit but then he cleaned up his act and opened some businesses that hired felons. The kids told me that he was into politics and I'd seen some of his social media promoting various causes. That's who I thought he was. But it seems as if something from his past could've come back to haunt him.

"Nickel for your thoughts," Nilanti said.

"I was just thinking about my kids. I put them through something similar with the police when they were babies."

"Why you went to prison?"

"Yeah."

"I read your file. You don't seem like the young man that did all those robberies."

"That's the point of going to prison. I figured out that I needed to make changes and made them. Educated myself. Worked on my speech."

"Five robberies. Man, you were busy," she whistled.

"That was all that I was caught for. Jacking was my thing. I wasn't a good drug dealer so I robbed people. And just when I thought police were a thing of the past, Benny gets locked up."

"Hopefully da kids are just shaken up a bit and won't need counseling. I feel bad for dem."

We became silent again. Didn't speak until I pulled up to her house.

"So, when can I see you again?" I asked, spinning to face her.

"I will keep in touch, Mr. Smooth Operator," she smiled, playing hard to get.

Torn Between a Gangster and a Gentleman

"I'm not what you think I am, Nilanti. I don't lie. I don't play games. And I'm definitely not into breaking hearts."

"But you are not ready for a woman like me. I fall fast and hard. I don't play around wit my heart."

I could hear the seriousness and vulnerability in her voice and see it on her face, and it made me want her even more. "And what if I also fall fast and hard?"

"When you drop da playa card, den we will talk."

"I don't like card games," I grinned.

"Bye, Ray. Tank you for dinner," she smiled before getting out of the truck.

My eyes followed every bounce of her big bouncing booty as she walked to her house. *Damn, I couldn't wait the tap that!*

***

There was no sign of the police when I pulled into the driveway of Brianna and Benny's house. I looked up and down the block as I climbed from the truck. The streets were deserted for the most part. I walked past Benny's green Jaguar, up a short walkway with manicured hedges, and onto the front porch. That's when I seen sings of the police. There was a big dent in the middle of the expensive white door and the knob was hanging by a few wood splinters. Seeing the door brought back memories of when the police came to get me. After the reverie, I rang the doorbell.

Junior answered a few moments later. "Hey, dad. You heard about Benny?" he asked, appearing unaffected by the police kicking in the door.

"Yeah, Brittany told me. How are you? You good?"

"I'm good, dad. I thought it was raw! The police came in like they do in the movies. Brittany and mama was crying though," he explained, excitement flashing in his eyes.

"Like a movie, huh?" I chuckled. "Where the girls at?"

"They in the family room. Come in."

Since Benny was in jail and they had gone through a traumatic event, I decided to take my son up on the invitation and stepped past

85

him and into their house for the first time. Their house was enormous. Looked like something out of an interior design magazine. Big plants, fluffy brown furniture, the shiniest floors I had ever seen, and an expensive looking barely used fireplace.

"You shoulda seen it, dad. The police had on bullet proof vests and big guns. It all happened so fast. They was in and out quick," Junior explained while leading me through the house.

I noticed a family picture hanging on the mantle. The kids, Brianna, and Benny. They were all smiles. Looked like a happy family. Seeing the photo of my family without me in it caused a small fire to build in my chest. "Nice picture."

"Yeah. That was Christmas a last year," he said nonchalantly.

After going down a hallway, Junior led me to a room as big as the living room that had more big ass furniture. Big blue sofa set, think white carpet, a giant TV on the wall, and one of the biggest fish tanks I had ever seen.

"Daddy!" Brittany yelled, jumping up from the couch and crashing into me for a hug.

"Hey, baby girl!" I greeted, kissing her forehead.

Brittany was a splitting image of her mother. Same light-colored skin with a bronze tint. Same brown eyes. Same long curly hair. Looked like Brianna had cloned herself. Junior was my twin and Brittany was hers.

"Thanks for coming to check up on us," Brianna said as she got up and walked over. Her hair was wild like a lion's mane and eyes puffy. Looked like she had been crying a lot. She was dressed in a white T-shirt and leggings. In her hand was a strong drink.

"It was no problem. I—" I stopped talking when Brianna reached around Brittany and hugged me. I wasn't expecting it. Besides the kiss at Mom's house, which was a mistake, this was our only physical contact in 13 years. I wanted to pull away from her, but didn't. No need for the kids to see our issues. This was a trying time for them all so I returned the hug. Damn, she felt good. "It was no problem," I continued. "I know y'all must've been scared."

Torn Between a Gangster and a Gentleman

"I was, daddy. They had guns and everything. I thought they was going to shoot us," Brittany said, her arms still wrapped around me.

"It has to be some kind of misunderstanding. Benny is a good man."

"I hope so. He said the same thing, that it was a misunderstanding. But how do they mistakenly arrest you for murder?" Brianna asked, looking to me for answers.

"I don't really know how to answer that. Guess you have to wait and see what his lawyer says. Hopefully he gets a bail in the morning and you can talk to him about it. Worrying won't change anything. You have to go through the process."

She gave a stressed look and ran a hand though her hair. "I guess you're right. I'm going to make another drink. You want one?"

"Yeah. Sure," I accepted.

"I'll be back. Sit down. Make yourself at home."

"I need a hug, daddy. Can you cuddle with me?" Brittany asked, dragging me over to the giant couch.

"For sure, baby. I'll hold you forever," I said, pulling her into my embrace as we were swallowed by the couch.

"This is your first time in our house, huh, daddy?"

"Yeah, it is. You have a really nice house, too."

"Why you never wanted to come in?" Junior asked.

I didn't want to tell them the truth. That I couldn't stand being around Brianna and Benny. So, I lied. "I don't know. Guess it felt kind of weird."

"Why would it feel weird?" Brittany asked.

"I don't know. That's just how I felt."

"It's because of Benny, huh?" Junior asked.

I didn't like being interrogated by my kids. "C'mon, y'all. What's up with all the questions?"

"Oh my God! This is way too cute!" Brianna gushed when she walked in the family room and seen me cuddling with Brittany.

"I'mma hold on to her forever," I said, giving my daughter a squeeze.

"No, daddy! You squeezing me too tight!" Brittany whined.

I kissed her on the cheek. "I'm sorry, baby."

"Ohh! C'mon, daddy. Let me show you my room," Brittany said, dragging me from the couch. "And you can listen to my new songs."

I hung out with my kids and comforted them as best as I could. They fell asleep around 11 o'clock so I sat in the family room and hung out with Brianna. I agreed to stay until the locksmith showed up in the morning.

"When they took him, it reminded me of when they took you. It felt like déjà vu or something," she said, telling me the story of Benny's arrest.

"Benny didn't kill nobody. Had to be some kind of mistake. I can't see him as a shooter," I said, keeping the rumors I'd heard about Benny back in the day to myself. Brianna looked fried and I didn't think she could handle any more bad news. So, I told her comforting words while sipping the fine brandy. I was on my third glass and buzzing good.

"That's what I was thinking. He's into politics and reads business magazines. He donates to charity and hangs out with judges and smokes cigars. He's not a street nigga. He is nothing like y—" She stopped talking and froze up.

"Like me," I finished.

We were sitting across the room from each other, but I could see the regret in her eyes. "I'm sorry, Ray. I didn't mean it like that."

"It's cool, Brianna. I knew what you meant." We were silent for a few moments. A question that I had always wanted to ask her burned on the tip of my tongue. "Is that why you married him? Because he wasn't like me?" As soon as the words left my lips, I regret asking the question.

Brianna gave the question some thought. "Yes and no. But I don't think about it like that. When you left, I went searching for you. Tried to find pieces of you in other men. You were all I knew and all I wanted. My first everything. Then when Benny came along, he was different. People feared you and they respected him. And when he started showing me things I've never seen, I fell in love."

Torn Between a Gangster and a Gentleman

I knew she loved Benny but hearing her say it burned like someone poured a burning liquid down my throat and it got stuck in my chest. I downed the rest of the brandy trying to put out the fire and keep me from saying something stupid. Neither one of is spoke for the longest time. We just listened to the music playing from the radio. A couple of songs went by before Brian McKnight's *Anytime* came on. The liquor had also kicked in and I could feel the room spin. I was so drunk that when I closed my eyes, it felt like I was riding the music. And then my lips started moving.

J-Blunt & Miss Kim

CHAPTER 11-Brianna

"When I used to hear this song on the radio while I was in prison, it made me think about you." The sound of Ray's voice made me jump a little. After I answered his question about Benny, he closed his eyes and became quiet. I thought he had fallen asleep. "I remember this used to be our song." I smiled, going down Memory Lane. "Remember when we stayed with Tamar in the back room? You listened to this song every night for a month." I laughed.

"*Do I ever cross your mind, any time. Do you ever wake up reaching out for me,*" Ray sang.

I bust out laughing. He was murdering the song.

"*Still have your picture in the frame. Mmmhh. Hear your footsteps dooo-oown the hall. I swear I hear your voice, driving me insane. How I wish that you would call to saaaayyyyyy!*" He yelled.

"Ray, you're screaming." I laughed, going over to cover his mouth with my hand.

"C'mere," he said, gripping my waist and pulling me onto the couch next to him.

"Ray, you're making me spill liquor on the couch!" I protested weakly. Truth was, I didn't care about Hennessey being wasted on the couch. I would pour the entire bottle on the couch to be next to him.

"You know what?" he asked, head jerking forward, eyes opening a little bit. "You supposed to be my wife. You wasn't supposed to marry that nigga," he slurred.

I thought he was going to say more but didn't. Just stared at me for a moment before closing his eyes and laying his head back. All I could do was shake my head and laugh. Liquor was the ultimate truth serum. A week ago, he hated my guts and now he was in my house cuddling with me and telling me that I'm supposed to be his wife. And the crazy part about it all was this is what I wanted. Even though I was mentally and emotionally fried from the police kicking in my door and taking my husband to jail, in Ray's arms was the only place I wanted to be. I downed the rest of my drink and moved to sit my glass on the table.

"Don't leave, Bria!" Ray called, eyes popping open while gripping my waist tighter.

"I'm not going anywhere. I just want to sit my glass down."

He gave a drunken smile before laying back. After sitting the glass on the table, I lay my head against his chest. Being so close to him felt good. Like I was supposed to be there. And when he let out a satisfied sigh, I knew that he felt the same. I couldn't resist the urge to rub my hands over his chest, stomach, and arms. His muscles were tight and hard. Then I remembered that he had just called me Bria. Nobody called me that name except him. For us, it was my pet name. Like when lovers call each other baby or honey. My mind began drifting down Memory Lane and all of the old feelings began bubbling up. I had always loved Ray. Never stopped. Had never loved Benny as much as I loved him.

I tilted my head to look at him. I was always attracted to him. He was a handsome man and he wasn't conceited. I liked that about him. But now that he was older, he had become sexy. His jawline. The muscles. His lips. Made me wonder if he was a better lover. The kiss in front of my mom's house flashed in my head. It was deep and passionate. Thinking about it made my body grow warm, nipples get hard, and pearl twitch. I wanted to taste his lips again. So, I did. But just a peck.

Excitement shot through my body when my lips touched his. A voice in my head told me to stop but another voice from another part of my body egged me on. I listened to the horny sistah between my legs and began sucking his bottom lip. And then he came alive. He kissed me passionately, pushing me onto my back and climbing on top. He forced his way in between my legs and began grinding. I could feel the hardness through his jeans, threatening my mother pearl with a kind of loving that I hadn't had in a long time. I needed to feel him. I wanted him deep inside of me. I was thirsting to feel his passion and love. I stopped thinking and went with the flow. I tugged at his shirt and it flew off in a single motion. His body was hard and defined. Before I could take it all in, he began grabbing at

Torn Between a Gangster and a Gentleman

my shirt, aggressively pulling it over my head. His lips were against mine again, but the kisses were no longer passionate. They were rough. Almost mean. I wasn't sure where this was going but I was in too deep to back out now. I tugged at his waistband and his pants came off along with his boxers. I barely had enough time to take off my leggings before he was on me again. And without warning, he penetrated me. Deep.

"Huuuhhh!" I gasped, sounding like a mix between a drowning woman and a wounded animal.

It felt like he tore me open, but Ray didn't seem to notice my pain. He also didn't seem to feel my nails digging into his shoulders and back as he thrust into me like a wild man.

"Ray. Please. You're. Hurting. Me," I whined, wrapping my arms around his back and locking my body against his to try and slow him down.

He acted like he didn't hear me. Started grunting like a wild animal and humping harder. Then he started biting me. Not nibbles but bites that broke the skin. My chest. Shoulders. The top of my breasts.

"Ray, stop!" I said forcefully, trying to push his head away from my body.

It was no use. He didn't stop biting or thrusting. It seemed as if my cries and attempts to stop him only fueled him, making him bite harder and dig deeper. Every time his body came down on mine, our pelvises slapped, making a loud noise. And then I realized what was happening. The liquor had released his truth. His anger. His hurt. He was taking all of his pain out on me for leaving him. I wasn't strong enough to stop him so I stopped struggling and let him have his way. He grabbed one of my thighs, digging his nails into my skin, forcing my legs open wider. I wanted to fight him. To scream. Tell him to stop. But I didn't. I just cried and endured until he came. After he erupted inside of me, we just lay there. Breathing heavy. Sweating. He had made me feel his pain. And it hurt all over.

"I'm sorry, Ray," I cried, holding him and kissing his neck.

He didn't respond. Just lay in top of me breathing heavily.

"Get up. Come with me."

93

When he pushed himself up, the light from the TV allowed me to see his face. It was wet but I couldn't tell if it was sweat or tears. Or both.

"Come with me."

When I reached for his hand, he wrapped his around mine and allowed me to lead him through the house and to my bedroom. I stopped at the door to look in his eyes. Questions, confusion, passion, and pain swirled in his drunken eyes. I answered one of the questions when I took off my wedding ring and let it drop on the floor. He watched the ring fall and then looked back at me.

"Tonight, I want to be your wife."

After kissing him, I took him into the room I had been sharing with my husband. He had used his body to show me how much I had hurt him. Now I was about to use my body to show him how sorry I was and show him that I still loved him.

Torn Between a Gangster and a Gentleman

CHAPTER 12- Brianna

Knock, knock, knock.
"Mom, Benny on the phone!"
I shot up in bed when I heard Brittany's voice on the other side of the door. I wanted to stop her from coming in the room. Ray had also shot up in bed, alarm in his eyes as we watched the door open. Damn. We were too late.

"Mom, Benny—" she stopped talking and eyes grew wide when she seen her father in my bed.

Ray put a finger to his lips. "Shhh."

I reached for the phone, my eyes pleading with hers to keep this a secret. "Gimmie the phone."

Brittany smiled as she handed me the phone, amusement showing in her eyes as she looked back and forth from me and her father.

"Get out. And be quiet," I told her, covering the phone.

She continued wearing the same smile while leaving the room.

My heart raced like I was having a heart attack as I put the phone to my ear. The guilt from cheating with Ray was already starting to eat at me. "Hello? Benny?"

"Hey, baby. You okay?" he asked, sounding surprisingly upbeat.

"Yes. We're fine. What about you? How are you doing? Where are you?" I asked, hoping he wasn't on his way home.

"I'm still in jail, baby. But I'm being arraigned in a few hours. Should get bail. I need you to be here."

I could feel Ray's eyes on me so I turned so that he couldn't see my face.

"Okay. I'm on my way. Do you need me to do anything? Pick up anything? Call anybody?"

"No. Just be here for me. I'm sorry we have to go through this but it's all a mistake. I'm going to make it go away. I promise."

"Okay. I'm about to get in the shower and then I'll be on my way."

"Okay, sweetheart. Again, I'm sorry about putting you and the kids through this. I love you."

J-Blunt & Miss Kim

For the first time since I fell in love with Benny, I didn't want to tell him that I loved him back. I could feel Ray's eyes upon the back of my head. But I knew that if I didn't tell my husband that I loved him, that would open up another can of worms. "I love you too, Benny."

I felt the bed move as I hung up the phone. When I turned my head, Ray was climbing out of bed. "I need something to put in," he gruffed angrily.

"Benny's cloches are in that drawer," I pointed.

He mugged me. "I'm not putting on that nigga's clothes."

"I have sweats in my dresser. Second drawer."

I watched his muscular butt sway as he walked across the room and dug through my drawer. His naked body was a sight to see. Looked like he should be in a fitness magazine. Arms, chest, back, shoulders, and legs all chiseled like Black Onyx. "Brittany seen us. What should I tell her?" I asked.

"I'll talk to her and Junior," he said, putting on a pair of my black sweatpants. They fit him like skinny jeans.

"Okay then! Work it." I giggled.

"What you laughing at?"

"You." I laughed. "You look funny in my pants."

"Don't be laughing at me. Need to be worried about those," he said, looking at my chest.

I looked down to what he was talking about. When I saw the marks, it felt like I was going to have a heart attack. Red welts, bruises, and hickies were all over my shoulders and the top of my breasts. "Ray! Look what you did?" I screamed, shooting out of bed to look in the mirror. I checked my naked body in the mirror, not caring that Ray was seeing me nude. I cared more about the marks on my body. They looked really bad. No way I was going to be able to hide these from Benny.

"My bad." He smirked.

"You did this shit on purpose!" I yelled, pushing him. "Oh my God, Ray! Benny is going to kill me!"

"Considering the charges he's facing, I doubt it." He chuckled.

Torn Between a Gangster and a Gentleman

I wanted to throw something at him. I looked around for something hard enough to knock him out with. By the time I grabbed a hairbrush, he was walking out of the room. "Shit!" I cursed, throwing the brush at the door.

If Benny saw these marks, it was going to be hell to tell the captain. When he figured out Ray was the cause of the marks, there was a strong possibility that the police would be called to our house again. Divorce was guaranteed. This was bad. What in the hell was I thinking? Shit! I ran to the shower in the master bedroom hoping that soap and water would help the marks fade.

A few moments later Ray called me from the bedroom. "Brianna, they both know. They seen our clothes in the family room. Brittany was filling Junior in on what she seen when I came downstairs. I told them nothing happened and to keep their mouths closed."

I turned off the shower and covered up with a towel. When I walked in the bedroom, Ray was half dressed. He ogled my wet body, looking like he wanted to tear me up. And for a moment I considered letting him. Our situation couldn't get any worse than it already was. *Stop, Brianna!* I lectured. I had more important things to worry about than an orgasm. "Did they believe you?"

"No." He laughed. "They're teenagers. They know."

"Shit, Ray. This is bad," I breathed.

He continued to stare at me.

"So, what now, Ray?" I asked, wanting to know if last night meant anything.

"What do you mean?"

"I mean last night. What do we do now?"

He searched my face for a long time. "You're married, Brianna. We were drunk. Let's not make something out of nothing."

Ouch! I wanted to shrug the words off but couldn't. They cut really deep. I was crushed. "But what about the things you said? That I'm supposed to be your wife? Don't you remember?"

"I was drunk, Brianna. I passed out and the next thing I know is I'm waking up in your bed. I think it would be best if we both just forget about last night."

I wanted to hit him. I jeopardized my marriage and now he was treating me like a fly by night hoe. He was being cold and uncaring again and it hurt. Especially after I took his pain and gave him my love. We just stood in the middle of my bedroom staring at one another. I couldn't hide the hurt in my eyes, and he looked to be satisfied that he caused me pain. Now he was waiting to see how I would react. He wanted me to cry and curse him out. And as much as I wanted to cry and curse him out, I couldn't give him the satisfaction. I had to remain strong. I had to hold my composure. I had to play it cool and play his game.

"Yeah, you're probably right, Ray. It was a mistake. I don't know what I was thinking about cheating on my husband, especially after he has done so much for my family. Last night made me realize how much I love him. You are right. This can't happen again."

Something flashed in Ray's eyes. He wasn't expecting my response. I had chinked his armored heart and it felt good. He looked like he wanted to respond but didn't. Gave me a long and angry leer before leaving the room. *Got his ass good.*

When he left, I dressed in a purple pantsuit that covered me from my neck to my feet. By the time I finished putting myself together, Ray had already left. After kissing the kids and making them promise to keep their mouths closed about their father spending the night, I headed to the courthouse. I got to the Safety Building a little after 8 o'clock. Everything in the building was shiny. Polished floors, whitewashed walls, bright lights, silver, gold, and bronze accents. Looked like crime did pay. Extremely well. I followed the signs until I found the commissioner's court. Benny's lawyer was waiting outside the door. A woman stood next to him.

"Mrs. Boston! Glad you could make it. How are you?"

Donald Warren was a tall and slim older white man with brownish gray hair and big brown eyes. He wore a dark tailored suit and carried a briefcase. The woman with him was a gray-eyed brunette that looked to be in her early thirties.

"I'm fine, Donald. Better than I was yesterday," I said, flashing a weak smile.

Torn Between a Gangster and a Gentleman

"Good. He'll need you to be strong. This is my associate, Lyda Silverman. We're going to try to get your husband bail. This proceeding should be relatively short. With any luck, his bail should be around fifty to a hundred thousand dollars."

I was surprised at the amount but went along. "Okay. That's fine. When does the hearing start?"

"In about ten minutes. You showed up just in time. Follow me."

When I followed Donald into the courtroom, the first thing I noticed was the press. Men and women with cameras and microphones were everywhere. A murmur went through the crowd when they noticed me.

"Ignore them. They're gutless hounds chasing a story. I'll speak to them when this is over," Donald assured, leading me to the first pew.

There was a woman seated at the end of the pew, but I didn't acknowledge or pay her any mind. I was too worried about Benny and the press. When this aired on the news, it was going to create a social nightmare for our family. Then there were also the marks all over my body. Still wasn't sure how I was going to explain that one.

"Hey, Brianna," the woman at the end of the pew spoke, pulling me from my thoughts.

I looked over and got a surprise. It was my husband's secretary. "Hey, Ciarra. What are you doing here?"

"I came as soon as Mr. Boston called. I've been here for almost an hour."

I didn't like Ciarra. Never had. There was something about her that I couldn't put my finger on that rubbed me the wrong way. She gave me bad vibes. I was also wondering why Benny called one of his employees from jail. That didn't seem right. "Okay. They said he should be coming out in about ten minutes," I managed.

"I know." She grinned. "Donald told me."

Now I definitely didn't like her. She was too familiar with Benny's business. She had even talked to his lawyer before I did. I really didn't like that. And since I didn't have anything nice to say, I took the advice my mother gave me when I was a little girl and didn't say nothing at all.

Benny came out a few minutes later and just like Donald said, the hearing was over in less than 5 minutes. His bail was set at 75,000 dollars. As soon as we left the courtroom, the press was all over us.

"No comment! No comment!" Donald and Lyda called as we walked the hallway.

After a certain point, they stopped following.

"Mrs. Boston, Lyda will take you to pay your husband's bail. I'm going to talk to the press. It'll take at least an hour for them to process him out. I know a place that serves pretty good food that's close by. You up for Italian breakfast?"

After paying my husband's bail I went with Benny's lawyers to get breakfast, making sure to leave the secretary behind. An hour later we walked back to the Safety Building to await his release.

10 minutes into the wait, Benny walked out. "Man, am I happy to be out of there!" Benny smiled.

I ran over to get a hug and kiss. "Hey, baby! I missed you so much. I was worried about you."

"I missed you, too. Hey, Donald. Thanks for everything, man," Benny said, breaking our embrace to greet his lawyer.

They walked a few feet away to have a private conversation.

While I was waiting for him to wrap up the conversation with his lawyer, Ciarra appeared out of thin air. "Hey, Mr. Boston!"

Benny looked surprised to see her. "Hey, Ciarra. What are you doing here? I thought I told you to run the place until I came in."

"I know. I told Sergio—"

"But, Ciarra, I told you, not Sergio. If I wanted Sergio in charge, I would've called Sergio and told him. I called you," he lectured.

I loved watching Benny check her ass. I was hoping that he would fire her.

"Yes, sir. I'll get right over," she said demurely, leaving without another word.

Benny turned back to his lawyer for a few more words before they shook hands and parted ways. "Honey, I need to get home and get this jail smell off me. Let's get out of here," Benny said, walking over and wrapping an arm around my shoulder.

Torn Between a Gangster and a Gentleman

"I don't like your secretary," I admitted.

"She's harmless, baby. And a good worker. Hard to find good help these days."

"But she rubs me the wrong way. And she calls me by my first name. I don't want her calling me Brianna. We're not friends."

"She is one of my best workers and has been with me since I started the company. I can't just fire her because she gives bad vibes. But I'll talk to her. I promise. From now on, she'll address you as Mrs. Boston," he assured as we walked to my truck.

Feeling better about Ciarra being put in her place, I addressed his charges. "So, what about the charges against you? Did you do what they say you did?"

Benny removed his arm from my shoulder, stopping in his tracks. "Are you serious?" he asked incredulously. "Of course I didn't kill anybody. What kind of question is that? I told you it was a mistake when the police arrested me. I didn't do this, Brianna. I'm innocent."

I wanted to believe him, but the entire situation didn't sit right with me. I couldn't just forget about the police kicking in our door and taking him out in handcuffs. I couldn't let it go so easily. "How do they mistakenly arrest you for murder?"

"If I knew, I would tell you. That's what the lawyers are for. But I'll make it go away. I promise."

"I want to believe you, Benny. I do. But I have so many questions. If you're involved in something, you can tell me. I'm not naïve. I've been through this before with Ray."

He exploded. "Don't you ever compare me to some lowlife stick up kid, you hear me! Never ever compare me to Ray again! There is no comparison. I am Benny Boston. A respected man. I didn't live to be forty-six years old by being stupid. I told you this is all a mistake. I did not do this. Don't worry about my legal situation. I will make it go away," he snapped before walking toward my truck.

I cocked my head to the side and watched him walk away. I knew he was angry, frustrated, and probably a little scared about being arrested for murder and spending the night in jail. But what I didn't expect was for him to snap at me like that for asking questions. I didn't even compare him to Ray, but he snapped like I had. I'd never heard him talk about my kids' father like that. This wasn't the Benny I knew. Made me wonder if he really had something to worry about. But instead of confronting his ass like I really wanted to, I turned up my own attitude and followed him to the truck.

The ride home was silent. Benny was lost in his own thoughts and I was lost in mine. I gave a little more thought to his legal situation, wondering if he was telling the truth about the arrest being a mistake. I wasn't fully convinced that he was telling the truth but there was nothing I could do about it. I had to wait for him to open up. After coming to terms with Benny's case, my thoughts jumped to my bruised coochie and the marks on my shoulders, chest, and breasts. If Benny wanted to have sex later, I was going to have to figure out a way to deny him. He knew my periods came at the beginning of the month so I couldn't play that card. My only options were to get mad or play sick.

When I pulled into the driveway, I was relieved to discover that we had a new door. I continued to keep my attitude as we walked in the house, deciding that anger might be the best way to keep Benny's hands off me for the night.

"Brianna, will you bring me a drink to the bedroom?" Benny asked.

I stopped to give him a head-to-toe look. "Really, Benny? After you just talked to me like that, now you want me to be your bartender?"

"Brianna, please," he said weakly, letting out a stressed breath. "I just spent the night in jail for the first time in my life. Don't fight me today. I just want a drink, a bath, and a little time to figure some things out. Can you please make me a drink?"

I gave him a lingering stare before heading to the bar in the basement. "I'll be up in a minute." I went to fix him a Hennessey on the rocks before taking it to our bedroom. When I walked in, Benny was sitting on the bed naked. *Uh oh!*

"Thank you so much, sweetheart. I'm sorry for snapping at you the way I did. I'm so stressed out. How about you take those clothes

Torn Between a Gangster and a Gentleman

off and join me in the shower. Let me make up for snapping at you by putting my face between your legs for as long as you want."

Shit! I thought I got away, but this fool was about to pull it. So, I did the only thing I could to kill the mood. "Are you serious, Benny? You want me to fuck you after you had the police terrorize me and my kids? Are you kidding me!"

The burst of anger left him momentarily stunned. "Now, that ain't no way to talk to your husband, Brianna. I said it was all a mistake and I'm sorry. But you won't be talking to me like that in my house."

I rolled my neck and put a hand on my hip. "Your house! You mean our house, right? Because my name is on the deed, too. The same house the police kicked the door in, right? The house they humiliated us and treated us like criminals in, right? That house?"

A snarl spread across Benny's face and he sat the drink on the bed. "I just told you about talking to me like that, Brianna. Lower your voice. I know you're mad but you not about to be disrespecting me."

I turned it up a notch. "You didn't say that to the police when they kicked in the door, screaming and pointing guns at us. You didn't have to explain to Brittany that they weren't going to shoot us. You didn't feel the humiliation that I felt from our neighbor's dirty looks. But now you want me to get on my knees and fuck and suck your dick, huh?"

Benny threw this drink across the room. "I don't have to listen to this bullshit! You acting real stupid right now. I just spent the night in a fucking jail cell and now you want to come at me with this bullshit! Fuck you!" he yelled before scrambling into his clothes and storming away from the room.

CHAPTER 13-Benny

"Where are you?"

"On my way to B&B Global," Ciarra said flatly, a hint of anger in her voice. She was still mad about the way I treated her outside the courthouse.

"Chang of plans. Meet me at your house. I'll call Sergio and tell him to look after this company."

Ciarra's attitude perked up a bit when I told her to meet me at her house. "Yes, daddy. I'm turning around right now."

After ending the call with Ciarra, I called Sergio.

"Hey, boss."

"Sergio, I'm taking the day off. You're in charge."

"Say less. You know I got it," he said pausing. "I heard you got arrested last night. You good?"

I let out a long breath. "Yeah, I had to spend the night in jail. Some bullshit from the old days is coming back to bite my ass."

"You need my help?" he offered.

"Not right now. I have to go through the legal process. But there may come a time when I will need your services. Stay ready."

"I stay ready so I won't have to get ready."

I chuckled at the cliché response. "That's my boy. I'll catch you later."

After ending the call with Sergio, I reflected on my night in jail as I weaved the Jaguar through traffic. Jail was truly the worst place on earth. It stunk, the inmates stunk, and the guards all seemed to have a pole stuck up their asses. If jail was that bad, I could only imagine that the prison was 10 times worse. I couldn't go back. Jail and prison were no place for me. I couldn't understand how Ray had done 13 years when I had a hard time doing 13 hours. How people constantly went in and out of jail was a mystery to me. It sounded insane. I couldn't go back. I had to find a way to get to Red Fox and silence his ass. And I knew just the man for the job.

After figuring out a way to deal with Red Fox's bitch ass, my thoughts turned to Brianna. In the 11 years that I had known her, she had never talked to me like that. No woman had. Brianna knew her place. Had she been any other woman I would've slapped this shit out of her and choked her until she passed out. But I gave my wife a pass. She was my trophy. Congressmen, senators, alderman, and businessmen had all seen and drooled over her. She was from a rare pedigree. A beautiful woman who knew how to handle herself in the presence of powerful men. I trained her myself. She helped my public image. And if I would've kicked her ass all over that bedroom like I wanted and the police got involved, I would've automatically been indicted by the public as guilty of murder and domestic abuse. I needed Brianna more than she knew. But that still didn't excuse her tongue. She had lashed out strongly. Made me wonder if she was trying to hide something. But what?

When I pulled up to the curb outside of Ciarra's eastside home, I pushed all thoughts of Brianna from my mind. I needed rest and time to think. I couldn't be concerned with an emotional wife at a time like this. So, after hitting the alarm, I made my way up the walkway. Ciarra lived in a brown brick one story house in a working-class neighborhood. I bought her the house 5 years ago for $180,000. It was the perfect place to chill for the rest of the day.

"Hey, Benny!" Melvin greeted when I walked in the house. Melvin was the oldest of Ciarra's 3 children. He was 12. His father was locked away with life in prison. Melvin had never met him.

"Hey, Benny!" the second oldest, Darius, greeted. Darius was 10 and didn't know his father either. Got killed in a shootout with the police while Ciarra was pregnant.

"Hey, boys! Why y'all ain't in school?" I asked, stopping to check out that video game they were playing.

"Covid-19 outbreak. Our school is closed for 2 weeks," Melvin answered happily.

"Going back to virtual learning," Darius echoed.

"Okay. You boys take care. Where is Benny Jr?" I asked, heading toward the back of the house.

On cue, little Benny came running out of Ciarra's sister's room.

"Daddy! Daddy!" he screamed.

"Hey, baby boy! What you up to?" I asked, scooping up my little man and giving him a kiss. Benny Jr was my 3-year-old son.

"Nothing. Watching a movie with my tee-tee. I wanna be a race car driver," he squealed.

"A race car driver! Really? That's pretty cool, man. I'mma have to buy you a race car then. You want to be a NASCAR driver, right? How that sound?"

"Yeaaahhh! I wanna be a NASCAR race car driver!" he squealed.

"Okay. Go back in there with tee-tee and finish watching the movie. Daddy has to take a bath."

"Okay, daddy. Bye, daddy!" he said before taking off running down the hallway.

I followed my boy down the hallway and past Ciarra's sister's room. She was the live-in mooch-slash-babysitter. She didn't do anything, go anywhere, or own anything. Just sat around and ate and got fat. About the only thing she was halfway good at was sucking dick. I let her hit me off every now and then. "Hey, Shandra," I waved as I walked by.

"Hey, Benny. You staying over?"

"Yeah. Your sister is on her way home," I called as I walked into the bathroom. After closing the door, I ran water in the tub and got undressed. I didn't want a shower, not after a night in jail. I needed to soak. No sooner than I had climbed into the water, the bathroom door opened.

"Hey, daddy!" Ciarra smiled.

"Hey, baby. You are just in time," I said, puckering my lips to receive her kiss.

"I thought you were mad at me for coming to court. I just wanted to be there for you, daddy," she said, walking over and grabbing the body wash and a towel.

I liked when she took the initiative. There was something sexy about a woman that didn't need to be told what to do. I loved a woman that catered to her man. After spending the night in jail and arguing with Brianna, this is exactly what I needed.

"I know you wanted to be there for me, baby girl. I know. But I told you to go to work. You have to listen to what I say. You can't always trust your emotions. They can mar your judgement sometimes. You have to believe in me and trust in my vision. In the sixteen years that I've known you, have I ever let you down or steered you wrong?"

"No, daddy," she answered while rubbing the towel across my shoulders and chest.

"And I won't start now. Things will get rough for me with this murder wrap hanging over my head and I'm going to need your support. Can I count on you for that?"

"Yes, daddy. I will do whatever you need me that do."

"Good. Now last night was hard on me. I need to release some frustration," I said before standing to my feet.

When Ciarra saw my dick pointing at her like a missile, a gleam of excitement flashed in her eyes. "Yes, daddy."

***

"I need this nigga dead yesterday!" I said, leveling my eyes at my houseguest. We were sitting at the table in Ciarra's kitchen smoking a joint of Exotic and drinking cognac.

"I understand your dilemma, old friend. And I got the perfect people for the move." The Candy Man smiled.

The Candy Man that I was sitting across the table from looked nothing like the man in the movies. The real Candy Man was short, portly, with eyes that never stopped searching. He was also black as night with skin that looked tough as leather. I had known him for about 20 years. Back in the day he was a ruthless killer. A hired gun and lose cannon that made people's problems go away for a fee. These days he retired from getting his hands dirty but was still in the killing business. He managed killers. Had a troupe of assassins on call almost anywhere in the United States.

"Make suew this nigga is in a box. He all they got. If he can't talk, I'mma free man," I expressed, stubbing out my joint roach in this ashtray.

"So, how do you even know this clown? I heard he was snitching a long time ago. Why would you link up with a nigga like that?"

Torn Between a Gangster and a Gentleman

"I met that nigga in '98. He used to be over on 20th and Atkinson. His brother was one of my runners. Nigga name Ivan. Well, Ivan got knocked moving five bricks for me. Took the wrap. All he asked was for me to pay his legal bills and take care of his family. The Feds gave him forty. Something happened while he was in and Ivan got poked to death. I reached out to his family and met his little brother Red Fox. He was a small-time pimp with a bad coke habit. Ended up owing a nigga five grand and couldn't pay. They came to collect with guns blazing. He called me and we went and took care of it. Now the bitch ass nigga wanna roll over on me."

The Candy Man shook his head. "Damn, that's fucked up, B.B. Damn snakes are vicious. I'mma take care of it for you. Since it's an inside job and will probably take more than one man, it will cost fifty. These niggas ain't ever getting out so their families will need to be compensated."

"No problem. Shit, I'll give you an extra ten when it's done. I need this done right so that it won't get back to me."

"Confidentiality is a must, B.B. I'll need twenty-five up front and twenty-five when it's done."

"No problem. Give me the account information and I will have it transferred as soon as possible."

J-Blunt & Miss Kim

CHAPTER 14-Ray

"Dad, don't nobody listen to those rappers no more. Scarface, JAY-Z, and Rick Ross are old and played out. Est Gee, 42 Dugg, and Lil' Baby are what's hot right now," Junior said before taking a bite of pizza.

I had taken Brittany and him to Rocky Rococo's. I made sure to take them out every weekend to hang out and spend time. I loved kicking it with my kids. Interacting with them was fun. I also loved teaching them. Had to show and tell them all that mom and dad never told me.

"See, that's the problem with y'all youngins. Don't know history. You can't talk about 42 Dugg and Lil' Baby being hot if you don't know nothing about Tupac and Biggie. They are GOATS."

"They died before we were born, dad," Brittany cut in. "That's old school. We're new school."

"But what about you and singing? You know who Whitney Houston is. Now, who is better than her?"

"Nobody. Whitney is a legend. But singing is different. It's timeless. Rap isn't."

"Well, it is to me."

"That's because you old, dad!" Junior laughed.

"Yeah, I'll show you old. If I'm so old, how come you can't beat me at basketball?"

"Oohhh!" Brittany rubbed it in.

"Shut up, Brittany," Junior said, mugging his sister before turning to me. "I'mma beat you, dad. I promise."

"Dream on, lil' man." I laughed.

"So, did you start looking for your mom yet?" Brittany asked.

"No, not yet. I'm really not sure that I want to meet her."

"Why not?" Junior asked.

"For starters, she gave me up when I was three. I think she made her choice back then."

"But, what if she changed? What if she wants to see you?"

"You changed," Brittany added.

I thought about their words. "Y'all kind of made some points."

"I think you should find her, dad. What if she rich or famous? Don't you want to know? I do," Brittany said.

"I have always been curious about who she is. But I don't even know where to start looking for her."

"They have apps that can find people, dad. All you have to do is download one of them and answer some questions."

"Really?"

"Yes, daddy. Stop being stuck in the 90s. There is an app for everything. Duh." Brittany laughed, making me feel stupid.

"You know I been in prison for the last thirteen years, girl. Cut me some slack."

"Oh yeah. I forgot. Was it scary in there?"

"Not really. When I first got to Waupun prison I had to watch my back a little because of some of the things I did to people before I got locked up. I made a few enemies back in the day and some of them wanted their lick back. But after a couple of fights they left me alone."

"Dang, dad. You a beast!" Junior said, looking at me like I was Black Panther.

"I wanna know if you and mama are getting back together," Brittany blurted.

I gave her a puzzled look. "How do we go from talkings about me being in prison to me and your mother?"

"Because I wanna know. When Benny went to jail, you spent the night with mom. Are y'all getting back together?"

I paused to think of a response. The last thing I wanted to discuss with them was sleeping with their mother or us getting back together. "I thought I told you to forget about that."

"No. You said nothing happened and don't tell Benny that you spent the night," Junior cut in.

I gave him the Ice Cube mean-mug. "Didn't nothing happen and I don't know want y'all talking about."

"Dad, we're not stupid. We're teenagers. We know about sex," Brittany said.

"You don't know nothing about nothing, lil' lady. You're too smart for your own good. We didn't do nothing."

Torn Between a Gangster and a Gentleman

"Dad, I'm about to be fourteen, not five. Plus, I know Mommy still loves you."

That got my attention. "How do you know all of this, Ms. Psychic?"

My daughter let out a frustrated breath and rubbed her temple. "Tell him, Junior."

"We seen how she looked and acted when you used to call while you were locked up. And when you come to pick us up, she watches you from the window. I think you make her happy. Like she was the night Benny got locked up. She acts different around you," my son explained.

"You guys are very perceptive."

"Do you love Mommy?" Brittany asked, her eyes lighting up with hope and expectation.

"I will always love your mother. She blessed me with you two. But no, I'm not in love with her and we won't be getting back together."

Brittany looked deflated.

"But what if Benny goes to jail?" Junior asked.

"Man, it sounds like y'all gave this way too much thought." I laughed. "Where is all this coming from? I thought y'all loved Benny?"

"We do. But he's not our dad. We want a real family, huh, Junior?" Brittany said, gaining her brother's support.

"Yep."

I went silent for a moment. They were hitting me with tough questions and I didn't want to disappoint them. "I don't know, y'all. Let's just see what happens."

***

After dropping my kids off, I headed home. I plopped down on the recliner and thought about what they said about finding my mother. I did want to see her. I wanted to know where I came from, who she was, and why she gave me up. So, I decided to look for her. After a Google search, I found a people finding app and downloaded it on my phone. There were 25 questions to answer. I did the best I could. When I finished, a message popped up saying I would get an email with the results.

As I sat in this chair, I began to think about my aunt Michele. She was my dad's sister. I hadn't spoken to her since I was about 10. Our family wasn't close knit. Everyone lived separate lives and I don't ever remember going to a family reunion. When I got out of prison, I didn't contact any of my father's family. They left me in prison to rot so I didn't see a need to reach out to them when I came home. But something inside of me made me want to reach out to her. So, I did a Facebook search and found her in a few minutes. She wasn't active so I sent her a friend request.

I was about to sit my phone down when it began vibrating. Nilanti sent a text.

Mother Africa needs tending. ;-)

***

"Do you honestly tink dat da movie Da Notebook could be real? Like a man would really go tru all dat for a woman?" Nilanti asked, wearing a cynical look while leaning back against the passenger door of my truck. She was stretched across the cab with her feet in my lap. I was giving her a foot rub as I drove. We had just come back from a stepper's club. This was our fifth date.

"Absolutely. True love and the display of it wasn't monopolized by women. You don't think that men are capable of being loving and tender?"

"Yeah. In the movies." She laughed.

"What do you think about me? About the way I treat you? Do you think this is a game to me?"

She studied my face for a few moments. "To be honest, I tink you are a good man. You have almost restored my faith dat dere are good men out here. But for every one of you, dere are ten playa-playas."

Torn Between a Gangster and a Gentleman

"Well, thank you for the compliment. I know that was hard for you," I joked.

"But you still scare me a little."

"Why? You think I'm the Boogey Man?"

"You are almost too nice. You seem too good to be true. Like one day I will wake up and dis will all be a dream."

I pinched her foot.

"Ouch! Why did you do dat?" she squealed, kicking me.

"To show you this isn't a dream."

"Much betta way to do dat den pinching my foot. The dream ting was a figure of speech."

"I know that. I was just playing. But what are we going to do now that you know I'm real?" I asked while parking the truck in front of her house.

"What do you mean?"

"I mean where do we go from here?"

She was silent. Looked at something down the street for a few moments before turning back to me. "What do you want from me, Ray?"

"Everything that you have to offer."

"I don't want to be hurt again. And I don't just sleep around."

I should've let her go. Should've drove away and never looked back. But I couldn't. Nilanti was irresistible. The more she gave, the more I wanted. And I wouldn't be satisfied until I got it all. "Nilanti, I want you. Us. I'm serious."

"But what about the others?"

I told her about my friends. "When you say the word, I will delete them from my life. They were all temporary until I found what I was looking for."

"What're you looking for?"

"You."

Silence filled my truck. Nilanti removed her feet from my lap and sat upright. "I'm scared."

I reached out and grabbed her hand. "Don't be. I won't hurt you. I promise."

She stared at me, her dark eyes reflecting mixed emotions. I made my move. When I leaned in for a kiss, she closed her eyes and met me halfway. Our first kiss was a good one. She had the softest lips. Like brand new pillows. And when she got into the kiss, her truest desires confessed themselves in her moans and the way she grabbed my body. And then she stopped.

I searched her eyes for why.

"I have been hurt, Ray. Very bad. I have baggage. Can you handle dat?"

"Yes, I can. Now come here," I said before leaning in for another kiss.

She put a hand on my chest to stop me. "Wait, Ray. Listen. Just hear me out."

I didn't want to listen to anything but the sounds of her moans while I was deep in them guts. But the look on her face told me that I needed to listen. "Okay. I'm all ears."

"When I was nineteen, da man I loved and supposed to have married slept wit my sister. It hurt really bad when I found out. Like I told you, I fall hard. I really-really love dis man. Well, after I found out what he did, I tried to kill him. Cut him wit a machete. Tried to chop off his head. I missed and cut his shoulder. Den he beat me and raped me. Put me in hospital for two weeks. Dis is why I'm scared. When I'm in love, I can't control myself. When I fall in love, it has to be forever. Dat is da only way I love."

The look in Nilanti's eyes was serious. This was a warning. She told the story to let me know she didn't play with her heart. And even though it was a scary ass story, it wasn't enough to deter me. I had already cashed in my chips. I was all in.

"Nilanti, whoever that man was, I'm not him. I will not hurt you. Have you heard the saying, 'You never know what you're missing until it arrives'?"

"Yes." She nodded.

"You have become a need."

She searched my face and eyes, looking for the truth. Then she smiled. "Come with me."

Torn Between a Gangster and a Gentleman

After gathering her heels from the floor, she climbed out of the truck. A smile as big as the Atlantic Ocean spread across my face as I cut the engine and followed the sway of her hips. I felt like a climber that reached the top of Mount Saint Helen.

When we were standing outside her door, she spun to face me. "You know dere is no turning back once we are inside?" she asked, a sexy and dangerous look in her eyes.

"I am where I want to be."

"And you know dat if you hurt me, you will pay?"

It was another warning. And I ignored it again, closing this distance between us, placing my hands upon her hips. "It has always been my dream to visit the motherland."

Our lips met again. The second kiss better than the first. After a brief tongue wrestling match, she spun around to unlock the door. I swooped her into my arms and carried her across the threshold, kissing the entire way. I kicked the door closed behind us and we fell onto the nearest piece of furniture; a black loveseat with embroidered rose petals. How appropriate. When she tugged at my black sports jacket, that came off along with my T-shirt. Then she pushed me onto my back and straddled me, rubbing my chest and abs. She let out a sexy moan while kissing my lips, down to my chin, and pausing at my neck. From my neck, she worked her way down to my chest, to my nipples. She ground her sex on my lap as she bit down. Felt like I had been electrocuted.

"Ssss! Ahh!" I groaned.

She giggled.

"Take this off," I said, tugging at her dress.

She stood in front of me and pulled the straps of the yellow evening gown past her shoulders. The dress pooled at her feet and she was stark naked underneath. Her body was beautiful and amazing. Charcoal black and curvy. Just the way I imagined. Her breasts were big and round and firm. Her areolas bigger and blacker than any I had ever seen. Looked like they tasted like chocolate. I let my eyes travel down her torso, across her stomach, small waist, massive hips, and to the neatly groomed V between her thick thighs. It looked delicious!

"Let me see you," she requested.

I stood next to her, kicking off my shoes while unbuckling my belt. She watched me like a lioness stalking prey. I slipped my boxers and pants off in a single motion. She let out a gasp when I stood up.

"Dat is going to hurt," she gasped, eyeing my magic stick.

"No pain, no gain," I cracked before kissing her again.

She lay back on the couch and opened her legs. Our tongues continued to twist as I climbed on top. Instead of going right into the action, I kissed my way down her body, stopping to give her big, beautiful breasts some love. She rubbed my back and moaned, sounding like she was humming a favorite tune.

"Make love to me Ray," she moaned, opening her legs wider and thrusting her hips.

I kissed my way back up her body. When I was between her legs again, she grabbed my meat and put the head in. Her insides felt like a silky waterfall.

"Mmhh! Wait. Wait," she moaned, putting a hand on my chest to stop me from going deeper.

I was halfway in. Her womb felt so good that I wanted to thrust my entire body inside.

"You have to be gentle with me. I haven't made love in a long time."

I gave her a reassuring kiss while giving slow, half-strokes, waiting for her walls to adjust to me. When she began moving her hips, that was my signal that she was ready.

"Okay. I'm ready. Do me, Ray."

That sounded like music to my ears. I went slow and steady, being as gentle as I could while stroking deeply. Nilanti made the sexiest moans. Even started speaking Arabic. That shit had me so geeked that I bust sooner than I wanted to. After a round on the couch, she led me to the bedroom for more. She became more vocal and uninhibited once we were in the bedroom. I made sure that she got hers before I busted again.

Torn Between a Gangster and a Gentleman

When we had gotten all the lust out of our system, she snuggled up had to me, wrapping her arms around me. "You are a very good lover, Ray," she moaned, kissing my cheek.

I didn't answer right away. I was too busy kicking my own ass for sleeping with her. Now that it was over, I wanted to leave. Laying next to her felt awkward. This wasn't going to work out. She didn't fit.

Torn Between a Gangster and a Gentleman

CHAPTER 15-Ray

I was nervous as hell.

When Aunty Michele got back to me on Facebook, I was excited about meeting the family I had never known. But now that I was here, the excitement had turned to jitters. I had just parked in front of a black and white house in the middle of the block on 24th and Capitol. There were about 15 people standing and sitting on the porch. Men, women, young, and old. They were eyeing my truck like a celebrity was about to pop out. After cutting the engine, I ended their suspense.

"Is Aunty Michele in there?" I asked the crowd.

A tall, dark-skinned brother with a nappy 'fro stood and walked toward me. He looked to be around my age, dressed in a black T-shirt, blue jeans, and a pair of Nike's. In one hand was a bottle of Old English 800. The other was stretched out to greet me. "Ray? You Reggie son, Ray?" he asked, flashing 2 rows of gold teeth.

"Yeah. What's up? Who are you?"

He grabbed my hand and pulled me in for an aggressive hug. "Awe shit! Sup, nigga! You look just like Uncle Reggie. I'm Trip. We cousins. Michele is my mama. Hey, er'body, this Ray!"

The people on the porch mobbed me like I was Yeesus. I shook hands and hugged everybody as they made introductions. There were 5 cousins and 7 friends. One of the friends was Trip's soon to be baby mama.

"C'mon in the house, cuz. Mama waiting to see you."

I followed Trip in the house and found aunty Michele sitting in a docking chair in the living room. She looked nothing how I remembered when I was 10. Back then she had long hair, a pretty face, and a shapely figure. Today she looked like a stage 4 cancer patient. Dark blotchy skin, heavy bags under her eyes like she never slept, and short gray, uncombed afro. There were oxygen tubes in her nose, the tank within arm's reach. She looked like death was moments away.

"Hey, Ray!" she whispered hoarsely, smiling and showing 2 rows of purple gums. Didn't have a single tooth.

"Hey, Aunty Michele!" I greeted, going in for a hug.

She was all skin and bones and felt fragile. Like if I hugged her too tightly, she would break. And she smelled like weed. The good shit. "Look at you, nephew. Boy, you look just like yo daddy!"

"I was just telling him that, mama. Look like Reggie spit this nigga out," Trip chimed in.

"Sho' do. Have a seat. Have you met everybody? We have a big family but they at work or too busy. You know how folks is nowadays. Only sit still when they go to sleep."

"They bourgeois, cuz. We got a lot of bourgeois family members that won't step foot in this house or go to the hood."

"Don't talk about the family like that. They got they own lives live."

"I'm just keeping it real. When the last time Major, Aunty Kelly, or Uncle Steph came over here? Ain't seen none of 'em in at least ten years. Moved to the suburbs and didn't look back. Know my mama sick but they didn't even reach back. That's bogus. They shunned yo pops after he went to the bing the first time. That's why didn't nobody know where you was or what happened to you all this time. They straight up bourgeois."

I was surprised by the information. I had no idea my father got shunned by his family. "Don't seem like I should be concerned with reaching out to them, huh?"

"Nope. Forget them, cuzzo. How you been? What's been up with you? You want something to drink? Beer? Henny? Do you smoke? You know Mama keep that medical on deck for her cancer. Pharmaceutical grade. One hitter quitter."

"Boy, you bet not be fucking with my weed!" Aunty Michele warned.

"Nah, I'm good on the smoke." I laughed. "I gotta lil' legal situation. But I'll take a beer."

"Lady, go get Ray a beer," Trip told the young dark skinned woman who's stomach was as big as her booty.

"That's yo cousin. You do it," she sassed, rolling her eyes and smacking her lips.

"Bitch, go get my nigga a beer before I slap the—"

Torn Between a Gangster and a Gentleman

"Hey! Y'all not about to be fighting up in here!" Aunty Michele yelled before breaking out in a fit of coughing. "And you betta watch yo mouth, Trip. Stop calling that girl out her name."

Trip mugged his mother and soon to be baby's mother as he got up from the couch. "I got you, cuz. That's what I get for fucking with these W-2 ass thots."

When Trip left the room, I turned to Aunty Michele. "So, how are you doing? Is the cancer going away?"

"No, baby. Too much smoking and drinking. Don't know how long I got left. Started in my lungs and been spreading. Normally be in a lot of pain but today is one of my good days."

I shook my head. "I'm sorry to hear that, Aunty."

And I was. I couldn't imagine how it felt to know that death was right outside your door and there was nothing you could do about it. I often thought about how my dad felt when he found out he was dying.

"Don't be sorry for me, nephew. I lived sixty-four years and done seen and done it all. I made peace with Jesus. I'm ready to go whenever He comes to get me."

I seemed to be the only one saddened by the news. When I looked around the living room, everyone seemed more interested in me than hearing about a dying woman.

"Here you go, cuzzo," Trip said, coming from the kitchen and handing me a cold bottle of Old English.

"Good looking, man," I said before turning back to Michele. "So cancer must run in the family, huh?"

"I think so. But me and your daddy the only ones to get it from our generation. Couple people on your mother's side had it while we was growing up."

"That cancer ain't no joke, cuzzo. But that medical keep her right. You say you don't smoke, huh? You on papers or something?" Trip asked.

"Yeah. Gotta couple years on parole."

"Damn, my nigga. You a felon too, huh? Where you do yo time at? I was in Green Bay back in 2012. Did a nickel."

123

"I just finished doing thirteen. Did most of it in Waupun and Portage."

Gasps came from the friends and family.

"Damn, Ray. You was bitin', my nigga. What, you caught a body?"

"Nah, some robberies. They gave me a hundred years but I got back on appeal," I said before taking a sip from the bottle of malt liquor.

"That's what's hannin'." Trip nodded. "I met a lot of good niggas that ain't never coming home. Free the guys."

"Free the guys," I saluted before turning back to Aunty Michele. "So, when was the last time you seen or heard from my mother? I was hoping to reach out to her."

She thought for a moment. "Damn, Ray. I haven't seen your mother in over twenty years. Last time I kicked it with Carla, you was a baby. She wasn't doing too good either. That's why she left you with Reggie. She had a habit. The last time I seen her, I think she was over there turning tricks on the eastside."

Hearing that my mother was a dope fiend hoe stung a little bit.

"Don't look like that, cuzzo. Er'body gotta dope fiend in they family. That's how it is in the hood. Shit, mama didn't stop hitting that horn until about five years ago. Kept smoking even after she found out she had cancer."

"I'm still sitting here, boy," Aunty Michele reminded. "Don't be putting my business out there like that."

"I know. You know we ain't got no secrets, mama. Ray is family. Ay, cuzzo, come outside and lemmie holla at you. I know you tired of er'body just staring in yo face."

I looked around at everybody after Trip put them on blast for staring at me. None of them would look me in the eyes. "All right."

We stepped onto the porch followed by cousins Dink and Man-Man. As soon as the door closed, Trip began rolling a blunt. "My bad about Lady, cuzzo. Lil' bitch in training. I'm try'na show her how to be a woman. She only sixteen so she got some more growing to do."

Torn Between a Gangster and a Gentleman

I looked at Trip to see if he misspoke when he said her age. He appeared unphased. Kept rolling the blunt. I glanced at Dink and Man-Man to see if they would react to Lady's age. Nope. "You said she sixteen?" I asked, thinking of Brittany.

"Yeah. Lil' bitch lied about her age, talking bout she was eighteen. Turned out she was only fifteen. I didn't find out her real age until she got pregnant. Her OG kicked her out when she found out she was pregnant. I moved her in with me and moms. Now I got the lil' bitch in training."

"Damn," I mumbled, not knowing what else to say.

"But fuck that lil' bitch, cuzzo. What up with that bag unc left you from that life insurance?"

I frowned, wondering how he knew. "What you talking about?"

"C'mon, fam. Moms told me." He chuckled. "Said Reggie left you a hunnit Gs. I can tell by the look on yo face that it's true. Hook a nigga up, fam. I ain't got no job, we about to lose the house, mama need help with them medical bills, and I got a baby on the way. We need some help, man."

This was what I didn't want to happen. I had seen movies and heard comedians crack jokes about family that you never met asking for money when they found out you had it. Now it was really happening to me. "My hands kinda tied up right now, Trip. I'm locked in some investments."

"C'mon, Ray. We ain't no mooches or leeches, my nigga. We need some help. The rest of the family shitting on us. Don't act like them mu'fuckas. We family."

"Um, listen, I'mma see what I can do," I stammered. "But I gotta go. I'mma check with you and aunty later."

He looked disappointed. "So, that's how it us, cuzzo? Gon' treat us like the rest of them bourgeois niggas?"

"My word is my bond, Trip. I'mma see what I can do. I'mma call you when I figure something out."

***

"R-Sun! What up, fool!"

"What's up, Cray? Lemmie get a Budweiser."

"Okay. Cold one coming right up." He grinned, opening the cooler and grabbing the beer. "What brings you to my neck of them woods? I thought all the stockbrokers hung out on Wall Street," he cracked.

"I needed somewhere to chill and collect my thoughts for a minute. I just came from meeting some of my pop's people."

Cray gave a look of concern as he sat the beer on coaster in front to me. "You went to see Reggie's people? Who?"

"Aunty Michele and some of my cousins."

"Oh, well that's a good thing, right? How is Michele doing? I haven't seen her in a while. She still on that shit?"

"Nah, she ain't on dope no more. But she ain't good either. She got cancer. Could die any day."

Cray looked saddened by the news. "Nah, man! Michele, too? Damn, Ray. That shit runs in your family."

"Yeah, apparently. Her son try'na hit me up for some money to help them out. Medical bills, the mortgage, and help his pedophile ass take care of him and his sixteen year old baby mama."

"They didn't waste no time hitting you up for the green, huh? And what's up with this pedophile shit?"

"Trip is about my age. His girl is sixteen. He training her how to be a woman."

Cray's eyebrows bunched as he frowned. "What the fuck kinda Jerry Springer, Maury Povich shit they got going on over there?"

"I don't know. I'mma cut 'em a check for ten thousand and wash my hands. Too much shit going on in that house."

"That's pretty generous. I wouldn't give they ass shit. You don't know them. They didn't help you during those thirteen years you spent in the pen. But since you feeling generous, I need a couple thousand to pay some bills."

I gave Cray a *'You gotta be kidding me'* look.

"I'm just messing with you, Ray." He laughed. "I don't wanna do nothing that will make you bring R-Sun back out."

"You crazy, man." I laughed.

"That's why they call me Cray."

Torn Between a Gangster and a Gentleman

"Hey, man, what is the streets saying about Benny Boston? You know he got locked up a couple weeks ago?"

"Oh shit! Yeah, man. I seen that on Facebook. Said he killed some nigga named T-Mac back in the day. Some pimp nigga bust his head to get some Fed charges dropped."

The news surprised me. "Damn. Seriously?"

"Yeah. This what the streets saying. You know, Benny used to be a cold muthafucka back in the day? Had a couple blocks on the Eastside. Used to be a major supplier before he went legit. Now this fool all at Senator Ron Johnson parties. He did it how it's supposed to be done. Turned that dirty money clean. Word is, if you need something moved, for the right price, Benny's trucks will move it."

"Damn, Cray. I didn't know Benny was plugged in like that. Why you just now telling me this? My kids in the house with this nigga."

"I don't know, Ray. It never came up. I figured you always knew about Benny. Plus, you never wanted to talk about Brianna. But shit, the way things is looking, he might not be in that house much longer. He might be headed to the big house."

"I heard rumors about him in the streets, but I thought they were just rumors. You know how that shit be. But I didn't know he was on that Big Meech shit."

Cray shrugged. "Ain't really nothing you can do about it now. Gotta just sit back and see how it plays out. How does Brianna feel about all this? She knew about his past, right?"

Normally conversations about Brianna were off limits but I made an exception. "She don't got a clue about this nigga's past. She think he Bill Cosby or Uncle Phil off Fresh Prince."

"Maybe that's for the better. Maybe Benny is trying to protect her and your kids. No sense in telling her about his demons. That's a conversation between husband and wife. Sometimes silence is golden."

"Yeah, I know. I wasn't going to say nothing to her. It ain't my place. She put up with me and my shit back in the day so she'll be okay. She is a soldier," I said before taking a sip of beer.

127

"This the most I heard you talk about her since you came home. You and Brianna good now?"

I paused a moment to think of a response that didn't reveal too much. "Yeah. We talked the night Benny went to jail."

Cray gave me a searching stare.

"Why you looking at me like that?" I smiled.

His eyes got as big as hot air balloons. "Oh shit! You fucked Brianna!"

I tried to contain the smile. "C'mon, Cray. You know me and Brianna don't get down like—"

"Bullshit! You ain't got that joker grin on your face for no reason. All this time you been acting like you hate her and you still in love. You a slick muthafucka, Ray!"

"It was an accident, man. I was drunk. I told her I didn't even remember."

"But you did!" Cray laughed.

"I might've. But that's as far as it's going with her. I'm seeing somebody new right now."

"Yeah, whatever." He waved me off. "Who is the new girl? Is it really Brianna but you just don't want to tell me?"

"Nah. It's my P.O."

Cray's eyes got bigger than they did when he found out I was sleeping with Brianna. "Get the fuck outta here! You fucking your parole officer?"

"Yeah. She from Africa. Built up like a stallion."

"Damn, Ray! I wish I could be you for one day." Cray whistled. "Got you something from the motherland, huh? Bet you ain't gotta ever worry about getting revoked for a violation."

"I don't know, man. I think I bit off more than I can chew with this one. I thought I wanted to be with her. She cool. Down to earth. Educated. Sexy as hell. But now that I got her, I'm not really feeling her like that. I enjoyed the chase more than I'm actually enjoying her. Plus, she don't fit."

"Damn, Ray. You one of those men that enjoy the hunt better than the kill. You shouldn't have led her on, brotha. She has your freedom in her hands. And what do you mean she don't fit? What is that supposed to mean?"

"When we sleep together it don't feel right. It's like trying to stick a square in a hole that's meant for a circle."

Cray lifted his hands, confusion showing on his face. "What the hell are you talking about, Ray? Do her breath stank? Do she snore? She got fucked up feet that scratch your legs when you sleep?"

"Nah, man. None of that. You know how women like to sleep. Cuddling and spooning. It don't feel right with Nilanti. I don't want to hurt her feelings because she's fragile. Probably a little crazy, too."

"Awe, hell, Ray, just sleep at the other end of the bed then. You talking all metaphorical with squares at circles and shit. If you don't wanna cuddle with her, just tell her."

I laughed and shook my head.

Cray watched me for a moment. "Hey, Ray. I got another question. It's a about Brianna. Does she fit?"

J-Blunt & Miss Kim

Torn Between a Gangster and a Gentleman

CHAPTER 16-Brianna

"So, how is everything at home? How is Benny?" my mom asked, looking at me over the rim of her coffee cup.

"He's holding up pretty good considering everything that's going on. Some of his friends in politics are turning their backs on him, but that's to be expected," I explained, playing in the apple pie that I thought I wanted but no longer had an appetite for. I was at my mom's house. My mom, Tamar, Sarita, and I were sitting at the kitchen table talking.

"I can't believe he got arrested from murder. That don't even seem like him. Ain't he try'na to be a Mayor or something?" Tamar asked, feeding Sarita a bite of pie.

"You would think, right? Especially since he done drug me to all them fundraisers and luncheons. I don't know what to think about this murder. I don't know if Benny is capable of killing somebody. I mean, maybe we all can kill if forced to. I would do anything for my kids and my family. He just doesn't seem like the kind of man that just goes around killing people. But I don't know how to explain the police kicking in my door and pointing guns at us. Was that really the mistake that Benny says it was? He says it's all a misunderstanding and that somebody is trying to set him up. But why would somebody want to set him up? He doesn't have any enemies."

"People will always find a reason to hate, Brianna. Especially somebody that is doing as good as Benny. I don't believe he did it. They love to see successful black men locked up and in jail. It has to be a mistake. Benny ain't no killer. I bet you any amount of money it's a hater trying to bring him down. Benny is one of the good guys," Tamar said matter-of-factly.

"I don't know if he's a good guy, but I don't know if I would go so far as to call him a murderer," mom cut in.

"What are you talking about, mom? Benny is a good man," I defended.

"I didn't say he wasn't a good man. I think he's a wonderful man to you and to the kids. He's a good provider and respected businessman. I said, I don't know if he's a good guy. He may have wooed you and Tamar with his smooth talk, expensive clothes, and nice stuff, but not me. The devil is a smooth talker, too. Everything that glitters ain't gold. Don't be surprised if he has enough skeletons in his closest to fill up a graveyard."

"Where is all of this coming from? Why are you calling my husband the devil?"

"I'm not calling him the devil, Brianna. I used that as an example. I just don't believe that everything with him is straight up. When most people smile, you can see it in their eyes. Not Benny. I always thought that was strange."

"Why didn't you tell me of these strange things when I asked you if I should marry him?"

"Because I didn't have a reason to."

"What does that mean?"

"It means he wasn't facing a murder charge back then. Plus, Ray was gone."

I was getting irritated now. "What does Ray have to do with this?"

"Everything." Mom smirked.

There were so many hidden meanings behind her response that even Tamar picked up on it. "What are you talking about, mom?"

"Ask your sister."

Tamar turned to me. "What is she talking about?"

"I don't know. This isn't even about Ray. We're supposed to be talking about Benny."

"You didn't tell her about the kiss?" mom blurted.

I gave the woman that gave me life this meanest look I could muster.

Tamar looked at me with wide eyes. "You kissed Ray!"

"Why would you do that, mama?" I asked, wishing I could get her back for putting my business out there.

Mom responded with laughter.

"You and Ray kissed?" Tamar pressed.

I didn't answer but mom had no problem spilling the beans. "She sure did. Right in the middle of the street."

Torn Between a Gangster and a Gentleman

Tamar looked like she a watching a Lifetime movie. "When was this? Why didn't you tell me, Brianna?"

I invoked my fifth amendment right and stayed silent.

"About a month ago," Mom continued. "Both of them was over here acting like they didn't want to be around each other. She knows she still loves him and he still loves her."

"Oooh-weeee! Ray and Brianna, sitting in a tree, k-i-s-s-i-n-g!" I broke my silence. "Really, Tamar? You going all rhyme time on me? Really?"

Her and mom bust out laughing.

"Chill out, girl. We all know how you feel about Ray. We're just teasing. Maybe Benny going to prison is a way for y'all to get a second chance."

Mom perked up, eyes growing wide. "That's what I was thinking!"

I thought about what Ray said the morning after we slept together. That it was a mistake and we should forget about it. "Y'all are reading into this way too much. Ray has his own life and I have mine."

"Look at you acting like you wasn't at my house telling me love stories about your baby daddy. Now you try'na front in front of mama."

"I'm not fronting. I just don't want y'all dissecting my love life. Why don't you tell mama how your baby daddy came over and pulled a gun on us?"

My mother's face scrunched, her eyes blazing anger. "Armani pulled a gun on y'all?"

Tamar looked like I had just told her deepest secret. "Why would you tell her that, Brianna?"

I ignored the look on her face as dove into her business like they had done mine. "Yep, mama. He kicked in the door because Tamar wouldn't let him see Sarita. Benny had to come save us."

"Why didn't you tell me about this, Tamar?" Mom asked, giving my big sister a scolding look.

"Because I didn't want you to worry. Benny handled it. You wrong for this, Brianna."

133

***

I hung out with my mom and sister a little while longer, exposing some more of Tamar and Armani's relationship before heading home. A feeling of dread came over me when I saw Benny's car in the driveway. Things around the house had been tense ever since he got arrested. He was stressed out all the time and we barely spent time together. Arguments were constant. Sex was just a word that neither of us knew the definition of. We had hit a rough patch in our marriage, and I wasn't sure what direction we were headed. After parking beside the Jaguar, I let myself in through the backdoor and found Benny in the kitchen.

"Well, don't you look lovely this evening." He smiled, floating over to give me a kiss.

The greeting surprised me. "Hey, Benny. You're in a good mood. What's up?"

"I woke up this morning and had an epiphany. Every day that I wake up is a blessing. Sometimes we can take the seemingly small things for granted. Breathing is a miracle, but we don't recognize that. Why? Because we are too caught up in ourselves to pay attention to the small things. I realized that I've been so caught up in my problems that I haven't been tending to the most important person in my life. My wife. It's been over a month since we made love and I can't remember the last time we went out. So, c'mon. Let's go. The kids are with Ray and we have the rest of the night to ourselves."

I was beyond surprised. He seemed like a new man and it left me speechless. "Are you okay? What's going on, Benny?"

He wrapped his arms around my waist and stared lovingly into my eyes. "Everything is fine, sweetheart. I did some reflecting and put everything in perspective. I've been off ever since I got arrested and you've suffered as a result. I want to make it up to you. I want to make things right. Will you let me take you out tonight?"

"Go where? When?"

"Right now. I have everything planned. All I need is you."

Torn Between a Gangster and a Gentleman

I looked down at my clothes. I was wearing a T-shirt, jeans, and Nike Cross Trainers. "Wait. I need time to shower and change clothes."

He put a finger on my lips. "Shhh. Everything is taken care of, Brianna. Let's go."

I stared into his eyes for a moment, trying to make sense of this overnight change. Benny's eyes were dark and unreadable. My mother's words about his unsmiling eyes popped into my head but I didn't have the time to dwell on it. Benny wanted to work on our marriage, and I wanted my husband back. "Okay. You lead and I'll follow."

Benny used the rest of the evening to remind me why I fell in love with him 11 years ago. He was the perfect gentleman during our meal at Ruthcris. Not only was his chivalry on full display, but he actually listened to me and was very interested in my life and day to day affairs. This side of him was rare since he was being pulled in 10 different direction on any given day. Most of the time, he only had time for himself. So, for them couple of hours that the spotlight was on me, I enjoyed it.

After dinner at the steakhouse, Benny took me to the beach. It was a little past 10:00 at night so we had the beach to ourselves. The weather was a perfect 75-degrees and I loved the way the moon and stars were reflecting on the water. We walked the shoreline hand in hand, the romantic atmosphere being a perfect way to end the evening. It felt like I was in a movie.

"Are you happy, Brianna?" Benny asked.

"Yes, I'm happy. Everyone is safe and healthy. I couldn't ask for more. I'm more worried about your case than anything."

"Will you let me know if you ever become unhappy?"

I stopped to look at him, trying to get a read to see where these questions were coming from. All I got was the moonlight reflecting in his emotionless eyes. "Why are you asking me this?"

"Because you mean the world to me and your happiness is very important. I'm committed to you for life, Brianna, and if you're unhappy, that means I'm not doing my job. Missing you is my hobby, caring for you is my job, making you happy is my duty, and loving you is my life. I've spent most of the day reflecting on my life and you are a big part of it. So, the question still remains. Will you let me know?"

I was touched by the words. They were loving and sincere. "Yes. I will let you know, baby," I said before moving closer to suck on his lips.

"Good. Because we are meant to be together. You are my soulmate. The last thing I want to do is push away something that was meant for me."

When Benny said the S-word, only one man came to mind and it wasn't my husband. Luckily something glowing in the distance grabbed my attention. "Oh, Benny, that is so sweet. What is that?"

He looked at the flickering light ahead before turning back to me. "That's a surprise for you. C'mon. This is where we will be spending the rest of the night."

Benny's surprise turned out to be a blanket, lamps, and picnic basket filled with goodies. After pouring glasses of champagne, we cuddled on the blanket and looked up at the stars.

"You get a lot of romantic points today, husband. I feel so special." I sighed, sipping champagne while laying my head against Benny's chest.

"You are special. Tonight is just a literal manifestation of just how special."

"Thank you for showing me. It's been long overdue," I cracked. "I noticed that we've been talking about me all night. How are you?"

"I am well. I just wanted to make sure I spend some time with you. I'll probably be out of town most of next week, so I wanted to make tonight all about you."

"What about your case? What are the lawyers saying? Who is that confidential informant?"

"We still don't know who the informant is but my lawyers are working hard to get the case thrown out. There is no evidence connecting me to anything. It's just someone saying I did something that I didn't do. I'm going to make this go away."

"Why would somebody try to set you up of murder?"

136

Torn Between a Gangster and a Gentleman

"I wish I knew the answer to that question. But everything in the dark will come to light soon enough. But enough about me. Tonight is your night. How about I show you what I learned online about going down on you with a cough drop in my mouth."

All the wounds from my night with Ray had healed and I wasn't about to deny myself the pleasure of Benny's lips on my lady parts.

J-Blunt & Miss Kim

CHAPTER 17-Ray

"Hello?"
"What's up, cuzzo? How you been?"
I tried to place the voice. "Trip?"
"Yeah, this me. What's good?"
"I'm good. I didn't recognize your voice. How you doing?"
"Everything good on my end. I'm calling because I seen somebody that you probably wanna see. I knew a text message wouldn't do."
I took a moment to think about someone that I wanted to see. We never ran in this same circles and I don't remember mentioning to him that I was looking of somebody. "Who is it? Where are they?"
"I seen yo ol' girl."
The world around me stopped. "You seen my mother?"
"Yeah."
"When? Where?"
"Over on 27th and Wisconsin. I was taking moms to the doctor when we seen Carla on the bus stop. Well, moms the one that knew it as her because it was my first time seeing her."
"Where is she now?"
"I don't know. But I got her info. She live on 14th and Hampton. You ready for the address?"
"Yeah. I'mma put it in my phone." My hands shook as I typed the address.
"And just lil' heads up, cuzzo. She don't look like she doing too good. You gotta be ready for that."
"Okay. Thanks, Trip. I owe you big time for this."
"Nah, man. I owe you. That ten Gs you gave us really helped out a lot. I'm forever indebted to you, my nigga."
"Don't mention it, Trip. We family."
"A'ight, cuzzo. I gotta run. My bitch in training acting up and I gotta check the bitch. Holla at you later, my nigga."
After hanging up the phone, I reclined my chair and began staring at the wall. I couldn't believe that I had my mother's address. I

139

had dreamed about this moment for as far back as I could remember. I had so many questions. The most important one being why didn't she come back.

I don't know how long I sat in that chair staring at the wall, but I eventually jumped in my truck and made the drive to find my mother. 20 minutes later I pulled up to a black and white duplex, second house from the corner. The lawn out front was mostly dirt and the house looked like it could've used a fresh coat of paint 5 years ago. I parked directly across the street and sat there from a moment. I wanted to get out and knock on that door, but I didn't. I was scared, and that surprised me. I had kicked in the doors of drug dealers, survived shootouts, and done 13 years in prison; yet I was scared to go see my mother.

I sat for a couple of minutes trying to gather my thoughts and courage when there was movement at the front door. It opened and a tall, skinny man with an uncombed graying afro walked out. He had very dark skin, a full beard, and looked to be in his 50s. The T-shirt that he wore was wrinkled, the jeans were stained, and the white Nike's on his feet looked like he got them from a landfill. He closed the door behind him and began a quick step. Before he could make it to the street, the door opened again, and a woman stepped outside. She was short, brown skinned, and very skinny. Her short, permed hair was unkempt, some sticking in the air and the rest going wildly in all directions. She wore a black T-shirt, dark skinny jeans, and no shoes on her feet. It looked like she was chasing the man. Like they were arguing. I got out to investigate, keeping my eyes on the woman. Something in my gut told me she was my mother.

"Get yo ass back here, Frank! Quit running like a lil' bitch!" the woman screamed.

"I done told you to watch yo mouth, woman! Call me another bitch and I'mma make you kiss the ground."

"Bitch, bitch, bitch, bitch, bitch! You a punk ass, scary ass, bitch ass bitch, Frank!"

Torn Between a Gangster and a Gentleman

The man spun on his heels, violence in his stride as he walked toward the woman. "I told you about disrespecting me, Carla. I'm going to jail tonight because I'm about to whoop yo ass!"

When he said her name, my heartrate increased, and I felt suspended in time. There she was. The lady that gave me life. And just like Trip said, she didn't look well. I knew without a doubt that she was a crackhead. And I also knew that if I didn't intervene, Frank was about to kick her ass.

"Yo, Frank!" I called.

He spun to face me, a question lighting his eyes. "I know you?"

I looked from him, to Carla, and then back to him. "Not yet. But I'mma make sure you don't spend the next couple days in jail."

"Who is you?" Carla asked, giving me a suspicious look.

"I'm Ray. I need to talk to you."

Carla covered her mouth, her eyes growing as wide as full moons.

Frank became defensive. "What do you want to talk to my woman about?"

I kept my attention on Carla, reading the disbelief in her eyes. "She knows."

Frank turned to Carla. "Who is he?"

Carla ignored Frank as she walked toward me, her body trembling with every step. "Ray! Is that really you?"

"Yeah. Hey, Carla."

"Oh my God! I can't believe it's you!" she said, trembling as she wrapped her arms around my waist. "I can't believe you found me."

I didn't want to hug her. I don't know why, but I didn't want her to touch me. So, I kept my hands at my sides and stared down at the top to her head.

"Who is this nigga you got coming to my house?" Frank asked, sounding like a jealous lover.

Carla looked up at me with tears in her eyes. "This is my son, Frank. This is Ray."

Frank looked back and forth to me and Carla like we were playing a prank. "Yo son? What do you mean yo son? You never told me you had no kids."

Carla ignored Frank, staring up at me like she was trying to memorize my face. "You are so handsome. Look just like Reggie."

I didn't know what to say because I couldn't return the compliment. So, I said the only thing that came to mind. "Thanks."

An awkward silence came and stood in between us. I wanted to ask where she was all my life and why she gave me up but now that I was standing in front of her, those would have been stupid questions. She looked like she was having a hard time taking care of herself. No way she could have done anything for me.

"Do you want to come in? I know you probably have a lot of questions."

That was an understatement. "Yeah. Sure."

Frank walked away while Carla and I stepped in the house. Their living room looked like a poorer version of mine. The TV was the same clear 13" flat screen that I had when I was in prison. It was sitting on a stack of 4 blue milk crates. The furniture consisted of 3 mismatched wooden chairs around a small black kitchen table. There was an ashtray on the table filled to the rim with cigarette butts.

"Do you want something to drink? All we have is water and Four Loco."

"I'm good on the drink. Is this where you live?"

"Yeah. It ain't much but it keeps us sheltered. We learned to live without all the fancy stuff. Just got what we need."

Another understatement.

"It's okay. I live the same way. Learned to get by with the basics."

Another pause passed between us.

"Have a seat. Do you smoke?" she asked, pulling out a pack of Kools.

"Nah. I don't smoke."

"Well, I need one. Michele mentioned you yesterday. She told you where I lived, huh?"

Torn Between a Gangster and a Gentleman

"Yeah. Her son, Trip, called me a lil' while ago. I always wanted to meet you."

She lit a cigarette and took a puff. "Hope I didn't disappoint you too bad," she cracked.

I just stared at her.

"I heard about Reggie. I'm sorry to hear that. I didn't even know he passed until Michele told me. I've been living under a rock so..."

"Listen, Carla. I know this is probably a stupid question but I gotta ask. Why did you leave me?"

She took a long drag on the cigarette, a faraway look in her eyes. "Look, Ray, I been on dope since right after you was born. Reggie went to prison and while he was in, I met a nigga that turned me out. I knew I couldn't take care of you. I didn't know how. You cried too much and needed too much attention. All my attention was going toward Monte and getting high. I couldn't take care of you, so when Reggie got out, I dropped you off with yo daddy." There wasn't an ounce of regret, sorrow, or love in her voice. She sounded like the story was about strangers instead of her and her son.

"So that was it? You dropped me off and kept going? Didn't look back? Didn't think to check up on me?"

She got mad. "What do you want from me, Ray? Why would I check in on you? I couldn't do nothing for you. I did the best I could by dropping you off with yo daddy."

I got mad. "So you chose dope and a nothing ass nigga over your own flesh and blood?"

She didn't have a response. Took another long drag on the cigarette as tears rolled silently down her face.

I wanted to verbally assault her ass but seeing the tears made me hold back. "Do I have any brothers or sisters?"

She shook her head. "No. You was enough for me. I didn't want no more kids."

Hearing that she turned her back on her only child pissed me off even more. I wanted to give her the business so bad. But I held back. Instead, I was going to shame her. "I have two kids, Carla. Ray Junior is fifteen and Brianna is thirteen. I could never turn my back on them, no matter what I'm going through in life. They are the reason that I'm still alive. They are the reason that I didn't give up when the judge gave me a hundred years in prison. I would never turn my back on my kids."

Carla was quiet. Stared at the floor while puffing the cancer stick.

"So that's it, huh?"

She looked at me again, her eyes red, face tear-stained. "What else do you want me to say? I'm a fifty-four year old dope fiend. I don't got nothing, Ray. I told you everything."

"How about, 'I'm sorry for abandoning you, Ray'? How about taking responsibility? How about showing some remorse?"

"I'm sorry," she mumbled.

I wanted to laugh but I didn't. Just stared at her. She looked pathetic. I didn't feel anything for her. No love. No sympathy. Nothing. Kind of wished I would've let Frank beat her ass. "I'mma get out of here," I said heading for the door.

"Wait!" she shrieked, grabbing my arm.

"What, Carla?"

"Um... I was wondering if I could hold twenty dollars? I can pay you back tomorrow."

I couldn't hold back my laugh this time. Laughed so hard that tears came to my eyes. Laughed all the way out the door and to my truck.

CHAPTER 18-Ray

Nilanti and I had officially been together for a month. Most of the time we were inseparable. I had either spent the night at her house or she spent the night at mine. Sleeping with her was still uncomfortable because she always wanted to cuddle, but sex with her was fun. She was still inexperienced in some areas since I was only her third boyfriend and man she slept with, but she was a quick study and fast learner. She had also gone through some sort of transformation. The confident, man-eating feminist alter ego had vanished, being replaced by a vulnerable, kind of needy, and sometimes insecure version. But I still liked her. Liked her enough to deal with the overnight change and even allowed her to buy me some dishes and a table set for my kitchen. I was currently using those dishes to cook dinner.

The meal was simple. Pork chops, spaghetti, corn bread, and carrots. Nilanti had called me about 10 minutes ago to let me know she was leaving work. I had just pulled the cornbread from the oven when the doorbell rang.

"*Can I come over? Can I? Come over? To see you?*" I sang along with Aaliyah while grabbing Nilanti's glass of wine and heading for the door. "Hey, baby!" I sang while opening the door.

To my surprise it wasn't Nilanti. It was Brianna. And she was crying.

"Brianna, what are you doing here? And why you crying?"

"Can I come in?" She sniffled.

"Yeah. Sure. Come in," I said, making room for her to pass while looking down the block for Nilanti's car. No sign of her. After closing the door, I spun toward Brianna. "What's going on? Why the tears? Did something happen at home?"

She didn't respond right away. Just stood in the middle of my living room with a spaced-out look in her eyes. Like she just found out that Benny was guilty of murder. "Mama's dead," she choked before breaking into tears.

It felt like I had been punched in the chest by Mike Tyson. I had trouble catching my breath and became lightheaded. "Wait. What? You serious?"

She nodded, wiping away tears. "I just left the hospital. She died in her sleep this morning. Brain aneurysm."

I couldn't believe what I was hearing. It had to be a mistake. "I just seen her a couple days ago. She was good. Now you saying she gone?"

And that's when the front door opened.

"Hey, you." Nilanti smiled. When she seen Brianna's tear-stained face, her smile vanished.

"Hey, baby," I said weakly.

She loomed back and forth from me and Brianna. "Who is dis? What tis going on?"

"This is my kids' mother, Brianna. Brianna, this is Nilanti."

They didn't speak to each other. Just exchanged stares.

"Nilanti, can I talk to you for a moment?" I asked, stepping outside.

She gave an uncertain look as she followed, closing the door. "What tis wrong? Did someting happen?"

"I'm sorry, baby, but I have to cancel this evening. Her mother died."

Anger flashed in her eyes. "Why do we have this cancel our plans? What does dat have to do wit you? Wit us?"

"She was like my mother, too. I have to deal with this."

Nilanti wasn't hearing it. "But she was not chur mum. And *she* has a husband."

"I don't want to fight about this, Nilanti. I'll call you later. Just let me deal with this. Please."

She stared at me for a few moments. "Every time she needs you, will you go?"

"Nilanti, it's not what you think," I said, reaching for her hand.

"No! Don't touch me!" she yelled. "Run to your kids' mudder," she said before walking down the steps.

"Nilanti!"

She never broke her stride. Got in her car and fled away. That's when I realized I was still holding the glass of wine. I chugged it before walking back in the house.

"I didn't mean to mess up your night," Brianna mumbled.

"It's fine. She'll be okay. You want something to drink? Hungry?"

"I don't have an appetite. I'll take a drink though." She followed me into the kitchen where I poured her a glass of wine and offered a seat. "I see you bought more furniture," she commented.

"Yeah. Nilanti did this."

"She is pretty. Where is she from?"

"Africa."

"Is she your girlfriend?"

I didn't want to answer the question, so I asked some of my own. "When did you find out she died? Why didn't you call so I could come to the hospital?"

"Tamar found her this afternoon. They were supposed to go to a baby shower, but mom wasn't answering the phone, so she went to check up on her. Found her in the bed, still."

I shook my head, unable to comprehend that she was really gone. "Where are the kids? Do they know?"

"Yeah, the kids know. We all went to the hospital together. They are with Tamar. I wanted to come tell you in person. I wanted to see you. Benny is out of town."

"Damn. I can't believe she's really gone, Bria," I mumbled, reaching for the bottle of wine. I took a long chug, trying to drink away the sadness that was filling my body.

"Me either. I miss her already. I don't know what I'm going to do without my mother," Brianna said, her voice breaking as the tears spilled.

I cried alongside her as thoughts of Mom filled my head. I was really going to miss her. And then it hit me. Mom was a Jesus loving, super saved, church all week-long kind to woman. "To be absent from the body is to be present with the Lord," I said, quoting one of her favorite verses.

"She said that all the time," Brianna mumbled.

"I know. I don't think she would want us to sit around crying. She always talked about going to heaven one day. She probably looking down on us right now wondering why we sitting in this kitchen crying. We should remember the good times."

"Yeah. You're probably right. Pass me that bottle," Brianna said before downing her glass.

"I remember the first time I met her, right after we found out you were pregnant with Junior. She came in the living room mugging me like she wanted to hit me." I laughed.

Brianna poured another glass of wine and passed the bottle back to me. "Should've seen how mad she got when I told her I was pregnant. Scariest moment of my life. I thought I was going to die at sixteen." She laughed.

"I'mma miss her." I sighed.

"Me too," Brianna echoed.

Silence filled the kitchen for a moment as we sipped wine and thought about Mom. Then I thought about Carla. "I met my mother yesterday."

Brianna looked at me with wide eyes. "Your real mother?"

I nodded.

"Where is she? How did it go?"

"Not good. She a dope fiend."

"Oh, Ray! I'm sorry to hear that. Can she be helped? Is she out there bad?"

"Yeah, it's bad. She wasn't even remorseful about giving me up. Said she did the best she could by giving me to pop."

"Well, if she was out there bad, that might've been her best choice."

"I know she made the right decision by giving me to pop, but I guess I was expecting her to be sorry and apologize. I expected her to at least pretend like she wanted to keep me and giving me up was hard. But I didn't get none of that. She even got mad because I was asking questions. Then had the nerve to we me for twenty dollars before I left."

Brianna bust out laughing.

I gave her a dead ass stare. "Not funny."

Torn Between a Gangster and a Gentleman

"I'm sorry, Ray. It's kinda funny though." She giggled.
I laughed with her.
Moments later the laughter turned to tears. "I miss my mom, Ray. I can't believe I won't be able to see her again. It hurts," Brianna sobbed.
I reached across the table and grabbed her hand. "C'mere."
She didn't protest as I led her around the table and onto my lap. I sat the bottle of wine on the table and wrapped my arms around her, holding her tight. Brianna sat her glass down and wrapped her arms around me, laying her head on my chest. It felt like she was supposed to be there.
"Can I stay with you tonight?" her voice quivered. "I don't want to be alone."
Images of Nilanti and Benny popped into my head. If I allowed her to sleep over and either one of our partners found out, shit could get ugly. But when I thought about the night I spent with her while Benny was in jail and the way she felt in my arms while sitting on the chair, I knew I couldn't deny her request. "Yeah. You can stay. I don't want to be alone tonight either."
"Thanks," she said, giving me a squeeze and kissing my neck.
Then, almost as if she forgot something, her lips returned the same spot on my neck. She kissed it and licked. Sucked and nibbled. I lowered my head to taste her lips. Kissing Brianna was like eating cotton candy. Her lips felt like fluffy clouds that melted against mine and her tongue tasted like sweet wine. Kissing her felt familiar and brand new. Her moans were like music to my ears. Things between us heated up when she straddled my lap. My hands moved under her shirt to unhook the clasp to her bra and then I found what I was looking for. Her nipples were hard as gumdrops. She moaned when I squeezed them. We stopped kissing long enough to remove our T-shirts. When she took off the bra, I stared at the breasts I used to know so well. Her big and beautiful 34Ds had minimal sag. The large dark areolas were begging to be in my mouth.
"Mmmh!" she moaned, rubbing my head, neck, and back as I sucked a nipple in my mouth.

I gripped her booty and hips while moving my mouth back and forth from each breast. When I felt her hands traveled down my torso and stop at my belt, I knew what time it was. She got up to take off her pants and I did the same. When I sat back on the chair, Brianna didn't waste time getting what she wanted. She grabbed hold of me and eased down slowly.

"Oh, Ray!" she moaned, biting my ear as she impaled herself on my sword.

The only word that I could use to describe how her womb felt was 'heavenly'. I wanted to stay there forever. When I was deep inside her and we were pelvis to pelvis, her lips found mine again. Her kisses were greedy. Like she was trying to find my soul and lay claim to it. And when she started rocking her hips, I found myself wanting to lay claim to everything inside of her. She rode me like a mad woman on that kitchen chair, testing it's sturdiness as we thrashed around until we came. That was round one. For round two I knocked everything off the table and threw her on top. She put her legs on my shoulders and let me go as deep and as hard as I wanted. Round three was in my bed. We made love. It was slow and passionate and fulfilling. When we finished, we were spent. Exhausted and satisfied. She cuddled next to me, her head on my chest. A perfect fit.

***

"Ray."

I stirred. When I opened my eyes, Brianna was sitting up in bed fully dressed. "Hey. You leaving?"

"Yeah. I have to pick Benny up from the airport," she said, stroking my cheek tenderly.

I didn't want her to leave. "You talked to him?"

"Yeah. About an hour ago. I've been sitting here watching you sleep."

"That's kinda creepy," I joked.

"Shut up!" She laughed, slapping me on the shoulder. "Come walk me to my truck."

Torn Between a Gangster and a Gentleman

"Okay. Let me get dressed."

Brianna watched me as I went to my drawer to put on a pair of underwear and shorts. "Was she your girlfriend?"

I laughed. "Does it matter?"

"Not really." She shrugged. "I figured since you were making dinner and drinking wine that she must mean something to you. She bought you a kitchen table, too. People don't buy furniture unless there is something there. Is she?"

"Yeah. We're dating. Been about a month."

"That's good." Brianna nodded. "Thank you for letting me spend the night."

I slid into my slippers. "You made it hard to say no."

"And you're making it hard for me to leave," she said, getting off the bed and standing in front of me. There were a myriad of emotions showing in her eyes and written on her face.

"You good?"

"I'm sorry for leaving you, Ray. And for hurting you."

I continued staring into those cinnamon brown eyes, right to her soul. There was sorrow, guilt, pain, and shame. "I know."

"And I still love you, Ray. I mean, in love with you. I never stopped loving you. I swear."

The words reached deep down inside of me and quenched the fire that had been burning since she left. "I know that, too."

"So, can we be cool, now? Like friends or...?" Her words trailed off, but I knew what she was trying to say.

"Yeah. Let's be or," I cracked, pecking her lips.

"Silly." She pushed me.

We left the bedroom, and I led her outside. I seen it as soon as I stepped on the front porch.

"Fuck!" I cursed, anger bubbling up inside of me.

"Oh, Ray! I'm sorry!" Brianna apologized.

Her words did nothing to erase the rage that was building inside. My truck had been vandalized with white spray paint. *Cheater* was spray painted on the passenger side in large letters stretching from the headlights to the taillights. *Liar* was sprayed on the driver's side.

151

The final insult was spray painted on the hood in capital letters: *DOG*.

CHAPTER 19-Benny

I caught them sneaking peeks at each other!

I was at home, standing in the kitchen. Our house was filled with Brianna's friends and family, gathering to celebrate Earlene's life. Tamar, her kids, nieces, aunts, uncles, a few cousins, and friends that we hadn't seen since we got married filled the house. And then there was Ray. He mingled with Brianna's family and friends like he shared their bloodline.

The get together was being held in our backyard. I was grabbing extra meat from the kitchen which overlooked the backyard when I noticed Ray smiling like a lesbian in the shower in a woman's prison. I looked across the yard to see why he was smiling. Brianna stood next to her aunt Glenda staring in Ray's direction, wearing the same smile. Their smiles were those of secret lovers sharing a moment. They had probably been sneaking glances all day, not thinking anyone noticed. But I caught them. And seeing their little moment made me think of the argument that me and Brianna had when I came home from jail. She had snapped. Wasn't like her. She had never talked to me like that. And come to think about it, she didn't snap until I asked for sex. I had fallen for the oldest trick in the book. She used anger to mask the guilt and cover up her indiscretion.

"Bitch," I mumbled, grabbing the pan of meat and heading back outside.

My blood was boiling. After everything I did for her and those kids. Ray left them high and dry and I took them in. Gave them a good life. And this was my repayment. Betrayal. Chris Brown was right. These hoes ain't loyal. But I had a trick for both of their asses. They were playing chess with a grandmaster and I was about to go for the checkmate.

"Hey, Ray! You wanna give me a hand, brotha?" I called across the yard.

He walked over wearing a smug ass grin. I wanted to slap that smile clean off his bitch ass face along with his lips. "What's up,

Benny? Man, you working this grill. Got the whole neighborhood smelling good."

"Thank you, brotha. You know it's all about the seasoning when you're barbecuing. But, hey, I need you to take these tongs and flip the meat on the top rack. Gotta keep an eye on that chicken. Sometimes it sticks."

"No problem, Benny. What kinda grill is this? You got five racks and all kinds of extreme compartments. This is a nice piece of machinery," he said, sitting his bottle of beer on the attached countertop as he worked the meat.

"Grill Master 3000. She is a beauty, isn't she? Be careful though. You know what the good book says about coveting another man's things," I sneered.

Our eyes locked for a moment. His stare was even and cool. Mine was hard and cold. Then he seemed to catch the true meaning behind my words. Suddenly cooking barbeque became very tense.

"How are my mother's only two sons doing?" Brianna asked, popping up behind me and Ray, wrapping her arms around each of our shoulders.

"Fine, honey. Just grilling with Ray." I laughed, continuing to give him a hard stare as I placed more meat on the grill.

"We good, Bria. Benny was just giving me some pointers on scripture. Apparently, he's a student of the Bible." Ray smirked before walking away.

I had gotten under his skin. Good.

"What was that about?" Brianna asked, catching the sarcasm in his tone.

"Nothing, sweety. Just a guy thing." I smiled.

"Oh, okay. Well, I'mma go grab a drink. Want me to bring you one?"

"Uh, no. I'm fine. But I noticed that you and Ray seem to be getting along well. When did he start calling you Bria?" I asked, curious about the name. In all the years I had known her, no one had ever called her Bria. Sounded like a pet name.

She gave a nervous giggle. "Um... He's actually the only one that's ever called most that."

Torn Between a Gangster and a Gentleman

"Bria, huh? Pretty name," I said, acting nonchalant. I didn't want to show my hand now. Not until I had all the cards. Not until I had proof they were sleeping together.

"Okay, baby. I'mma go get mom's cake ready. Find me when your done with the meat. Love you," she said, giving me a peck on the lips before walking away.

Thoughts of revenge popped into my head after my wife walked away. And that's when I noticed that Ray left his beer on the counter. Oh, did I have something for his ass! I made sure to grab the bottle with my apron, not getting my prints on it as I stashed it in one of the grill's compartments. If he was fucking my wife, I would make sure that I got the last laugh.

After finishing the meat, I decided to amuse myself with a game of cat and mouse. I was the cat. Ray was the mouse. I was going to be his shadow for the rest of the evening. Show him that he was no match for me. I was bigger and better than him on every level. I beat the same streets that he had fallen to. Cost him 13 years in prison, the love of his life, and he didn't get to raise his children. And I still had one more trick up my sleeve. The highest card in the deck. This Ace of Spade! But until I played my trump card, I was going to have fun at Ray's expense. He was currently standing in a group with his son and some of Brianna's cousins. I was about this crash that party.

"What! Y'all crazy. Giannis is going to lead the Bucks to another championship. Watch and see. He's the best player in the game and he continues to get better," Ray was saying.

"Yo, Benny? Tell Ray's dreaming ass that the Bucks ain't got shit coming. They got they shot last year. That 2022 title is going out west," Brianna's cousin Demarco said.

"I like The Greek Freak. I think he's super talented. Another championship, I don't know. We'll have to see what kind of talent they continue to surround him with. We'll also have to see if he will remain loyal to the city and the team that made his dreams come true. You'd be surprised how many people bite the hands that feed them or flip the script when they experience success. Some people just don't understand loyalty. Lebron leaves the Cavs for the Heat then goes back to Cleveland and now he's a Laker. It's like women who leave their husbands and the good life only to go back to the losers they got away from in this first place," I said, keeping my eyes on Ray while I spoke.

"Lebron is chasing greatness so I don't blame him," Junior said. "It's all about that jewelry."

I decided to use the boy's comments to further incite his father. "See, Junior. Let me teach you something about loyalty. Being loyal to someone means making sacrifices. It's being the ultimate team player. A morally righteous thing. It has nothing to do with accolades or praise. It's about doing the right thing and letting all the people that took a chance on you know that you appreciate them. Take you for instance. Don't you appreciate the things I've done for you? The video games, clothes, and all that?"

Junior nodded.

I looked at Ray and could see steam coming from his ears. I loved this shit! "Now if somebody told you to steal from me or lie to me, would you do it?"

Junior shook his head. "No."

"See, that's remaining loyal. And when you get to the NBA, like I know you will, you should remain loyal to those people that were loyal to you. Did I tell him right, Ray?"

Ray looked like he wanted to fight me. "Yeah, that was good advice, Benny. But, Junior, what Benny didn't tell you is that sometimes the people that you think are loyal to you really aren't loyal at all. Sometimes they have hidden agendas and want you to remain loyal while they are being disloyal to you the entire time. You have to watch for that. Lebron wasn't disloyal to Cleveland. He gave them some of the best years of his life. Nobody was talking about Cleveland before the King. He built that entire state's economy. Then he left to pursue his own goals. After winning those championships in Miami, he went back to Cleveland and won them a championship to make up for leaving. He went back because he was homesick, and home is where the heart is. It's the reason why some wives give their old flames another shot. They realize their mistake and try to make up for it, huh, Benny?"

I was definitely fucking this nigga up when I got the chance!

Torn Between a Gangster and a Gentleman

"Is we still talking about basketball?" Demarco asked, picking up on me and Ray's hostilities.

"Yeah. We're just teasing about basketball. Brianna is about to cut the cake. Y'all ready for dessert?"

A few moments later the family and friends gathered the picnic table. Brianna came outside with the $300 red velvet cake with her mother's face on it. "Benny, I forgot the knife. Can you grab it for me?"

"No problem, honey," I said, concocting a plan as I went to grab some knives from the kitchen. "Okay, everybody. This is a special occasion to celebrate the life and passing of Earlene Swear. We all know that she is in a better place now, smiling down on us from above. And I know that this going away party is exactly the kind of party she would want. Dry eyes and lots of laughter. So, in the name of everything good, I want everybody to get a piece of this cake. Think of it as Earlene's body, like a Communion. Ray, would you mine cutting the first piece?"

He looked surprised that I had asked him to cut the first piece. "Alright, everybody. Let's celebrate mama," he said, grabbing the knife and cutting a piece.

"I'll have that if you don't mind," I said, grabbing the knife and cake from Ray. "Brianna, would you pass Ray the other knife so he can finish cutting this cake?"

She handed Ray the knife and they worked as a team slicing and handing out cake. Nobody noticed me slip into the house with my cake and knife. I went to my office to sit at my desk and eat the sweet treat. It was delicious! Best piece of cake I ever had. After eating the dessert, I grabbed an alcohol pad to wipe the frosting from the knife's blade. When it was good and clean, I put the knife in a zip lock bag and stashed it in my safe. Then I picked up my phone to make a call.

He answered on the third ring. "Prosey Private Investigators. This is Matthew Prosey."

CHAPTER 20
-Ray

I hadn't talked to Nilanti in a week. I went to her house, but she wouldn't answer the door. She blocked my phone number so I couldn't call or text and she blocked me on Facebook. Had even gone so far as to get me taken off her caseload so that she was no longer my parole officer. My new parole officer, Robert Gilreath, was in an entirely different building at another sight. I met with him 2 days ago and he seemed pretty cool. He didn't say why I was transferred, just that I was his new client. Since me and Nilanti's relationship was unethical and probably illegal, I didn't bother asking questions. I really felt bad about the way things ended with her. I wanted to make it right, but she made it clear that she didn't want to see me. I had to respect that.

"Dad, I think I want to be the next American Idol," Brittany said from the backseat.

"That's a good idea. Are they doing tryouts in Wisconsin?" I asked, weaving my freshly painted truck through traffic.

"No. But they're in Chicago this fall. Will you take me?"

"Absolutely. They got a fine judge that I wanna take a look at," I cracked as images of Katy Perry popped into my head.

"I don't know why you worried about Katy Perry, dad. Ain't like you can get her number," Junior laughed from the passenger seat.

"Man, you still on that? Just so you know, I ended up getting more than my P.O.'s number. Shoot, you need to give me my money back."

"Yeah right, dad. You ain't gotta lie to kick it."

"You don't even know who said that first. You can't be using rap lines if you don't know who they came from."

"Silkk the Shocker," he said smugly.

I was surprised that he knew. "How you find out about that?"

"I been doing my homework on old school rap. Master P founded No Limit records. Silkk the Shocker is his brother."

I nodded. "That's good, man. Keep doing what you doing and one day you'll be as boss as I am."

"No disrespect, dad, but I'mma be more of a boss than you. I'm going to the NBA one day."

I lifted my hand to give him a high five. "That's right, son. That's what you was supposed to say. Oh yeah. I meant to tell y'all that I found my mother."

"For real?" Brittany and Junior asked in unison.

"Yeah. Met her about a week ago."

"So, what is she like? When can we meet her?" Brittany asked.

"I don't know if that's a good idea. She's not well."

"What does that mean? Why can't we see our grandmother?" Junior asked.

"Because she's on drugs, man. Bad. I don't want to take y'all around nobody like that."

"Dang, daddy. That's messed up. You sad about it?" Brittany asked.

"Nah, not really. I mean, I was at first because she didn't even apologize for giving me up. But now I realize it was for the best. Grandad was a better parent and he offered me a better life."

"You think she might get herself together one day? It would be kind of nice to have one grandparent."

Hearing the longing for his grandmother in my son's voice made me want to take them to meet my mother. Earlene's death left a void in all of our lives. Unfortunately, I knew that my mother was in no condition to fill Brianna's mother's shoes. Those shoes were too big for almost anybody, let alone a crack addict. "I don't know, man. She looks bad. But you never know what God has planned. If she gets her life together, I promise to take y'all to meet her."

"Okay," they agreed.

I was heading down 76th Street, about to cross the intersection at Good Hope, when the light turned yellow. I smashed the glass, trying to beat the light.

"Yellow means slow down," Brittany warned as my truck sped through the red light.

Torn Between a Gangster and a Gentleman

"Well, when you get your license, you can slow down. To me, yellow means—"

Whoop-whoop!

I looked in the rearview mirror as the black and white patrol car sped up to catch me, lights flashing.

"Awe shit!"

"Profanity is the sign of an ignorant mind trying to express itself."

I looked through the rearview mirror and gave her a look that let her know the comments were annoying. "Alright, y'all. Relax. Let me see how much this is going to cost," I sulked, pulling to the side of the road.

I went into the glovebox to grab my registration and insurance, watching the side mirror as the police officers got out their car. The black man approached my side, and the white woman took the passenger side.

"Good afternoon, sir. You know why we stopped you?" the man asked. He was a big guy. About 6'2" and 250 pounds with a bald head and no facial hair.

"Probably have something to do with that yellow light, huh?" I smiled nervously.

"Yep. License, insurance, and registration."

I handed him my papers and watched him examine them like they were fake.

"Sir, I'm going to do a background check. I'll be back in a moment," he said before walking toward the squad car.

"Where you guys coming from?" the female officer asked, leaning into the passenger window to look around the truck's interior.

"The movies," Brittany answered.

"Oh, yeah? What did you guys go see?"

"Top Gun part two."

"Oh, I saw that. Cool movie, huh?"

"It was okay. I don't really like army movies."

"What's up with you, handsome? How are you?" she asked Junior.

"I'm okay. Is my dad in trouble?"

161

J-Blunt & Miss Kim

She looked over at me before answering. "No, not really. Just some traffic stuff. Maybe a fine." When her radio began to chatter, she gave me a nod before walking back toward the cruiser. She had a few words with her partner before they approached my window.

"Mr. Preston, have you ever been to prison?" the man asked.

I was surprised by the question and wondered what it had to do with my traffic stop. "What does my record have to do with a traffic stop?"

"Sir, just answer the question," he said firmly. "Ever been to prison?"

His tone pissed me off. "Yeah, I have. Now why is that you're business?"

"Sir, may I have permission to search your vehicle?"

I became enraged. "What! Nah, you can't search my truck. Now, write the ticket and give me back my shit so I can take my kids home."

"Sir, you are on high-risk parole for a felony and you just committed a traffic crime. If you want, we can drag this out and I can call your parole officer and get permission to search your truck. Or you can just let me search. If everything is good, you are free to go."

I wanted to bust the cop in his shit. He was harassing me for no reason. And it really pissed me off that I was being harassed by another black man.

"Dad, just let him," Brittany said, sensing my hostility.

I looked at my kids and seen the fear for my safety and freedom in their eyes. I had gotten out of prison less than a year ago and they didn't want me to do anything that would send me back. Plus, they had recently seen Benny get dragged out of the house in handcuffs. I could only imagine what they thought the police would do to me.

"Okay, man. You wanna search? Go ahead."

My kids and I wore humiliated looks on our faces as we sat on the curb under the watchful eye of the female officer. Her partner had been in my truck for about 5 minutes when he came out holding a liquor bottle with a white rag coming out of the top.

I shot to my feet. "Oh, hell nah! That ain't mine!"

"Sit down, sir!" the woman yelled, gripping the butt of her gun.

Torn Between a Gangster and a Gentleman

"What is that, dad?" Junior questioned.

"That ain't mine," I repeated the cops.

"Sir, this Molotov cocktail was found under the backseat of your vehicle. This is considered a weapon. We're going to have to place you under arrest," the man said, sitting the homemade firebomb on the hood of my truck.

No way I was about to let them take me to jail for something I didn't do. I couldn't go back. I was innocent. "That ain't mine, man."

"Sir, put your hands behind your back and get on your knees," the woman ordered.

I turned around and sized her up. She was little 5'5" and maybe 120 pounds. I could probably knock her out with one punch. The man would be a problem, but I knew I could whoop his ass, too.

"I'm not going to tell you again, sir. Get on your knees and put your hands behind your back," the man said, pulling the taser from the holster.

I looked him in his eyes as he pointed the taser at me. He wanted to shock me.

"Daddy, do what they say," Brittany cried. "They gon' shoot you."

I looked over and seen the tears pouring down my daughter's face. My son looked terrified. As much as I didn't want to go back to jail, I also didn't want them to see me get tased and probably shot. So, I dropped to my knees.

"C'mon, man. Let's get this shit over with."

J-Blunt & Miss Kim

CHAPTER 21-Brianna

I couldn't believe that Ray was back in jail. And for a bomb! What the hell was he doing with a bomb in his truck? After all the time that he spent in prison, how could he be so stupid? It didn't make sense. And of all the weapons he could've drove around with, why a bomb? Was he planning to blow something up?

"Brianna Boston?" a woman called, interrupting my thoughts.

"Yes, I'm here," I said, jumping to my feet and heading for the check-in desk.

A middle-aged white woman with bad makeup and no sense of fashion addressed me. "You'll be in booth one. You have an hour. I'll give you a five-minute warning when your time is up."

"Okay. Thanks."

After leaving the desk, I walked down a short hall that opened up to a room with lots of cubicle style booths. I heard laughing, crying, and screaming coming from different booths. When I found booth 1, I sat in the maroon plastic chair and stared at the small monitor. Ray wasn't there yet. I was nervous to see him. Hadn't laid eyes on him since my mother's going away party a week ago. I had so many questions. Like, why he was riding around with a damn bomb while the kids were in the car! If he was on a suicidal kick, I was going to kill him myself.

A few moments later there was movement on the screen. Ray walked into the picture wearing an orange jumpsuit. He looked stressed and aged. When he saw my face, he didn't look happy to see me. "What are you doing here?"

I wasn't expecting that reaction. "Well, hey to you, too. And I should be asking you the same thing. Why the hell are you back in jail!"

"It's all a misunderstanding. What are you doing here?"

"I came to find out why the hell you were driving around with a bomb while you have the kids with you? Have you lost your damn mind?"

"It wasn't a bomb, Brianna. It was a liquor bottle with gasoline in it. A Molotov Cocktail."

165

"I don't give a damn what it is called. Why did you have it in your truck?"

"I don't know. I'm still trying to figure that out."

That sounded stupid. "What do you mean you don't know? They found it in your truck. How did it get there?"

"I just told you that I don't know. But I don't want to talk about that right now. How are the kids?"

I gave him the evil eye for a few moments. I didn't want to talk about the kids. I wanted him to tell me why the hell he had a firebomb in his truck. But since he looked stressed out and the kids meant the world to him, I decided to take the conversation where he wanted it to go. For now. "Two days ago they were crying and upset. Now they're worried and confused about your situation. Why haven't you called them? They've been waiting and asking about you every hour. And why the hell did you have a bomb in your truck?"

"I just told you it wasn't a bomb. And I haven't talked to anyone since I've been in. I don't want to put the kids through this again. Tell them I'll call them soon."

"What do you mean you don't want to put them through this again? It's too late for that. We're already in it. Not calling won't help. We have questions. Like why there was a firebomb in your truck."

He gave me an angry stare. "If I knew, I would tell you. It wasn't mine."

I stared back at him, searching his face for the truth. He looked frustrated and angry. I realized that being angry at him wasn't going to get me answers so I changed my approach and softened my tone. "You have to have to help me understand this, Ray. You're in jail and might go back to prison. What am I supposed to tell the kids? Let me in. Tell me what is going on. What happened?"

He exhaled heavily, shaking his head and looking away. When he turned back to me, I could see confusion in his eyes. "Honestly, Bria, I don't know what is happening. It wasn't my Molotov cocktail."

"Where did they find it?"

166

"It was in my truck, but it ain't mine. I swear. I think somebody put it there, trying to set me up."

"So, you're not suicidal or tripping out? You wasn't trying to blow up nothing?"

"What? No. C'mon, girl. You trippin'."

I gave him a long look, assessing his mental state. "Okay. Now this is the Ray I know. Tell me what you need me to do. How can I help?"

"No, Brianna. Stay away. I'll do this. If push comes to shove, I'll just do the two years I have on parole and get it over with."

I couldn't picture not being able to see him for 2 years. "No, Ray. I'm not leaving you again. I already made that mistake and I regret it. I'm here and I'm not going anywhere. I mean that."

He stared at me for a moment before a smile spread across his lips. "Bria," he groaned, closing his eyes and shaking his head.

"I'm here, Ray. I'm not leaving. Now think. Who would want to do this to you?"

He lowered his head for a moment. When he looked up, he told me his theory. "I think it was Benny."

Hearing him say my husband's name surprised the hell out of me. "Benny? Really?"

He nodded. "He knows we've been sleeping together."

It felt like I had been karate chopped in the throat. "What are you talking about? He hasn't said anything to me."

"Remember when you came over to the grill at mama's party and we were talking? When I told you he knew the Bible?"

I nodded. I remembered. "Yeah."

"Before you walked up, he made a comment about coveting another man's things. I think the 'things' he was talking about was you. And when I was by Demarco and Junior talking about basketball, he walked over and started talking about loyalty and women who leave their good lives and go back to their loser exes. Even Demarco had to ask if we were still talking about basketball. He knows, Bria. He was warning me. I seen it in his eyes."

It felt like I was about to throw up. "Oh shit, Ray! Oh my God! This is bad. I didn't want it to happen like this," I panicked.

"I know. But this is where we are. He knows."
My thoughts were all over the place. Arguments. Fights. Lawyers. Courts. Divorce. Moves. New schools. "This is bad, Ray. Shit. But Okay. It is what it is. I'll worry about my problems later. How can I help to get you out?"

"I need you to call my P.O. and tell him that we are sleeping together and that we think Benny set me up. Tell him I'll pay for the bottle to be dusted for fingerprints. I've never seen or touched that bottle."

I didn't like the place. I didn't want people, especially his parole officer, to know my business. But if it would get him out of jail, I had to do it. "Okay. I'll call him as soon as I leave. Call me and give me the number."

"Alright. Thanks. I really appreciate you helping me."

"You don't have to thank me, Ray. I owe you this. Thank you for letting me help you."

We stared at each other for a few moments when a question that demanded an answer popped into my head. "Do you really not remember any of the night you spent at my house the night Benny went to jail?" I stared at his face intently, my heart beating rapidly as I searched for the answer in his expression.

He stared back at me wearing a poker face. Then slowly, very slowly, his lips crept into a smile. "I remember every moment."

My heart felt like it was about burst as a smile as wide as the Atlantic Ocean spread across my face. I looked down at the ring on my left ring finger. It was beautiful. 2 karat princess cut set in platinum. But I knew that I wouldn't be wearing it much longer. "Did you mean it when you said I was supposed to be your wife?"

His smile grew wider.

***

After leaving the visit with Ray, I sat in my truck in the parking lot to wait for his call. The emotional high that I got from being able to emotionally connect with my first love had me walking on clouds. It pained me that I was going to have to end my marriage. I

Torn Between a Gangster and a Gentleman

loved Benny and I really appreciated everything that he's done for me and my family. Without him, I wouldn't be the woman I am today. I could never repay him for all that he has done for me. But I also couldn't deny my heart. It belonged to Ray. Now I had to figure a way to have this conversation with Benny. And according to Ray, my husband already knew that we had slept together so the cat was already out of the bag. I wondered why Benny hadn't brought it up yet? Why would he hide that he knew I was cheating? What was he waiting for? Damn, he was good at concealing emotions.

When my phone rang, I pushed all thoughts of my husband from my mind and listened to the instructions. I pressed 5 repeatedly until the robotic voice said we could talk.

"Hey, baby daddy. I miss you already."

"Girl, stop playing. You just seen me. And you still married."

"That's how it is, for real? We just spent a whole hour together and we spent the night together twice. Now you wanna get all brand new on a sistah?"

"You know I'm just playing, Bria. You gon' always be my girl, no matter who you married to."

I lifted my left hand to the steering wheel to look at my ring again. "Damn, Ray. I know this is wrong but it feels so right. I don't know how I'm going to tell Benny."

"You won't have much to say because he already knows."

"I wonder why he didn't confront me? What is he waiting for?"

"He was probably waiting to send my ass back to prison first, but hopefully that won't happen now that I figured out his plan. Take down my P.O.'s number. 871-1485. His name is Robert Gilreath. Make sure you tell him everything that we talked about."

"Okay. I'm going to call him as soon as you hang up. We need you home."

"Uh... Damn. I have to get off the phone, Bria. Shit. They shutting the unit down because these niggas about to fight."

"What! No! Okay. I'm going to call your P,O. Make sure you set up the Homeway and call—"

Click.

169

Talking to Ray on a jail call and having the phone hang up in my face was nostalgic. We went through the same thing 13 years ago. But I didn't allow myself to get caught up in the reverie because I had another call to make.

"Robert Gilreath. Probation and Parole."

"Um, hi, Robert. My name is Brianna Boston. I'm calling about Ray Preston."

"And this is concerning?"

"Well, I just came from visiting him and I think I have some information that could help him get out."

"Okay. I'm listening."

"Well... Um... We... I mean, we think my husband put the Molotov cocktail in his truck."

The parole officer was silent for a moment. "Your husband? Really? Who are you to Mr. Preston? What is your relationship?"

"I'm the mother of his children."

"Oh. I see. And why would your husband put a firebomb in his truck?"

"Well, see... We're having an affair and we believe my husband knows."

"Oh. Okay. I see. Well, that's definitely a motive. Can you prove that your husband did this?"

"Well, I was hoping that you could check the bottle for prints. Ray's fingerprints are not on that bottle. We'll pay for it. Ray is innocent. He's changed. He loves his kids. He didn't do this, Mr. Gilreath."

"Okay, Mrs. Boston. I can't make any promises, but I'll look into it. Ray seems like a pretty good guy, so I'll give him a fair shake. Do you have a number where you can be reached?"

"This is my phone."

"Okay. I'll save your number because I might have some follow up questions."

"Okay. Thanks."

"No need to thank me. I'm just doing my job. No sense in keeping an innocent man in jail."

Torn Between a Gangster and a Gentleman

I had just hung up the phone when it rang again. It was my sister. "Hello?"

"Where you at?"

"Now I know Mommy taught you to talk on the phone better than that."

"Sorry. I'm just frustrated. My stupid car broke down again. Sarita needs some Pampers and milk. Where are you? In need a ride."

I paused for a moment, wondering if I should tell her where I was. I closed my eyes and winced. "I... Um... Just finished visiting Ray."

"Oh, for real? Tell him I said what's up? Y'all cool now?"

"Um... I can't do that right now. He's in jail."

She got loud. "Are you serious! Ray back in jail!"

"Calm down. Yeah. On a P.O. hold. Somebody set him up."

"Are you serious? Him too?"

"Yeah. I just came from seeing him. He's been locked up for two days. I'm trying to help him get out."

"Damn. What are the chances that your husband and kids' father get locked up and both of them say they got set up?"

"I don't know. It's all crazy. But you wanna hear something crazier?"

"I don't think it can get much crazier unless them niggas are codefendants." She laughed.

"Ray thinks Benny set him up."

My sister didn't speak for a moment. "Wait. Stop playing, Brianna! What the hell are you talking about? Why would Benny set up Ray?"

I took a deep breath before spilling the beans. "Me and Ray have been sleeping together. Ray thinks Benny found out and planted a Molotov cocktail in his truck."

"OH MY GOD! OH MY GOD!" she screamed before busting out laughing. "You and Ray! Mama was right! This sound like some Lifetime movie shit. I'mma need you to hurry up and get yo ass over here and tell me more. And on the way, grab Sarita some Pampers and milk. Hah! I can't believe this shit. You and Ray?"

171

"Okay, okay. Calm down. I'm on my way."

"Hurry up, Brianna. Don't make no other stops. Just to get Sarita's stuff and get yo ass over here!"

After ending the call with my sister, I drove a few blocks to the Grand Avenue Mall. I managed to dash in and out in less than 20 minutes. Didn't even stop to buy anything for myself. And that was a miracle because it's hard to walk through a mall without buying anything. I was walking across the parking lot, carrying my niece's things when I saw a face that made me want to turn and walk the other way. And if it wasn't for my truck being about 50 feet away, I would've.

"Hey, Brianna!" Ciarra smiled, saying my name like we were besties. She was walking with 3 boys. 2 were preteens and the other a toddler.

"Hey, Ciarra." I smiled, giving her one of the fake smiles that I gave the people at Benny's political events.

"How is the family? I know things must be hard with dad... I mean, Mr. Boston going through that legal problem."

"Yeah, it's tough. But we're troopers. We'll be okay. Are these your boys? They're handsome."

"Yeah. This is Melvin. He's twelve. Darius is ten. And Benny Junior is three."

It felt like a bucket of cold water had been thrown in my face. I shook the dizziness off and stared at the boy's face. *No! Couldn't be!*

"You said, Benny Junior?" I asked, unable to take my eyes off the boy.

"Mmm-hhmm. Benny Junior. He's three," she repeated with a smile.

The smug look on her face told it all. The boy was my husband's son. And there was no need for a DNA test. The boy looked just like Benny. This is why she showed up to Benny's court hearing. They had more than a boss-worker relationship. They had an actual relationship.

"Well, it was nice seeing you, Brianna. Tell the family I said, hi."

Torn Between a Gangster and a Gentleman

I stood there paralyzed and flabbergasted, watching Ciarra and the smaller identical version of my husband walk away. I wanted to do something, but I didn't know what. I wanted to chase Ciarra, pull the wig off her head, and beat her ass but I couldn't move. Seeing Benny's son literally had me stuck. When I finally got my feet to move, I walked back to my truck feeling dizzy and lightheaded. Benny had a 3-year-old son with his secretary. I couldn't believe it. It felt surreal. Like the plot to a movie.

When I got to my truck, the tears came on strong. Benny had been cheating on me for years. Had another family. The betrayal burned inside my chest. I knew there was a reason I never liked Ciarra.

J-Blunt & Miss Kim

Torn Between a Gangster and a Gentleman

CHAPTER 22-Ray

Free at last, free at last! Thank God Almighty, free at last! It took 10 days and $750 to get out of jail. Some of the best money I ever spent. My P.O. dropped the hold and all charges had been dropped. Sometimes the justice system did work in favor of a black man. And it turned out Benny didn't set me up. The check for his prints on the bottle of rum came back negative. When I got the news that Benny's prints weren't on the bottle, it took another day for me to come up with another suspect. On a guess and a prayer I told Robert to check for Nilanti's prints. Came back a match. I didn't want to believe it but when I remembered some of the threats or promises she made to me if I broke her heart, I wondered why I didn't think of her first. I guess it was because I wanted sex and didn't think she would try to hurt me. But not only did she try to hurt me, she tried to send me back to prison. And she confessed to everything when her boss confronted her with the evidence. Since I was supposed to be in her care, I was a victim and wouldn't face any prosecution. I didn't know what the outcome would be for her, nor did I care. I was just happy to be free and have her crazy ass out of my life.

"Ray!"

I recognized the voice instantly and spun around to find her. Brianna came running toward me like a sprinter. She wore a green blouse, black pants, and heels, but she might as well had been wearing a tracksuit. Her hair along with all of her jiggly parts bounced as she ran at me full speed. When she was at kills feet away, she launched herself at me. I braced myself for a rough landing, stumbling backwards and almost falling as I caught her in my arms.

"I'm so happy to see you, baby!" she squealed, planting kisses all over my face.

"What are you doing here, girl?"

"Your P.O. called me. And told me. They were. Dropping the hold. I've been. Waiting out here. For two hours," she managed in between kisses.

"Wait, Brianna. We gotta be discrete. You're still married."

She stopped kissing me and gave a dead ass stare. "I'm leaving Benny. You know that. I'm not hiding anything. He has a son with his secretary. It's over."

"You still haven't told him yet, right?"

She unwrapped her limbs from around me and stood. "No. We agreed to see what happens with you first. Now that you're out, I'll tell him."

"Okay. But make sure you do it the right way. Benny ain't stupid and he's not who he pretends to be. He a gangsta, Bria. Let me know when you're ready to tell him so I can be there."

She smiled, closing the distance between us and staring in my eyes. "Will you protect me from him?"

"You already know that I will."

She leaned forward and bit my bottom lip before sucking it into her mouth. After a make out session that was too hot for TV, we came up for air.

"Let's get out of here before we get in trouble. Where you parked at? I need to get out of these clothes and take a bath."

She turned up her nose like I stank. "Mmmh! Sure do. You smell like jail. I'm parked down the street. Hurry up and get in the car before the funky police arrest you."

We laughed and joked all the way to her truck. Being around her felt good. She knew me so well and was unlike any woman I had ever met.

"Damn, so this is what the inside of a luxury SUV feels like. Being married to Benny has it's perks, huh?" I cracked while checking out the interior of her Lexus.

"Benny didn't buy my truck. I got two daycares, remember? And if you wasn't so cheap, you could buy your own luxury vehicle. It's not like you don't have the money."

"My F-150 is good. I have better things to do with my money than buy hundred-thousand dollar whips."

"Like what? Furniture? Oh, I forgot. You don't got none," she cracked.

"Hey, you better get off my spot. You know how people with money keep money? By not spending it."

Torn Between a Gangster and a Gentleman

"If you don't want me to talk about your being cheap then don't be talking about me having perks from being married to Benny. I won't go there if you won't."

"Okay. You got a deal. Truce."

"Good. So, what's going to happen to Nilanti? Is she going to jail for trying to set you up?"

"I don't know, and I don't care. I just want her crazy ass to leave me alone," I said, glancing in the side mirror. I wasn't sure but it looked like we were being followed by a black car.

"I hope she goes to jail. She was crazy. Did you love her?"

I could feel Brianna's eyes on me so I stopped looking at the side mirror and turned to her. "Keep your eyes in the road."

"Answer the question. Did you?"

"No."

"What about the other girls? You still talking to them?"

"No. I thought I wanted to be with Nilanti so I left the other girls alone."

Brianna smirked.

"What was that look about?" I asked.

"Ain't you glad I showed up the night mama died? Just think about what she would've done to you if y'all were really in love. She is crazy. I helped you dodge a bullet. You should thank me."

I gave her a sideways look. "You really feeling yourself right now, ain't you? Head getting too big for your car."

"No. I just think credit should be given where credit is due."

I looked out the window while giving her comment some thought. My eyes were drawn back to the side mirror. The car was still behind us. Four cars back. A black 90's model Ford Taurus. "Thank you, Brianna. I owe you."

She smiled like she won the prize on the gameshow The Wall.

"You're welcome."

We spent the rest of to ride talking about seeing the kids later and Benny's betrayal. I also regularly checked the mirror for the black car.

"What are you looking at?" Brianna asked, turning onto my block.

"Somebody is following us in a black car," I said turning to look out the back window as she pulled up to my house.

Sure enough the black Taurus turned onto my block a couple seconds later. I jumped out the truck to get a better look at the driver. A white man, clean shaved, dark glasses, and a ball cap. I would never be able to pick him out of a lineup, but I did get his license plate numbers.

"Who was he?" Brianna asked, getting out of the car a little too late.

"A white man. Did you notice anybody following you?"

"No. Why would somebody be following me?"

"I think that's one of Benny's guys. I told you he knows. He might've hired somebody to follow you."

She blew it off. "Oh well. I don't care."

"You should probably go home or to one of the daycares."

She cocked her head and looked at me like I was crazy. "Nu-uh. I'm coming in the house with you."

"C'mon, Brianna. We gotta be smart about this. You got people following you and Benny is suspicious. I don't think this is a good idea."

"You already know I'm leaving him, Ray. My marriage is over."

"Bria, we have to—"

"Do you love me, Ray?"

I wasn't surprised by the question, but I was surprised by the timing. We talked every day, a couple times a day, while I was locked up, but she never asked me if I loved her. She wanted to ask now that we could be busted by her husband and a Cheaters film crew. "Bria, you know—"

She cut me off. "Yes or no, Ray."

I stared into those beautiful brown eyes, getting lost in memories of us. I couldn't deny the truth. "Yes."

She gave an 'I knew it' smile. "Well, I'm definitely not leaving now."

As soon as I locked the door behind us, it was on! We kissed, groped, and rubbed each other's bodies, leaving a trail of clothes from this front door to the bathroom. By the time I sat Brianna on the sink, we were naked. I left her there long enough to turn on the shower. The steam began filling the bathroom quickly. When I turned around, she was watching me, biting her bottom lip, legs wide open, playing with herself. I checked her out for a moment, getting super turned on watching her stroke her kitten.

"You gon' watch me or join in?" she asked.

I went to her, kneeling on the floor and replacing her hand with my tongue.

"Ooh, Ray!" she moaned, grabbing at my head.

Her juices tasted like berries. I teased her with licks for a few moments before diving in. I sucked and licked her clitoris like it was the last Jolly Rancher on earth. Brianna went mad. Screamed and thrashed around the sink like she was having a seizure. When she was reaching her climax, she grabbed the back of my head and pulled my face against her love box. My nose was glued to her pelvic bone, making it hard to breathe. But I kept on licking and sucking.

"Oh, Ray! Ahhhh!" she screamed as the orgasm passed through her.

Her juices rushed out like an ocean tide, washing over my face. I wiped my chin as I stood, Brianna looking like she was in LaLa Land. Her eyes were low like she smoked a blunt, her breathing was heavy, and she was smiling like she was enjoying pure bliss.

"You good?" I asked, leaning forward to kiss her.

She responded by trying to swallow my face. Then she wrapped her arms around my shoulders and legs around my waist, pulling me in. Her insides felt like someone had wrapped the ocean in a tight hole. I lifted her from the sink and carried her into the shower. Ended up staying in the shower until the water turned cold.

Torn Between a Gangster and a Gentleman

CHAPTER 23-Benny

"What do you mean the shit went sour?" I asked, trying to keep my cool.

"My boys stuck him good, B.B. but he lived," The Candy Man said apologetically.

I didn't want excuses. I wanted Red Fox dead. "Why are you telling me this, man? Go get his ass again."

"Can't, man. Not only did I lose one of my boys in the scuffle, but they also put the Fox in protective custody. Ain't no getting to him now."

I exploded. "What the fuck do you mean ain't no getting to him now! I paid you twenty-five grand. My life is on the line, Candy Man."

"Ain't nothing in this business for sure, my man. You know that. We tried. You win some and you lose some."

He said that last part way too cool for my taste. I wanted him to be as pissed off as I was. "Give me my damn money back if you can't finish the job. I didn't pay for failure. You supposed to be the best out here. What the fuck happened?"

"C'mon now, B.B. I told you that my boys tried their best. And I lost one of my soldiers trying to get this nigga. The job didn't get finished so we'll leave things the way they are. I'll have to use that down payment to compensate my soldiers' families. I gave it my best shot, B.B."

"Fuck you, Candy Man. I should—"

"Watch yo mouth, B.B. I know you mad, but don't let your feelings fuck up your judgement. I don't take disrespect lightly."

Click.

"Fuck!" I snapped, slamming the phone on my desk. Red Fox survived the hit. Now he was in protective custody. There was no getting to him now. "Shit!" I exploded, slapping a stack of papers on the floor.

Ciarra ran into my office looking worried. "Are you okay, daddy?"

I got up from the desk and headed for this door. "I'm taking the rest of the day off. Cancel all my meetings and pick those papers up from the floor." I jumped into my Jaguar and drove around aimlessly. Thinking. I needed to find a way to shut up Red Fox. If I didn't, he would bring me down. I couldn't let that happen. I am Benny Boston! B.B. King! Respected everywhere from the streets to the Capitol. I couldn't let a low life pimp take me under. The vibrations from my phone pulled me from my thoughts. It was Matthew Prosey. "Hey, Matt. How are things going?"

"Hey, Mr. Boston. I've made progress. Can we meet?"

I got a tingle in my gut. More bad news was coming. I could feel it. "I'm out of the office right now so I'll have to come to you."

"I'm also out of the office. Over on the westside. You?"

"Northwest. Industrial Road. Meet me at the gas station on 76th. Can you do that?"

"ETA ten minutes."

"See you when you get there."

Took me 5 minutes to get to the gas station. I pulled on the side of the building to wait, thinking about what Matthew found. He said he made progress and that could only mean one thing. Brianna and Ray were fucking around. I was going to make sure I got the last laugh though. One thing was for sure; B.B. King always got the last laugh. Anxiousness washed over me when the black sedan pulled into the gas station. Matthew parked near a pump and jumped out wearing his usual get up. Black ball cap, dark shades, dark T-shirt and jeans. At 38 years old he was in good shape. Slim build, long limbs, and stood about 6 feet tall. He was carrying a tablet and a manila envelope.

When he hopped in the passenger seat, he got right down to business. "Sorry to be the one to tell you this, but your suspicions are true. I took these yesterday. His name is Ray Preston. He just finished doing time in—"

I cut him off. "Let me see the pictures."

He cut on the tablet and handed it to me. I scrolled through the pictures of Ray and Brianna. The one that caught my eye was a picture of her in his arms, her legs wrapped around his waist. They

Torn Between a Gangster and a Gentleman

were kissing in front of what looked like the county jail. There were words to describe the emotions I felt. But one thing was for sure; I would get the last laugh.

"Thank you, Matt. This is all I needed to see. Do you have some copies of these pictures for me?"

He handed me the envelope and took the tablet. "Sorry about this, man. Call me if you need anything else," he said before getting out of my car.

I left the gas station with thoughts of murder on my mind, heading straight home to see my wife. "Hey, kids," I smiled at Brittany and Junior when I stepped in the family room. The boy was playing a video game and Brittany was on the phone.

"Hey, Benny," they greeted.

"Where is your mother?" I asked, fighting to keep my emotions in check.

"I think she's in her room," Brittany answered.

As I walked up the stairs, I had to fight my urges to reveal everything that I knew and beat her ass silly. I wanted to grab the folder from the car, throw it in the bed, and laugh while she tried to explain what the pictures clearly showed. But I needed to control myself. I wanted to have some fun and toy with her like I had done with Ray at Earlene's party. The show was about to start in 3, 2, 1. When I walked into the bedroom, she was coming out of the bathroom. *Action!*

"Hey, Bria," I smiled, using Ray's pet name.

"Hey, Benny," she said flatly, cutting her eyes at me.

The energy in our house had been tense for a week. We only talked when necessary. She kept giving me these looks that I couldn't describe. Every time I asked her about it, she removed herself from my presence. But now that I had these pictures, I had the power. The chess match had tilted heavily in my favor.

"So, how was your day? Did you go to the daycares?" I asked, kicking off my shoes.

"I took the day off. They can run them without me. You home early. Why?"

183

"I had a meeting with an old friend. Found some interesting information."

"Oh yeah? Anything I should know about?" she asked, giving me the strange look as she walked over to the dresser. I couldn't tell if it was the look of guilt, an angry sneer, or something in between.

"No, no, no. Don't worry your pretty little head about it. I'm getting to the bottom of it as we speak," I said, watching her ass jiggle in the spandex as she bent over to dig in the drawer.

"Why would I be worried? I'm not hiding anything. Are you?" she challenged, giving me the look again.

Damn. She knew something. But what?

"You have a look in your eyes that I haven't seen before. It's sexy. Makes me want to do nasty things," I teased, unbuckling my belt. I didn't know why but her energy and the look on her face was turning me on.

"I bet it does." She smirked before heading back into the bathroom.

When I heard the shower come on, I took off my pants, planning to join my wife for some fun under the water. I got halfway across the room when the bathroom door opened.

"You forgot something?" I asked, sliding my briefs down.

She looked at my dick and then back up at me. A slight snarl spread across her lips and anger fired up in her brown eyes. "You want me to suck your dick, huh?" she asked while walking toward me.

"Yeah, baby. And I want you to suck it good."

She grabbed my dick aggressively and forced me over to the bed. It hurt and felt good at the same time. "You want me to suck it like I'm your hoe? Like I'm your bitch?" she asked, stroking me roughly.

We had never done the dirty talk or rough sex before, but I liked where this was heading. "Yeah, baby. Be my bitch."

She pushed me onto the bed and tried to swallow me whole. Sucked me hard. Felt good as hell! Ray was definitely teaching her good.

Torn Between a Gangster and a Gentleman

"Ouch! Ohh!" I moaned when she began to nibble at the head. Then she went back down on me. Sucked me angrily. My wife had never sucked my dick this good in all the time that I had known her. She was giving Ciarra a run for her money. Then she began working the head again. Sucking and nibbling while stroking me with her hand. When she sucked me back into her mouth, I bust my nut. Felt like my balls had been sucked into my stomach.

"Awe shit! Damn, Brianna!" I moaned as she sucked me dry. "Damn, Brianna. I don't know what has gotten into you, but you need to keep it." And I meant that. If she always sucked dick like that, I might let her and Ray keep sleeping around.

Instead of responding to my comment, she climbed on top of me and crawled up my body. When she was leveled with my face, she kissed me. It was forceful and rough. She used her tongue to pry my mouth open and that's when I felt something thick and slimy slip from her mouth into mine.

"Bitch!" I yelled, slapping her across the face and spitting the cum on the bed.

Brianna rolled off the bed and onto the floor. I jumped up, about to stick a foot in her ass. Wife or not, murder charges or not, I was about to beat her ass!

"Do you hit Ciarra the same way after she sucked your dick?" she yelled, staring up at me with hatred in her eyes.

The words stopped me in my tracks. That's what the looks were about. She knew. "What did you say?"

She stood and mugged me. "I seen your son, Benny! Your three-year-old son, Benny Junior. I seen him at the mall with his mother."

Shit!

"You don't got nothing to say?"

I said the only thing that I could. "I have pictures of you and Ray. You've been fucking him. Don't try to turn this around on me. You don't know what you're talking about. I have pictures of you with Ray in my car, Brianna. I got receipts!"

"Yes, I'm fucking Ray. I fucked him while you were in jail and I fucked him all day yesterday. And I love him, too. Always have.

But at least I'm woman enough to admit it. When are you going to be a man and admit that you've been fucking your secretary and had a baby with her?"

She loved him. Hearing those words cut deeper than I expected. "Get the fuck out of my house, bitch!"

She gave me a defiant look. "Your house! I'll show your ass! No, you get out! Unless you want me to call the police and show them what you did to my face," she threatened, showing off her blood-stained teeth when she smiled.

"Punk ass bitch!" I cursed, reaching for my pants.

Torn Between a Gangster and a Gentleman

CHAPTER 24-Ray

I was standing over the stove whipping up a pot of macaroni when the front door opened and my son walked in.

"Hey, man. Where is your mom and Brittany?"

"Hey, dad. Brittany behind me," he said, carrying what looked like an overnight bag.

"Hey, daddy. Mama outside. She need your help," Brittany said, also carrying a duffel bag.

"What is going on? What's up with all the bags?"

"We spending the night."

I looked at Junior. "What is she talking about?"

"Mom said we spending the night with you."

I walked outside and spotted Brianna struggling to carry luggage up the walkway. "What's going on?" I asked, grabbing the bags.

"Me and Benny had a fight. He knows about us. Said he had some pictures. I told him the truth and confronted him about Ciarra."

I noticed a bruise near her lip and leaned in for a closer look. "Did he hit you?"

"I'm okay. I'm leaving him. I want us—"

"I'm beating that nigga ass!" I said, dropping the bags and heading for my truck.

"No, Ray! No!" Brianna yelled, chasing after and grabbing me.

"Move, Bria!" I yelled, pushing her away. I wasn't about to let that nigga get away with hitting her. Hell nah! No way!

"Ray, stop. The kids are looking."

I looked toward the porch and seen Junior and Brittany watching us. That calmed me down a little. "Y'all not going back to that house."

She leaned into me, wrapping her arms around my neck. "I know. I don't want to go back. That's why we're here."

"We good. Y'all can go back in the house," I told the kids.

They gave us questioning looks before going inside.

"What did you tell them?"

"I didn't say anything. Just that we would be staying with you for a couple of days. I'm leaving the rest up to you. But they knew me and Benny were having problems. Things around the house had been tense ever since I found out he had a son."

"What did you say about your lip?"

"Brittany asked and I told her I put on some spoiled lipstick. They believed me."

"You a terrible liar." I laughed.

"I didn't know what else to say. It's not that bad, is it?"

"Nah, you good. Just a lil' boo-boo," I said, leaning down for a kiss.

"Ray, I want us to be a family again. I want another chance with you. I never stopped loving you and I swear to God I won't ever leave you again."

I could see the emotions in her eyes, the tears threatening to spill. I wasn't going to deny us any longer. Everything happens for a reason. Benny getting locked up and having a kid with his secretary wasn't an accident. Brianna was the love of my life and the universe made it so we could be together again. She was the only woman that I had ever given my entire heart. The only woman that fit perfectly next to me when I slept. "Okay, Brianna. Okay."

"Come and give me a kiss and tell me how much you love me." She smiled, reminding me of the lyrics in Lyfe Jennings song *Must Be Nice*: 'Smile bright enough to make the projects feel like a mansion.'

I pulled her into my arms and gave her swollen lips some TLC.

"That's what I'm talking about. Now help me get these bags in the house. I have a couple more in my truck."

When we walked in the house, Brittany and Junior were waiting, staring at us like they witnessed a miracle.

"What y'all looking at?"

"We seen y'all kissing." Brittany smiled.

"So. That's what grown people do."

"Are y'all getting back together?" Junior asked hopefully.

I turned to Brianna.

"You tell them," she said, putting the ball back in my court.

Torn Between a Gangster and a Gentleman

"Yeah. We getting back together. And y'all ain't going back to that house with Benny," I said as my phone began ringing. It was my cousin, Trip. "Hello?"

"Yo, Ray. I got some bad news, cuzzo," he said sadly.

Aunty Michele's face popped into my head. "What's up, cuz?"

"Carla in the hospital. A nurse called me a couple minutes ago looking for next of kin."

I didn't know what to think or how to feel. My birth mother, who really didn't love or care about me, was in the hospital. And it was probably serious since they were looking for next of kin.

"Ray? You there?" Trip asked, pulling me from my thoughts.

"Yeah, yeah. I'm here. What's wrong with her? Is it serious?"

"Yeah, brah. They said she had a heart attack."

I shook my head. "Okay. You know what hospital?"

"Mount Sinai."

"Alright. Thanks for letting me know."

When I hung up the phone, Brianna and the kids were staring at me.

"You okay? What happened?"

"That was my cousin Trip. My mom's in the hospital. She had a heart attack."

"Oh, no! Is she okay?"

"I don't know. They called him looking for next of kin. Then he called me."

"It sounds serious, Ray. Don't you think you should go see her?"

"I don't know. A part of me feels like I should, but another part of me doesn't want to care."

"But what about the kids? What if this is their only chance to meet her?"

I turned to Junior and Brittany. I could tell by the looks on their faces that they wanted to meet her. "Should I go?" I asked, already knowing how they would answer.

"Yeah, dad. I want to meet her," Brittany said.

"Me too," Junior echoed.

***

I wasn't a big fan of hospitals. The halls reminded me of prison corridors. Dodge Correction Institution to be exact. The over waxed floors, bright lights, cool temperature, and antiseptic smell. Stepping into Mount Sinai caused me to have a flashback of walking down the long prison hallways. After the trip down Memory Lane, me and the family found the nurses station. It was being manned by a middle-aged black woman wearing blue scrubs.

"Good afternoon, ma'am. I'm looking for Carla Legend. I think she had a heart attack."

"And you are?" the woman asked as she began typing at the keyboard.

"Uh... I'm her son." Saying the words felt strange.

"Okay. She's on the fourth floor. Check in at the nurses station to see what room they put her in."

"Alright. Thanks."

After a short elevator ride, we got off on the fourth floor. To the left was the nurses station. A chubby white woman sat staring at a computer screen. She perked when we approached. "Good afternoon. Can I help you?"

"Can you tell most what room Carla Legend is in?"

"One moment. Let most check the charts. Um... Who are you? Only immediate family can be here now."

"I'm her son, Ray Preston. This is my wife and children."

Brianna gave me a look when I called her my wife.

"Okay. If you can just have a seat in the family room for a moment and I'll get the doctor. We've been trying to find her immediate family since she arrived. The doctor will need to speak with you before you see her."

During the wait for this doctor, I was fidgety, nervous, anxious, and scared all at the same time. Brianna held my hand and tried to comfort me with soothing words but that did nothing. Even though I had only met Carla once, I felt some kind of attachment to her. I wanted her to by okay. I wanted her to live.

"Mr. Preston?"

Torn Between a Gangster and a Gentleman

I looked up and seen an older black man in a white coat walking toward me. He had a full beard, short afro, and was kind of chubby. Reminded me of the doctor from the TV show Grey's Anatomy. "Yeah. Is Carla okay?" I asked, standing and extending a hand.

"Hi. I'm Doctor Gableman," he introduced himself as we shook hands. "She is stable at this moment but it's mostly touch and go. What I have to talk to you about is sensitive. Can you come with me so we can talk?"

I looked toward Brianna and the kids. "I'll be right back."

"Go." Brianna nodded.

The doctor led the way from the waiting room, and we walked the hallway. "We've been trying to find her closest of kin all morning. You say that you're her son?"

"Yeah. Ray Preston."

"Forgive my skepticism, Ray, but we know Miss Legend pretty well around here. She has been in and out of our doors at least ten times in the last couple years. And all that time she's never mentioned having any family. Until today. A guy named Trip and a woman named Michele."

"That's my cousin and aunt on my dad's side. Trip called and told me Carla was here. Carla gave me to my father when I was a kid. I just seen her for this first time a couple weeks ago."

"Oh, okay." He nodded. "I guess that explain why she's never told us or any of the psychiatrists that she had a son. We—"

"Psychiatrists?"

"Yes. Um...there is no easy way to tell you this, Ray, so I'll just get right to it. Feel free to jump in and ask questions if you don't understand anything I say. Your mother is mentally and physically ill. Our psychiatrist diagnosed her as schizophrenic and bipolar. We've also recommended at least five mental health doctors for her to do follow ups with to help with her illness. She hasn't gone to see any of them. She also has a heart condition that causes murmurs. There is no cure for the heart condition, but she can take steps to prolong her life and stop her from coming to the ER so often. The main thing is to quit smoking cigarettes and crack, and take the medication we've prescribed. She hasn't been doing either. The reason

191

she is here now is because of a heart attack. It was severe. It almost stopped her heart. Caused by smoking crack."

When the doctors stopped talking, I just stared at him. I was shocked by everything that he told me. Carla was dying and didn't care. It was almost like she was trying to kill herself.

"I'm speechless, doc. I had no idea."

"I know. The reason I'm telling you all of this is because you might be the only person that can convince her to get help. The guy she's seeing, I think his name is Franky, is no help to her. If your mother continues heading down this path, she's going to kill herself. The next heart attack could take her out. To be quite frank, I'm kind of surprised that this one didn't. We have a rehab program with a Catholic church that can help her, but she has to consent to the help. I've talked to her about this on a few occasions, but she hasn't taken me up on the offers. I'm hoping that you might be able to talk her into saving her own life."

***

When I walked into Carla's room, the first thing I noticed were the tubes. They seemed to be everywhere. In her nose, mouth, and arms. She looked like she was sleeping. Her breathing machine made mechanical noises and the heart monitor beeped. Guess that meant she was okay.

"Carla?"

She didn't respond. Dr. Gableman said she with heavily medicated.

I walked over to her bedside and called her name again. "Carla, it's me. Ray."

Her eyes opened. After a fwq blinks they remained open. She looked surprised to see me.

"Hey." I smiled.

She continued to stare up at me with a surprised look.

"Trip called and told me that you were here. I came as soon as I could. I want to be here for you and help you."

Torn Between a Gangster and a Gentleman

Dr. Gableman told me that she wouldn't be able to talk from her being physically weak and the tubes in her throat. So instead of talking, she expressed herself with the tears that began pooling down her face.

I grabbed her hand and held it while wiping her tears. "Don't cry, Carla. It's okay. You'll be alright. I talked to Dr. Gableman and he said you'll make a full recovery. He said they have room for you in a rehab program and I want you to get that spot. I want to help you. I want to get to know you. I want my kids to know you."

The tears rolled in a steady stream as she gripped my hand tighter.

"The kids are in the waiting room with their mother. They want to meet you. I'm going to get them."

I tried to leave but Carla wouldn't loosen her grip. Her eyes showed fear of being left alone. She didn't think I would come back if I left.

"I'll be right back. I promise. I'm going to get the rest of the family."

She reluctantly loosened her grip.

"I'll be right back," I reassured one more time before going to get Brianna and the kids. We had to keep the visit short because Dr. Gableman said she needed to rest. But this wouldn't be the last time I seen her. If I could, I was going to help her. I wanted a second chance with my mother.

CHAPTER 25-Brianna

"How much longer does Granny have to be in the hospital?" Brittany asked from the backseat of my Lexus truck.

We had just come from visiting Ray's mother. She'd been in the hospital for a week. Her recovery was slow and steady, but at least she could talk and didn't have all of the tubes sticking out of her body like she had the first time we saw her.

"Doc says probably another week or so. Heart attacks are serious. This was her third one, so they want to keep an eye on her. Plus, they are waiting for the rehab center to accept her," Ray explained.

"I hope she goes into the church program. She seems cool. I want to be around her so we can get to know her."

"Me, too," Ray said, the yearning in his voice audible.

"Do you think they will let her come to my game this weekend?" Junior asked.

"I don't think so, man. They got hospital rules. But we can ask Dr. Gableman the next time we visit. I'm thinking about coming back tomorrow or the day after. Y'all want to come with me?"

"Yeah," the mix said in unison.

I took my eyes off the road to glance toward the passenger seat at Ray. He looked happy. The happiest I'd seen him since he came home. We had our family back together, plus one. I was surprised at how much he resembled his mother. He looked exactly like his father, but I could see Carla in his face, too. "You look like your mother. You have her nose and eyes. You have girly eyes," I teased.

"Really, Bria?" Ray asked, like he couldn't believe I had ribbed him. "You shouldn't be talking about nobody's body parts with those size eight in men's that you wear. I know you didn't get them feet from mama. She wore a six." Ray laughed.

"Ray!" I yelled, slapping him on the shoulder. "Don't be talking about my feet like that."

"Dang, mama! You wear a size eight?" Junior yelled from the backseat, adding fuel to the fire.

"I wear a seven in mens and a nine in womens. And just so y'all know, that is a normal size for a woman my height," I defended.

"Size eight for a five-foot-eight woman? Mmm-hhmm. Whatever, Big Bird feet." Ray laughed.

"How are you and your size twelves talking about the size of somebody's feet, daddy?" Brittany defended me.

"You taking your mother's side, Brittany? Do I gotta talk about that big ol' head you got?" Ray ribbed, spinning in the seat to face her.

"If I got a big head, I got it from you, chrome dome," Brittany shot back.

"You better get off my daughter," I warned.

"Or what? What you gon' do?" Ray challenged.

"I'mma pull this truck over and show you my alter ego. Think I'm playing?"

"Oohhh! I'm scared," he said, pulling out his phone and answering. "What's up, Cray?"

"Ray, I need your help, man! This bitch is crazy!"

The fear in Cray's voice grabbed my attention.

"What's up, man? You good?" Ray asked.

"Nah, man. She try'na shoot me. Irene is going crazy."

"What did you do? Why is she try'na shoot you?"

"I fucked up, Ray. I'm hiding at the bar. I'm in the basement. If she finds me, she's going to kill me. I need your help."

Hearing that Cray was about to be shot got me nervous. I didn't want Ray to get involved in nobody's shooting. We had just got back together. I didn't want him involved in anything that would take him away. Even if it was his dad's best friend. "Tell him to call the police," I said.

"Did you call the police?" Ray asked.

"Nah, man. I don't want to send her to jail. I need you to talk to her for me. Come on, nephew. I need you."

"Okay. I'm on my way," he said before ending the call. "Head over to 75th and Hampton, Brianna. I need to help him. I gotta stop Irene from shooting him."

Torn Between a Gangster and a Gentleman

"But, Ray, you just got out of jail a couple weeks ago. I don't want anything to happen to you. Why don't you just call the police?"

"You heard him. He don't want to send her to jail. Irene is his wife. Just head over there."

I gave Ray an angry look before turning the truck around and heading for Cray's bar. "What did he do that his wife wants to shoot him?"

"Knowing Cray, he probably cheated on her."

"I hope she shoots him before we get there," I said, thinking of Benny.

Ray gave me a look. "Why would you say that?"

"Because Cray is a dog. Dogs don't deserve to be saved."

Ray just shook his head.

It took 10 minutes to get to Cray's bar. It was a big brick building right off the corner with dark tinted windows. The sign out front said Gail's. The parking lot was almost empty except for 2 cars and my truck.

"Y'all stay here. I'll be right back," Ray said, about to get out of the truck.

"Wait. I'm coming with you."

"I got this, Bria. You gotta stay out here with the kids."

I turned to look at the kids. They wore fearful and confused looks. I couldn't leave them.

"Okay. But if you're not back in five minutes, I'm coming in."

When Ray left, I bit my nails and watched the bar door. I hated that I didn't know what was going on in there and that he went by himself.

"Mama, I'm scared for daddy," Brittany whined.

"Shouldn't we call the police if somebody got a gun?" Junior asked.

"Let's give him another minute. If he don't come out, I'm going in to get him."

Time seemed to slow down as I watched the bar. One minute seemed like an eternity. When I couldn't take the suspense any longer, I turned to the kids. "Listen. If I'm not back in five minutes, call the police. Don't neither one of you come to that door, you hear me?"

They gave sad nods. I hated to leave my babies and put myself in harm's way, but there was no way that I was leaving Ray hanging. I was prepared to ride and die with him.

I crept up to the bar and tried to look through the windows to get a look inside, but they were too dark. My only option was the front door. I opened it as quietly as I could and peeked inside. Ray stood by the wall with his hands in the air. A short older light skinned woman who resembled Tracy Ellis Ross was pointing a small shiny gun at him. She must've felt my presence because she turned to look toward the door. Ray used the distraction that I caused to rush her. The gun went off, scaring this shit out of me.

Pop!

"Ahhhh!" I screamed as a bottle of liquor exploded behind the bar.

"Irene, are you crazy?" Ray yelled, taking the gun and giving her a shove.

"Give me back my damn gun!" she screamed, charging at him. *Oh no she didn't!*

"Get your hands off him!" I yelled, running over and grabbing Irene. I pushed her back and stood in front of Ray, defending my future.

"What the hell is going on?" a man's voice called.

I spun around and seen Cray standing near the cellar door. I hadn't seen him in over a decade and he was a bit heavier with gray hair, but it was him.

"You son of a bitch!" Irene yelled, charging at him and letting her hands fly.

"Irene, stop! Hey, stop!" Cray yelled, trying to dodge the punches and slaps.

"Who did he cheat on her with?" I asked, wishing I could help Irene kick his ass.

"Her sister. You grab Irene and I'll grab Cray."

I was hesitant to grab her. I wanted her to get all of the licks she could get for him sleeping with her sister. When Ray jumped in and grabbed Cray, I waited a few moments to grab Irene. In those few seconds, Irene managed to draw blood from Cray's neck and forehead. I was proud of her.

"I'm going to kill you, Crawford! I swear to God I'm going to kill you!" Irene threatened as we pulled them apart.

"I'm sorry, baby. It was an accident. She didn't mean nothing to me. I love you, honey," Cray apologized.

"No, you don't. If you loved me, you wouldn't have done it. You don't love me. You love cheating on me."

"Irene, please, baby. Let's talk about this."

"No. You can save that conversation for the devil when I send you to meet him."

After those last words, Irene snatched away from me and stormed out to the bar.

"Damn, Cray. Her sister?" Ray admonished, letting Cray know he had gone too far.

"It was an accident, Ray. It only happened twice."

I rolled my eyes at him. I couldn't believe he just said that. And I definitely didn't want Ray hanging around a cheater. "Hey, Cray. I would say it's nice to see you again, but... This isn't a nice situation," I spoke up.

"Hey, Brianna. Long time no see. And even though the situation is what it is, it's good to see you again. So, y'all kicking it again?" he asked looking back and forth from me to Ray.

"We just came back from visiting Carla in the hospital. She had a heart attack and been in there for about a week," Ray explained.

"Damn. Sorry to hear about that, man. I hope she gets better soon."

"Yeah. Me, too."

I could tell that Ray and Cray wanted some time alone, so I excused myself. Plus, I needed to stop the kids from calling the police. "Ray, I'm going to go back outside with the kids. Cray, uh... Take care." When I climbed in the truck, the kids looked relieved to see me.

"Where is dad?" Junior asked.

"Everything is fine, y'all. He'll be out in a minute."

***

"When is this movie going to be over?" Brittany whined.

We were all sitting in Ray's living room on the furniture that I made him buy. Since he didn't want us going back to our house with Benny, I told him to make the house look like a home instead of a prison cell. He went and bought furniture, beds, and more dishes for the kitchen. And even though I liked how the house was coming together, there was no way that we would be sharing a 2-bedroom and 1-bathroom house much longer.

"Girl, relax. This is the best part," Ray said popping a hand full of popcorn in his mouth while staring intently at the screen. Across the room, Junior wore the same look. We were watching Snowfall.

"Don't be talking to my daughter like that," I said, pushing the side of his head and making him waste the popcorn that he was trying to shove in his mouth.

"Oh, you wanna muff me when I ain't looking?" he asked, looking down at the popcorn that dropped on his chest.

Before I could react, he threw the crumbs that were in his hand at me. They landed in my face and hair.

"Ray!" I yelled, running my fingers through my hair to get the popcorn out.

"Don't be throwing stuff at my mama!" Brittany yelled.

I looked up just in time to see a throw pillow sailing through the air. It hit Ray on the shoulder and sent popcorn flying everywhere.

"I'm messing you up!" he yelled, jumping up and ripping 2 pillows from this couch.

Brittany tried to run but Ray caught her and started beating her with both pillows. I snatched up a pillow and went to help my daughter.

"Get off my dad!" Junior yelled.

A pillow hit me upside the head and fell to the floor. I turned and seen Junior running at me swinging a pillow wildly. My son was bigger and stronger than me, but I had been having pillow fights long before he was born. I side stepped his wild charge and hit him

Torn Between a Gangster and a Gentleman

on the side of the head with my pillow. His momentum knocked him on the ground.

"Stay in your place, youngin," I celebrated.

"Get off my boy!" Ray yelled, hitting me with a pillow and ruining my celebration.

I turned to go at him, but he was already upon me. Beat me down with the pillows until I tapped out. After the pillow fight, we all sat around the popcorn covered living room breathing heavily.

"You and yo mama gon' clean up all of this in the morning since y'all lost," Ray told Brittany.

"Nope. Girls rule and boys drool," she said, sticking out her tongue.

"We will *all* clean up tomorrow," I said.

"Dang, man. Y'all made me miss the show," Junior complained.

"You can watch it again tomorrow. It's me and mama turn to pick something to watch," Brittany said. "We wanna watch Queen and Slim."

"Awe, man!" Ray and Junior whined.

By the time the movie was at the halfway point, Ray had his head in my lap, cocked slightly to the side, snoring. Junior sat on the couch across from us with his head titled back, mouth wide open, also asleep. Watching the urban love story made me want to take Ray in the bedroom and do nasty things. I was thinking lingerie and whipped cream. Problem was I didn't bring any lingerie. I left it at home.

After checking to make sure Ray was sleeping, I decided to take the trip to the old house to grab a few things. I knew I could make it there and back before he woke up. And I knew once he woke up and seen me in a corset, panties, and a bra, we would make love all night long.

"Brittany, I'm going to make a run to the old house. Do you need anything?" I whispered.

Her eyes lit up. "Yeah. I need my iPad and keyboard."

I looked at her like she with crazy. "I was talking about something small. It's late and I don't feel like carrying that big ol' keyboard."

"But I need it, mom. I thought we were just staying with dad for a couple of days. I didn't know we were moving in, otherwise I would have brought it."

She had a point. "Okay. I'll get it."

After sliding from under Ray's head I went over to wake Junior. "Keep your voice down. I'm going to the old house. Do you need anything?"

"Yeah. All my games and shoes," he said before closing his eyes again.

I turned back to Brittany. "If your dad wakes up, tell him I ran to the old house and I'll be right back."

I spent most of the drive to the old house praying that Benny wouldn't be there. I didn't want to see his face ever again. I hated him. I still couldn't believe he had another family. Damn, he was a good liar. Made me wonder what else he was lying about. He was probably guilty of murder, too. I didn't want anything from him when we got divorced either. None of his money, no alimony, or the house. He could keep it all. I had almost $60,000 in the bank and I owned 2 daycares. I didn't need his money or his drama. I just wanted to be free. I wanted my second chance with Ray.

When I pulled up to the house, I thanked God when I saw that the lights were out and Benny's car wasn't in the driveway. He was probably at Ciarra's house with his other family. Which was fine with me. I checked the mailbox as I walked upon the porch. There were a couple of things inside. Looked like Benny hadn't been by since I put him out. That was a good sign. Hopefully that meant he wouldn't fight the divorce. And since he was gone, I planned on packing as much of our stuff as I could into my truck.

After letting myself in the house, I began making the trips up and down the stairs, stuffing my Lexus with me and my kids' things. About 20 minutes into the packing, I was carrying Brittany's keyboard down the stairs when I thought I heard someone in the house.

Shit! Benny was home!

Torn Between a Gangster and a Gentleman

    I moved as quietly as I could, tip-toeing toward the front door. I was near the foyer when I thought I saw something move. All of a sudden, I was hoping that the movement came from Benny and not a stranger or wild animal. "Benny?" I called, pausing to listen.
    No one answered.
    I took a step toward the door when I heard something behind me. I spun around and saw someone running toward me. I threw the keyboard and tried to run. The next thing I remembered was falling but I didn't stay awake long enough to feel the floor.

J-Blunt & Miss Kim

CHAPTER 26-Ray

Something was wrong. I felt it as soon as my eyes opened. I looked around for Brianna, but she was gone. "Where is your mom?" I asked Brittany.

"She went to the old house. She said she would be right back."

I reached for my phone on the table, checking the time. It was 11:35. "I told y'all not to go back to that house without me. Why didn't you wake me up?"

"I don't know. She said she would be right back," she whined.

I ignored her whiny voice and called Brianna. The voicemail picked up. I hung up and re-dialed. Still no answer, so I left a message. "Brianna, call me." As I sat and thought about what to do next, I got a terrible feeling in my gut. "Hey, I'mma make a run. If your mother calls or comes back before I do, tell her to call me," I told Brittany as I headed to the room to grab a pair of shoes.

"Is mom okay?" she called after me.

I decided not to let Brittany in on my bad feeling. I didn't want her worrying or trying to come along with me. "Everything is fine. I just have to make a run."

I called and texted Brianna during the drive to their old house. She didn't answer. Something was definitely wrong. I raced to the Lake Shore Drive house, getting there in record time. I decided to park a few houses away just in case I needed the element of surprise. After parking, I studied the house as I approached. It was dark and there were no lights on. Brianna's truck was in the driveway and I didn't see Benny's car. I walked up to the front door about to try the lock when something inside my head told me to take a look around. I did. I was checking the yard for signs of trespass when I noticed a light coming from a room on the side of the house. It was the sitting room. I moved closer to see if I could get a peek inside. The curtains were drawn but there was a small gap between that allowed me to see inside. What I seen sent a chill through my body.

"Oh shit!" I mumbled, pulling out my phone.

"9-1-1. What's your emergency?"

"Send the police to 271 East Lake Shore Drive. Hurry up! There is a woman inside being tortured," I whispered.

"Sir, what? What's happening?"

"Listen. My name is Ray Preston. I'm at my children's mother's house on Lake Shore Drive. There is a man wearing a mask and dark clothes in her house. She is tied to a chair and he is hitting her. Send help right now!"

"Okay. I'm sending help. Can you see inside? How many people are in the house with her?"

"I can only see one but there could be more. It looks like a robbery. I don't know but I have to go. I'm going inside."

"Sir! Mr. Preston, do not go—"

I ended the call and pocketed my phone. I didn't know what was going on in the house, but I wasn't about to stand by and watch Brianna be killed. I walked to the back of the house, trying to open windows along the way. All of them were locked except the window for the half bathroom. The window was small. Maybe 12 by 12 inches. I didn't know if I would fit but I had to give it a shot. After snatching off the screen, I opened the window and climbed inside as quietly as I could. I looked around for a weapon. There was nothing in the bathroom but a plunger with a wooden handle. That would have to do.

I opened the bathroom door as quietly as I could, listening for movement. I had done my share of home invasions back in the day, so I knew the man with Brianna probably wasn't alone. I needed to find out who else was in the house.

I left the bathroom, creeping down the hall slowly with the plunger held high above my head. As I made my way toward the sitting room, I could hear a man's voice but was unable to make out what he was saying. Then there was a loud smack. Brianna screamed. I could hear her pleading with the man. I crept closer to the room, and when the man started talking again, I recognized his voice immediately.

I took a peek in the room and seen the masked man standing in front of Brianna with a gun in one hand and a knife in the other. It sounded like he was making some kind of confession. I ducked out

Torn Between a Gangster and a Gentleman

of view and pulled out my cellphone to record what he was saying. I wasn't shocked by some of them things that came out of his mouth.

"Aahhhhh!" Brianna screamed again.

It was a death scream. He had stabbed her. I was about to rush into the room when the man began speaking again. I held my ground outside the door, still recording. Then he mentioned calling me. And then the worst thing that could've possibly happened actually happened. My phone rang.

"Shit!"

J-Blunt & Miss Kim

Torn Between a Gangster and a Gentleman

CHAPTER 27-Benny

"Brianna! Brianna! Oh, wake up, sleeping beauty."

She was out cold. Asleep. Sergio had done better than I expected. Knocked her out, tied her up, and had her sitting here waiting for me when I arrived. He came by the house by coincidence. I needed him to pick up some things for me since I was staying with Ciarra. When he called and told me that Brianna was in the house alone, I hatched a plan, taking advantage of the opportunity that presented itself. Now I was going to get my revenge. The beer bottle with Ray's fingerprints sitting on the table would be the icing atop my pay back cake.

"Wake up, bitch!" I yelled before backhanding her across the face.

The impact of the slap sent Brianna's head flying violently to the left and she almost fell out of the chair. But she was awake.

"Please, man. Don't hurt me. I'll give you whatever you want," she pleaded, looking into my mask-covered face.

The terror on her face was golden. Wished I would have recorded the look so I could watch it whenever I needed a laugh. "Shut up, bitch. I don't want your money."

"Please don't hurt me. I'll do whatever you want. I have kids."

"I'm sorry, baby, but you have to die. How long did you think you would take me for a chump, Brianna? How long?"

She blinked rapidly while staring into my eyes. Recognition flashed upon her face when she realized it was me. "Benny?"

"In the flesh, baby!" I grinned.

"Benny, what is going on? What are you doing? Let me—"

"Shut up, Brianna," I whispered.

"Get me out to this chair. Untie me. Why are you doing this?"

"Shut the fuck up, bitch!" I exploded, punching her in the mouth.

Her lips split like exploding melons. The blood came quick. "What the fuck, Benny! Why are you doing this?"

I brought my face so close to hers that I could smell her makeup. And fear. The shit was intoxicating. "You wasn't crying when you

209

was fucking Ray, were you? You wasn't crying when you spit cum in my mouth, was you? Why the fuck you crying now?"

"Benny, please stop. What about the kids?"

I bust out laughing. "You hear this shit, Sergio?" I asked my trusted worker.

"That daughter is going to grow up to be a fine bitch. I want a piece of that pie." He laughed.

Brianna growled. "If you touch my daughter—"

"Shut up, bitch!" I roared, slapping her again. "I don't give a fuck about your kids. Not your bitch ass son or your bitch ass daughter who will grow up to be a hoe like you. Did you really think that you could fuck me over and I wouldn't get even? Well, let me tell you a secret, Brianna. I'm your worst muthafuckin' nightmare."

She looked up at me through a new set of eyes. Like she was seeing me from the first time. "My mother was right about you."

"Earlene? That old bitch. What did she say? That I was the devil or something like that? I ain't the devil but I'm just as bad. I'm B.B. King! The baddest muthafucka Milwaukee has ever seen. You thought I liked rubbing shoulders with those rich ass crackers? Bitch, is you stupid? That's what you call an insurance policy. Gotta have people in high places to have your back if you want to get on top and stay on top. How you think I made it this long?"

"Benny, please don't do this. I'm sorry for everything. I'm sorry," she whined.

"Didn't I tell you to shut the fuck up?" I yelled, reaching my arm back as far as I could before slapping Brianna's face. The blow left a welt from her ear to cheek. "Let me tell you just who I am, bitch. I'm B.B.-muthafuckin'-King. I been running the streets since yo ass was in grammar school. I'm bigger than the mayor. Shit, I'm the governor! And the bitch muthafucka they charging me with murder for, hell yeah I killed him. Shot him in the face twice. Buried him under a cement walkway. They would've never found the body if it wasn't for that bitch nigga, Red Fox. But don't worry, Bria. I'mma make sure they find your body. And guess who's going down for your murder?" I asked, pulling the knife from my waist. "Ray's prints are on this knife, baby. Remember when y'all was at

Torn Between a Gangster and a Gentleman

Earlene's party giving each other googly eyes? Y'all cut the cake and worked like a perfect team while I snuck away with everything I needed to send his ass to jail for life. Shit, he might be the reason they bring the death penalty back to Wisconsin. And I will push the courts to fry his ass if they bring it back."

"Don't do this, Benny," Brianna cried. "We can work it out. Please."

"We ain't working shit out. It's over. Matter of fact, I'mma make your daughter my new bitch. Pop her Cherry when she turns sixteen."

Murder flashed in Brianna's eyes. "Don't touch my kids, Benny! Don't fucking touch my kids or I'll—"

I plunged the knife deep into her thigh until it hit bone.

"Aaaaahh!" she screamed.

The sound of her pain was music to my ears. "Does it hurt, baby?" I asked with mock sympathy.

"Please, Benny! Don't do this, please!"

I left the knife in her leg while I grabbed her cellphone off the table. "You don't mind if I make a call, do you? I'm sending Ray a text telling him to come over. Should I make it a freaky text so he will hurry up? Maybe write how bad you can't wait to suck his dick? Yeah, that's it. I'm telling him to hurry up because you want to suck his dick. Is that how you say it?" I laughed while typing the message. "And when he gets here, he will find this knife in your body, that beer bottle with his prints on the table, and your blood everywhere. I'm going to call the police as soon as I finish texting Ray."

I could taste the sweetness of revenge as I sent the text. And then the damnedest thing happened. I heard a phone ring outside the sitting room door.

Hell nah! Couldn't be!

"Ray!" Brianna screamed.

"Fuck!" I cursed, tightening the grip on the Glock 9-millimeter as I spun toward the door.

211

J-Blunt & Miss Kim

CHAPTER 28-Ray

I ran into the room with the plunger held high, charging Benny. As I closed the distance between us, I seen a blur out the corner of my eye heading in my direction. Benny had a partner. I reached Benny before his partner could reach me, clocking him on the side of the head with the plunger. He stumbled backwards, squeezing the trigger wildly.

Clap, clap, clap!

I grabbed his arm holding the gun, trying to disarm him. The pistol continued to fire as we fought for possession of the gun.

"Ump!" Benny's partner grunted.

"Ahhhh!" Brianna screamed.

I used my peripheral to look around the room as I fought Benny for the gun. His partner had fallen to the floor and was clutching his chest. When I seen Brianna's chair flipped over and her lying on the ground, my knees went weak and my grip on Benny's arm loosened. He took advantage of my moment of weakness and elbowed me in the face. The blow dropped me to my knees, but I never let go of the gun. However, I was unable to protect myself from his fist and elbow. He rained down elbows on top of my head, opening up a wound. I could feel blood dripping down to side of my face. I had underestimated him. He was stronger than I thought. Dazed and bloody, my grip on the gun loosened as I fell to my hands and knees.

"You pussy ass nigga! I knew you was a bitch!" Benny taunted as he stood over me.

I grabbed at his ankles and knees, trying to pull myself up and shake away the dizziness.

"Yeah, that's right, nigga. Kneel at the feet of your master, bitch ass nigga!" he sneered, pressing the barrel of the gun to the back of my head. "You know what, Ray? I love fucking your baby mama. That pussy was fire. But I'mma love fucking your daughter better."

Brittany's face flashed in my head. I couldn't let him hurt my baby girl. The rage and strength that filled my body was instantaneous. It was nothing like anything I've ever felt before. I growled while grabbing Benny ankles and pulling.

Clap! The gun fired.

I could feel something burn in my shoulder and back as I lifted Benny high in the sky and brought him crashing down on the table. The table shattered and the gun flew from his hand. I climbed on top of him and began raining down blows on his face. I punched him until I could feel the bones in his face breaking, and then I punched him some more. The only reason I stopped was because the right side of my body was on fire and my arm stopped working. I looked down at my arm and seen blood soaking my shirt. The pain in my shoulder seemed to intensify once I realized I was shot. But I couldn't focus on my pain. I needed to check on Brianna.

"Brianna! Baby!" I called while crawling over to her.

She didn't answer me or move. Blood covered the front of her shirt, her eyes were closed, and face badly bruised.

"Brianna! Wake up, baby! Don't leave me, Bria! Please, don't leave me," I cried while untying her from the chair and pulling her into my arms.

The front door crashed open and I could hear the police screaming in the background.

"Brianna, wake up, baby. Please wake. Don't leave me baby. *SOMEBODY HELP!*"

Torn Between a Gangster and a Gentleman

Epilogue - 1 year later.

When she left, she took a part of me with her. It's been a year since she left but the pain still feels fresh in my mind and heart. Her passing created a wound that reopens every day that I realize I can't go see her or pick up the phone and hear her voice. As I stood over her grave, memories began to flood my brain. Her laugh, her smile, the way she smelled, and her cooking. I looked up into the sky at the bright blazing summer sun, hoping that she was up there in heaven smiling down on us.

"You think she in heaven, dad?" Brittany asked, staring up at me with tears in her eyes. She was standing next to me, my arm wrapped around her shoulder, looking more like her mother each day.

"Yeah, I do. And if by some chance she didn't make it, I don't want to go either."

"I believe she is," Junior said. "She was the best person that God ever made. If it wasn't for her, I wouldn't be here." Junior was standing on my right side, hugged up next to me in a similar way as Brittany. And he was looking down at me. The kid had grown 5 inches in the past year.

"No, Junior. I'm the reason you're here. Mama is the reason I'm here," Brianna cut in. She was standing next to Brittany looking just as beautiful as the day I met her. We were all standing in front of her mother's headstone.

"Well, mama, we just wanted to come spend some time with you. Let you know that we are still loving and missing you," I said.

"And that I audition on America's Got Talent next week!" Brittany added.

"And that I'm doing good in school and colleges are still trying to recruit me. Oh, and that I beat dad in basketball and now he doesn't want to play me anymore." Junior laughed.

"Because he cheated, mama. And I don't play cheaters," I clarified.

"And that we adding a new member to our family! I'm three months pregnant, mama!" Brianna screamed.

215

J-Blunt & Miss Kim

After one more round of goodbyes, we left Earlene's grave and headed home.

As I look back on my life, I can see that God has given me several seconds chances. A second chance at life. A second chance at love. And a second chance at being a father and raising my kids. There is still one more second chance that I'm looking forward to that hasn't happened yet. That is a second chance with Carla. She only lasted in rehab for a month. Never completed the program. After making a full recovery from the heart attack, she went back to smoking crack. Last I heard, she moved back in with Frank and they are continuing in their physically abusive crack-smoking relationship. I've washed my hands with her. Nothing I can do for someone that doesn't want to help themself. But whenever she is ready to kick the drugs and change her life, I'll be there for her. But the one thing I won't do is subject myself and family to her addictive lifestyle.

Our family has gone through a lot during the past year, good and bad. The good news being that Brianna is no longer Brianna Boston. The divorce from Benny was granted with lighting speed and I didn't waste time making her Brianna Preston. The baby we are expecting is the icing on the cake. Some of the low points came while attending Benny's court hearings. We had to testify at his trial for shooting us. It just wrapped up a few months ago. He was found guilty on 2 counts of attempted murder for shooting us and one count of reckless homicide for killing his worker, Sergio. The judge sentenced him to 100 years. And he is still facing time for killing Tracy Brown. The confession that I taped was used in his trial for shooting us and will be used in the Tracy Brown murder trial. Safe to say that we won't ever be seeing Benny again. Unless God decides to give him a second chance.

I don't know why God found me so worthy of a redo in life, but whatever the reason, I'm thankful for His mercy. It's been said that if you don't know what's in your future, you will be confused by your present. I agree. If your present produces pain, try not to dwell on it. Accept it for what it is and keep moving toward your future. Like child labor, pain is an indication that birth is getting close. The purpose of pain is not to kill you but to reveal your strength to you. You may not understand everything, but in order to grow, change, and progress, you must stand through everything. You have to go through something to get to something. And if God brought you to it, He will bring you through it; or give you a stronger back so that you can carry the burden.

The End.

Lock Down Publications and Ca$h Presents assisted publishing packages.

BASIC PACKAGE $499
Editing
Cover Design
Formatting

UPGRADED PACKAGE $800
Typing
Editing
Cover Design
Formatting

ADVANCE PACKAGE $1,200
Typing
Editing
Cover Design
Formatting
Copyright registration
Proofreading
Upload book to Amazon

LDP SUPREME PACKAGE $1,500
Typing
Editing
Cover Design
Formatting
Copyright registration
Proofreading
Set up Amazon account
Upload book to Amazon
Advertise on LDP Amazon and Facebook page

***Other services available upon request. Additional charges may apply
Lock Down Publications
P.O. Box 944
Stockbridge, GA 30281-9998
Phone # 470 303-9761

Submission Guideline

Submit the first three chapters of your completed manuscript to ldpsubmissions@gmail.com, subject line: Your book's title. The manuscript must be in a .doc file and sent as an attachment. Document should be in Times New Roman, double spaced and in size 12 font. Also, provide your synopsis and full contact information. If sending multiple submissions, they must each be in a separate email.

Have a story but no way to send it electronically? You can still submit to LDP/Ca$h Presents. Send in the first three chapters, written or typed, of your completed manuscript to:

LDP: Submissions Dept
Po Box 944
Stockbridge, Ga 30281

DO NOT send original manuscript. Must be a duplicate.

Provide your synopsis and a cover letter containing your full contact information.

Thanks for considering LDP and Ca$h Presents.

NEW RELEASES

KING OF THE TRENCHES 3 by GHOST & TRANAY ADAMS

JACK BOYS VS DOPE BOYS 3 by ROMELL TUKES

LIFE OF A SAVAGE 4 by ROMELL TUKES

CHI'RAQ GANGSTAS 4 by ROMELL TUKES

TORN BETWEEN A GANGSTER AND A GENTLEMAN by J-BLUNT & MISS KIM

J-Blunt & Miss Kim

Coming Soon from Lock Down Publications/Ca$h Presents

BLOOD OF A BOSS **VI**

SHADOWS OF THE GAME II

TRAP BASTARD II

By **Askari**

LOYAL TO THE GAME **IV**

By **T.J. & Jelissa**

TRUE SAVAGE **VIII**

MIDNIGHT CARTEL IV

DOPE BOY MAGIC IV

CITY OF KINGZ III

NIGHTMARE ON SILENT AVE II

THE PLUG OF LIL MEXICO II

CLASSIC CITY II

By **Chris Green**

BLAST FOR ME **III**

A SAVAGE DOPEBOY III

CUTTHROAT MAFIA III

DUFFLE BAG CARTEL VII

HEARTLESS GOON VI

By **Ghost**

A HUSTLER'S DECEIT III

KILL ZONE II

BAE BELONGS TO ME III

TIL DEATH II

By **Aryanna**

KING OF THE TRAP III

By **T.J. Edwards**

GORILLAZ IN THE BAY V

3X KRAZY III

Torn Between a Gangster and a Gentleman

STRAIGHT BEAST MODE III
De'Kari
KINGPIN KILLAZ IV
STREET KINGS III
PAID IN BLOOD III
CARTEL KILLAZ IV
DOPE GODS III
Hood Rich
SINS OF A HUSTLA II
ASAD
RICH $AVAGE III
By Martell Troublesome Bolden
YAYO V
Bred In The Game 2
S. Allen
THE STREETS WILL TALK II
By Yolanda Moore
SON OF A DOPE FIEND III
HEAVEN GOT A GHETTO II
SKI MASK MONEY II
By Renta
LOYALTY AIN'T PROMISED III
By Keith Williams
I'M NOTHING WITHOUT HIS LOVE II
SINS OF A THUG II
TO THE THUG I LOVED BEFORE II
IN A HUSTLER I TRUST II
By Monet Dragun
QUIET MONEY IV
EXTENDED CLIP III

J-Blunt & Miss Kim

THUG LIFE IV
By **Trai'Quan**
THE STREETS MADE ME IV
By **Larry D. Wright**
IF YOU CROSS ME ONCE II
ANGEL IV
By **Anthony Fields**
THE STREETS WILL NEVER CLOSE IV
By **K'ajji**
HARD AND RUTHLESS III
KILLA KOUNTY III
By **Khufu**
MONEY GAME III
By **Smoove Dolla**
JACK BOYS VS DOPE BOYS IV
A GANGSTA'S QUR'AN V
COKE GIRLZ II
COKE BOYS II
LIFE OF A SAVAGE V
CHI'RAQ GANGSTAS V
By **Romell Tukes**
MURDA WAS THE CASE III
Elijah R. Freeman
THE STREETS NEVER LET GO III
By **Robert Baptiste**
AN UNFORESEEN LOVE IV
By **Meesha**

MONEY MAFIA II
By **Jibril Williams**

Torn Between a Gangster and a Gentleman

QUEEN OF THE ZOO III
By **Black Migo**
VICIOUS LOYALTY III
By Kingpen
A GANGSTA'S PAIN III
By J-Blunt
CONFESSIONS OF A JACKBOY III
By Nicholas Lock
GRIMEY WAYS III
By Ray Vinci
KING KILLA II
By Vincent "Vitto" Holloway
BETRAYAL OF A THUG II
By Fre$h
THE MURDER QUEENS III
By Michael Gallon
THE BIRTH OF A GANGSTER III
By Delmont Player
TREAL LOVE II
By Le'Monica Jackson
FOR THE LOVE OF BLOOD II
By Jamel Mitchell
RAN OFF ON DA PLUG II
By Paper Boi Rari
HOOD CONSIGLIERE II
By Keese
PRETTY GIRLS DO NASTY THINGS II
By Nicole Goosby
PROTÉGÉ OF A LEGEND II
By Corey Robinson

J-Blunt & Miss Kim

IT'S JUST ME AND YOU II
By Ah'Million
BORN IN THE GRAVE II
By Self Made Tay
FOREVER GANGSTA III
By Adrian Dulan
GORILLAZ IN THE TRENCHES II
By SayNoMore

Available Now

RESTRAINING ORDER **I & II**
By **CA$H & Coffee**
LOVE KNOWS NO BOUNDARIES **I II & III**
By **Coffee**
RAISED AS A GOON I, II, III & IV
BRED BY THE SLUMS I, II, III
BLAST FOR ME I & II
ROTTEN TO THE CORE I II III
A BRONX TALE I, II, III
DUFFLE BAG CARTEL I II III IV V VI
HEARTLESS GOON I II III IV V
A SAVAGE DOPEBOY I II
DRUG LORDS I II III

Torn Between a Gangster and a Gentleman

CUTTHROAT MAFIA I II
KING OF THE TRENCHES
By **Ghost**
LAY IT DOWN **I & II**
LAST OF A DYING BREED I II
BLOOD STAINS OF A SHOTTA I & II III
By **Jamaica**
LOYAL TO THE GAME I II III
LIFE OF SIN I, II III
By **TJ & Jelissa**
BLOODY COMMAS I & II
SKI MASK CARTEL I II & III
KING OF NEW YORK I II,III IV V
RISE TO POWER I II III
COKE KINGS I II III IV V
BORN HEARTLESS I II III IV
KING OF THE TRAP I II
By **T.J. Edwards**
IF LOVING HIM IS WRONG…I & II
LOVE ME EVEN WHEN IT HURTS I II III
By **Jelissa**
WHEN THE STREETS CLAP BACK I & II III
THE HEART OF A SAVAGE I II III IV
MONEY MAFIA
LOYAL TO THE SOIL I II III
By **Jibril Williams**
A DISTINGUISHED THUG STOLE MY HEART I II & III
LOVE SHOULDN'T HURT I II III IV
RENEGADE BOYS I II III IV
PAID IN KARMA I II III

J-Blunt & Miss Kim

SAVAGE STORMS I II III
AN UNFORESEEN LOVE I II III
By **Meesha**
A GANGSTER'S CODE I &, II III
A GANGSTER'S SYN I II III
THE SAVAGE LIFE I II III
CHAINED TO THE STREETS I II III
BLOOD ON THE MONEY I II III
A GANGSTA'S PAIN I II
By J-Blunt
PUSH IT TO THE LIMIT
By **Bre' Hayes**
BLOOD OF A BOSS **I, II, III, IV, V**
SHADOWS OF THE GAME
TRAP BASTARD
By **Askari**
THE STREETS BLEED MURDER **I, II & III**
THE HEART OF A GANGSTA I II& III
By **Jerry Jackson**
CUM FOR ME I II III IV V VI VII VIII
An **LDP Erotica Collaboration**
BRIDE OF A HUSTLA **I II & II**
THE FETTI GIRLS **I, II& III**
CORRUPTED BY A GANGSTA I, II III, IV
BLINDED BY HIS LOVE
THE PRICE YOU PAY FOR LOVE I, II ,III
DOPE GIRL MAGIC I II III
By **Destiny Skai**
WHEN A GOOD GIRL GOES BAD
By **Adrienne**

Torn Between a Gangster and a Gentleman

THE COST OF LOYALTY I II III
By Kweli
A GANGSTER'S REVENGE **I II III & IV**
THE BOSS MAN'S DAUGHTERS I II III IV V
A SAVAGE LOVE **I & II**
BAE BELONGS TO ME I II
A HUSTLER'S DECEIT I, II, III
WHAT BAD BITCHES DO I, II, III
SOUL OF A MONSTER I II III
KILL ZONE
A DOPE BOY'S QUEEN I II III
TIL DEATH
By **Aryanna**
A KINGPIN'S AMBITON
A KINGPIN'S AMBITION **II**
I MURDER FOR THE DOUGH
By **Ambitious**
TRUE SAVAGE I II III IV V VI VII
DOPE BOY MAGIC I, II, III
MIDNIGHT CARTEL I II III
CITY OF KINGZ I II
NIGHTMARE ON SILENT AVE
THE PLUG OF LIL MEXICO II
CLASSIC CITY
By **Chris Green**
A DOPEBOY'S PRAYER
By **Eddie "Wolf" Lee**
THE KING CARTEL **I, II & III**
By **Frank Gresham**
THESE NIGGAS AIN'T LOYAL **I, II & III**

J-Blunt & Miss Kim

By **Nikki Tee**
GANGSTA SHYT **I II &III**
By **CATO**
THE ULTIMATE BETRAYAL
By **Phoenix**
BOSS'N UP **I , II & III**
By **Royal Nicole**
I LOVE YOU TO DEATH
By **Destiny J**
I RIDE FOR MY HITTA
I STILL RIDE FOR MY HITTA
By **Misty Holt**
LOVE & CHASIN' PAPER
By **Qay Crockett**
TO DIE IN VAIN
SINS OF A HUSTLA
By **ASAD**
BROOKLYN HUSTLAZ
By **Boogsy Morina**
BROOKLYN ON LOCK I & II
By **Sonovia**
GANGSTA CITY
By **Teddy Duke**
A DRUG KING AND HIS DIAMOND I & II III
A DOPEMAN'S RICHES
HER MAN, MINE'S TOO I, II
CASH MONEY HO'S
THE WIFEY I USED TO BE I II
PRETTY GIRLS DO NASTY THINGS
By **Nicole Goosby**

Torn Between a Gangster and a Gentleman

TRAPHOUSE KING **I II & III**
KINGPIN KILLAZ I II III
STREET KINGS I II
PAID IN BLOOD **I II**
CARTEL KILLAZ I II III
DOPE GODS I II
By **Hood Rich**
LIPSTICK KILLAH **I, II, III**
CRIME OF PASSION I II & III
FRIEND OR FOE I II III
By **Mimi**
STEADY MOBBN' **I, II, III**
THE STREETS STAINED MY SOUL I II III
By **Marcellus Allen**
WHO SHOT YA **I, II, III**
SON OF A DOPE FIEND I II
HEAVEN GOT A GHETTO
SKI MASK MONEY
Renta
GORILLAZ IN THE BAY **I II III IV**
TEARS OF A GANGSTA I II
3X KRAZY I II
STRAIGHT BEAST MODE I II
DE'KARI
TRIGGADALE I II III
MURDAROBER WAS THE CASE I II
Elijah R. Freeman
GOD BLESS THE TRAPPERS I, II, III
THESE SCANDALOUS STREETS I, II, III
FEAR MY GANGSTA I, II, III IV, V

J-Blunt & Miss Kim

THESE STREETS DON'T LOVE NOBODY I, II
BURY ME A G I, II, III, IV, V
A GANGSTA'S EMPIRE I, II, III, IV
THE DOPEMAN'S BODYGAURD I II
THE REALEST KILLAZ I II III
THE LAST OF THE OGS I II III
Tranay Adams
THE STREETS ARE CALLING
Duquie Wilson
MARRIED TO A BOSS I II III
By Destiny Skai & Chris Green
KINGZ OF THE GAME I II III IV V VI
Playa Ray
SLAUGHTER GANG I II III
RUTHLESS HEART I II III
By Willie Slaughter
FUK SHYT
By Blakk Diamond
DON'T F#CK WITH MY HEART I II
By Linnea
ADDICTED TO THE DRAMA I II III
IN THE ARM OF HIS BOSS II
By Jamila
YAYO I II III IV
A SHOOTER'S AMBITION I II
BRED IN THE GAME
By S. Allen
TRAP GOD I II III
RICH $AVAGE I II
MONEY IN THE GRAVE I II III

Torn Between a Gangster and a Gentleman

By Martell Troublesome Bolden
FOREVER GANGSTA I II
GLOCKS ON SATIN SHEETS I II
By Adrian Dulan
TOE TAGZ I II III IV
LEVELS TO THIS SHYT I II
IT'S JUST ME AND YOU
By Ah'Million
KINGPIN DREAMS I II III
RAN OFF ON DA PLUG
By Paper Boi Rari
CONFESSIONS OF A GANGSTA I II III IV
CONFESSIONS OF A JACKBOY I II
By Nicholas Lock
I'M NOTHING WITHOUT HIS LOVE
SINS OF A THUG
TO THE THUG I LOVED BEFORE
A GANGSTA SAVED XMAS
IN A HUSTLER I TRUST
By Monet Dragun
CAUGHT UP IN THE LIFE I II III
THE STREETS NEVER LET GO I II
By Robert Baptiste
NEW TO THE GAME I II III
MONEY, MURDER & MEMORIES I II III
By **Malik D. Rice**
LIFE OF A SAVAGE I II III IV
A GANGSTA'S QUR'AN I II III IV
MURDA SEASON I II III
GANGLAND CARTEL I II III

J-Blunt & Miss Kim

CHI'RAQ GANGSTAS I II III IV
KILLERS ON ELM STREET I II III
JACK BOYZ N DA BRONX I II III
A DOPEBOY'S DREAM I II III
JACK BOYS VS DOPE BOYS I II III
COKE GIRLZ
COKE BOYS
By Romell Tukes
LOYALTY AIN'T PROMISED I II
By Keith Williams
QUIET MONEY I II III
THUG LIFE I II III
EXTENDED CLIP I II
A GANGSTA'S PARADISE
By **Trai'Quan**
THE STREETS MADE ME I II III
By **Larry D. Wright**
THE ULTIMATE SACRIFICE I, II, III, IV, V, VI
KHADIFI
IF YOU CROSS ME ONCE
ANGEL I II III
IN THE BLINK OF AN EYE
By **Anthony Fields**
THE LIFE OF A HOOD STAR
By **Ca$h & Rashia Wilson**
THE STREETS WILL NEVER CLOSE I II III
By K'ajji
CREAM I II III
THE STREETS WILL TALK
By Yolanda Moore

Torn Between a Gangster and a Gentleman

NIGHTMARES OF A HUSTLA I II III
By King Dream
CONCRETE KILLA I II III
VICIOUS LOYALTY I II
By Kingpen
HARD AND RUTHLESS I II
MOB TOWN 251
THE BILLIONAIRE BENTLEYS I II III
By Von Diesel
GHOST MOB
Stilloan Robinson
MOB TIES I II III IV V VI
SOUL OF A HUSTLER, HEART OF A KILLER
GORILLAZ IN THE TRENCHES
By SayNoMore
BODYMORE MURDERLAND I II III
THE BIRTH OF A GANGSTER I II
By Delmont Player
FOR THE LOVE OF A BOSS
By C. D. Blue
MOBBED UP I II III IV
THE BRICK MAN I II III IV
THE COCAINE PRINCESS I II III IV V
By King Rio
KILLA KOUNTY I II III
By Khufu
MONEY GAME I II
By Smoove Dolla
A GANGSTA'S KARMA I II
By FLAME

J-Blunt & Miss Kim

KING OF THE TRENCHES I II III
by **GHOST & TRANAY ADAMS**
QUEEN OF THE ZOO I II
By **Black Migo**
GRIMEY WAYS I II
By Ray Vinci
XMAS WITH AN ATL SHOOTER
By Ca$h & Destiny Skai
KING KILLA
By Vincent "Vitto" Holloway
BETRAYAL OF A THUG
By Fre$h
THE MURDER QUEENS I II
By Michael Gallon
TREAL LOVE
By Le'Monica Jackson
FOR THE LOVE OF BLOOD
By Jamel Mitchell
HOOD CONSIGLIERE
By Keese
PROTÉGÉ OF A LEGEND
By Corey Robinson
BORN IN THE GRAVE
By Self Made Tay
MOAN IN MY MOUTH
By XTASY
TORN BETWEEN A GANGSTER AND A GENTLEMAN
By J-BLUNT & Miss Kim

Torn Between a Gangster and a Gentleman

BOOKS BY LDP'S CEO, CA$H

TRUST IN NO MAN
TRUST IN NO MAN 2
TRUST IN NO MAN 3
BONDED BY BLOOD
SHORTY GOT A THUG
THUGS CRY
THUGS CRY 2
THUGS CRY 3
TRUST NO BITCH
TRUST NO BITCH 2
TRUST NO BITCH 3
TIL MY CASKET DROPS
RESTRAINING ORDER
RESTRAINING ORDER 2
IN LOVE WITH A CONVICT
LIFE OF A HOOD STAR
XMAS WITH AN ATL SHOOTER

J-Blunt & Miss Kim